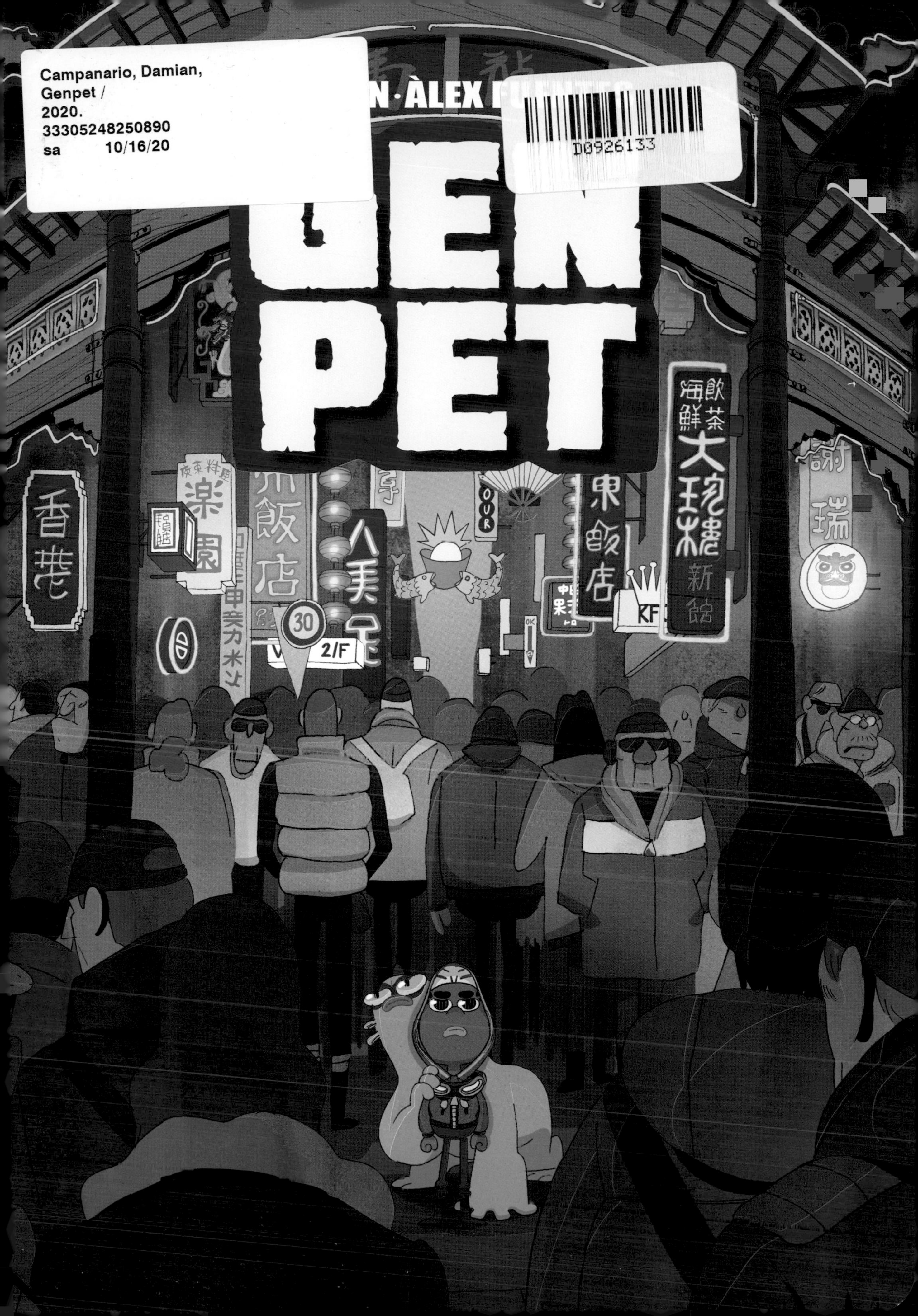
N·ÀLEX F
GEN
PET
30
2/F
KF
OUR

Written by
DAMIÁN

Illustrated by
ÀLEX FUENTES

Translation, Layout, and Editing by Mike Kennedy

MAGNETIC™

ISBN: 978-1-942367-76-5

Library of Congress Control Number: 2019918440

GenPet, published 2020 by Magnetic Press, LLC.
Originally published in French as *GenPet T01 Nat & Niko* © Ankama Éditions, 2016, by Damián & Àlex Fuentes and *GenPet T02 Nouveaux Héros* © Ankama Éditions, 2017, by Damián & Àlex Fuentes.
MAGNETIC™, MAGNETIC PRESS™, and their associated distinctive designs are trademarks of Magnetic Press, LLC.

10 9 8 7 6 5 4 3 2 1

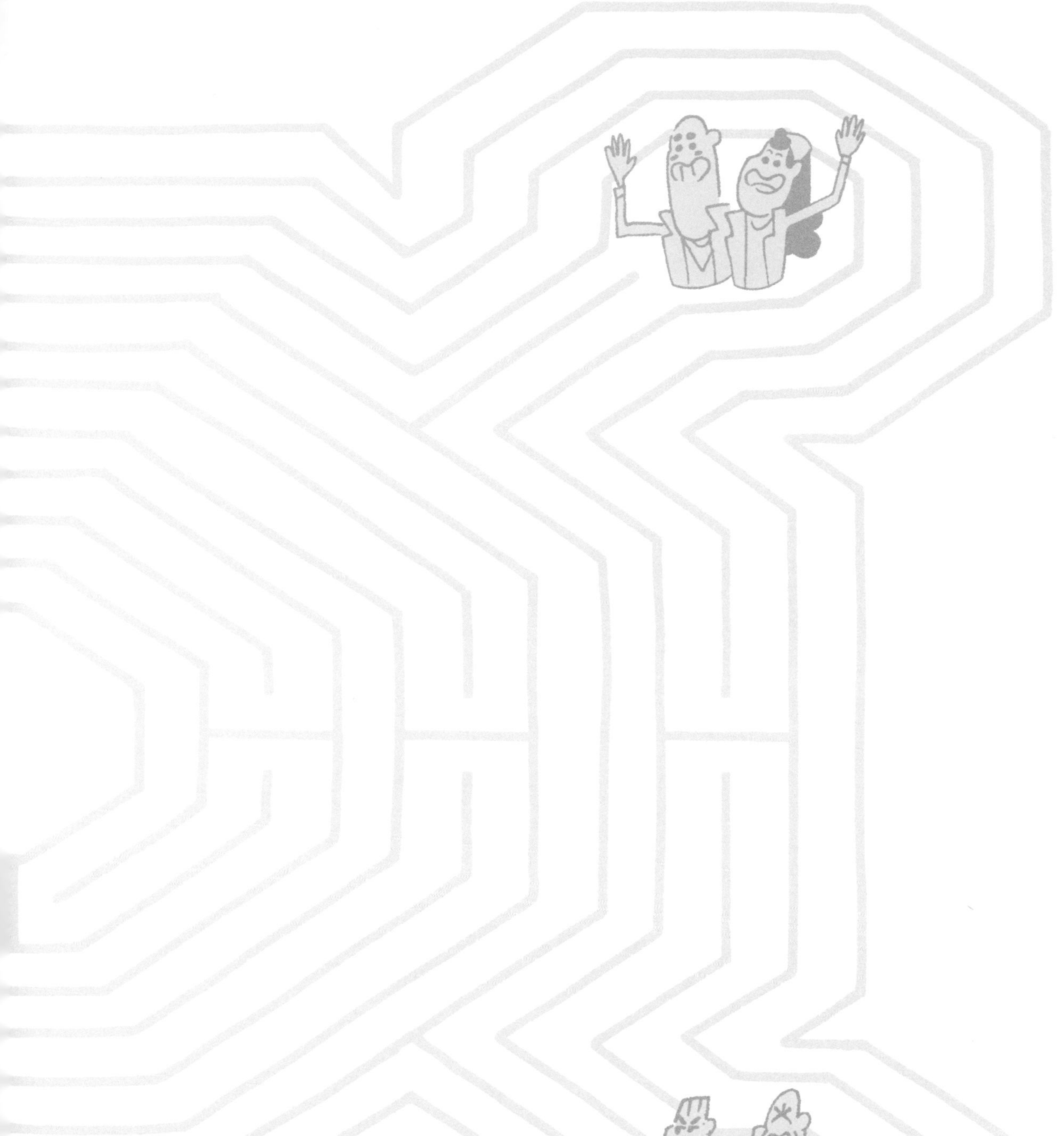

For Miguel, Pedro, Sergio, Unai, Helena, Lucia, Èric, Ana, and Andrea.

— Damián

To my parents, for always helping me when I needed it. To Raquel for helping me every day… and thanks to you, too, Jordi!

— Àlex Fuentes

Thanks to Élise for giving us this opportunity. We felt right at home.

— Damián & Àlex Fuentes

Chapter 1: Nat & Niko

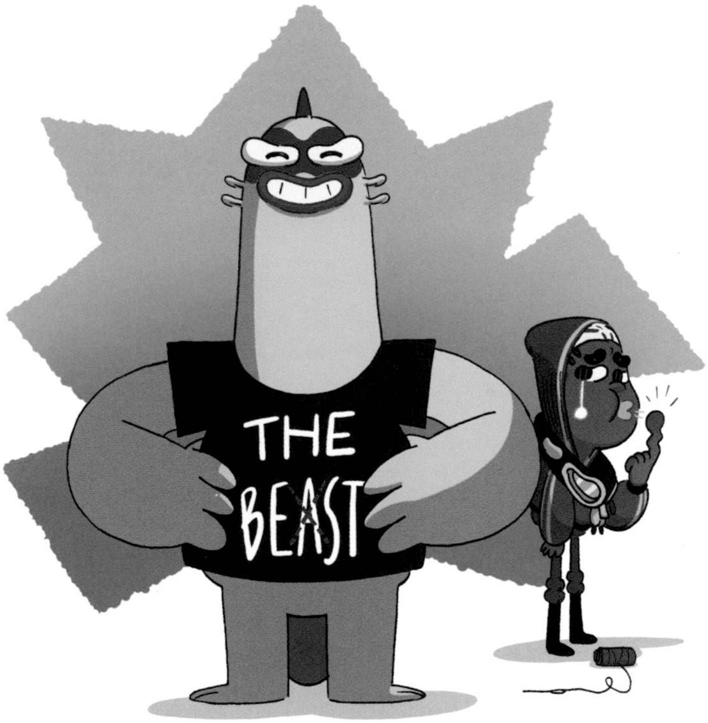
THE
BEAST

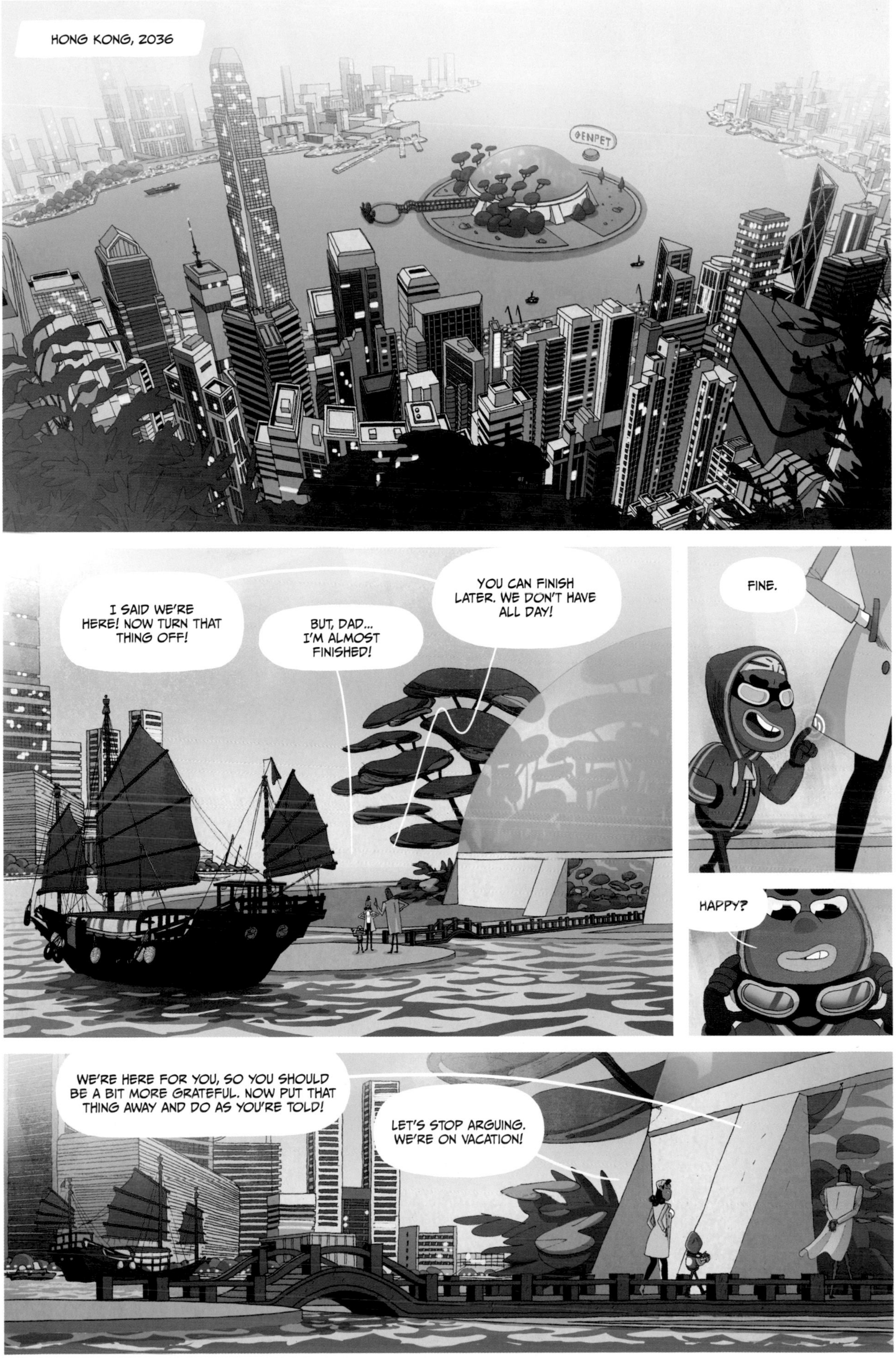
HONG KONG, 2036
GENPET
I SAID WE'RE HERE! NOW TURN THAT THING OFF!
BUT, DAD... I'M ALMOST FINISHED!
YOU CAN FINISH LATER. WE DON'T HAVE ALL DAY!
FINE.
HAPPY?
WE'RE HERE FOR YOU, SO YOU SHOULD BE A BIT MORE GRATEFUL. NOW PUT THAT THING AWAY AND DO AS YOU'RE TOLD!
LET'S STOP ARGUING. WE'RE ON VACATION!

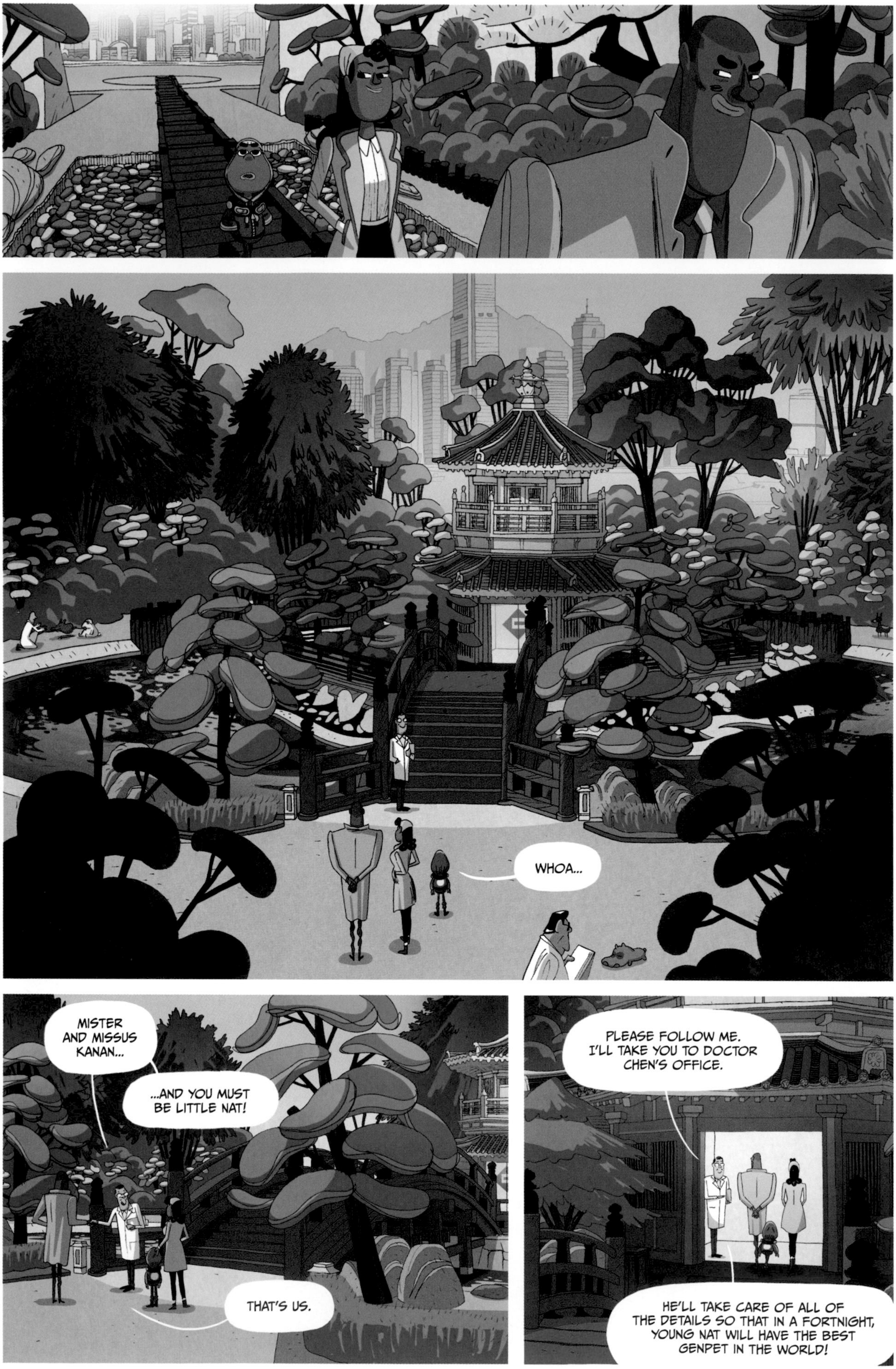
WHOA...
MISTER AND MISSUS KANAN...
...AND YOU MUST BE LITTLE NAT!
THAT'S US.
PLEASE FOLLOW ME. I'LL TAKE YOU TO DOCTOR CHEN'S OFFICE.
HE'LL TAKE CARE OF ALL OF THE DETAILS SO THAT IN A FORTNIGHT, YOUNG NAT WILL HAVE THE BEST GENPET IN THE WORLD!

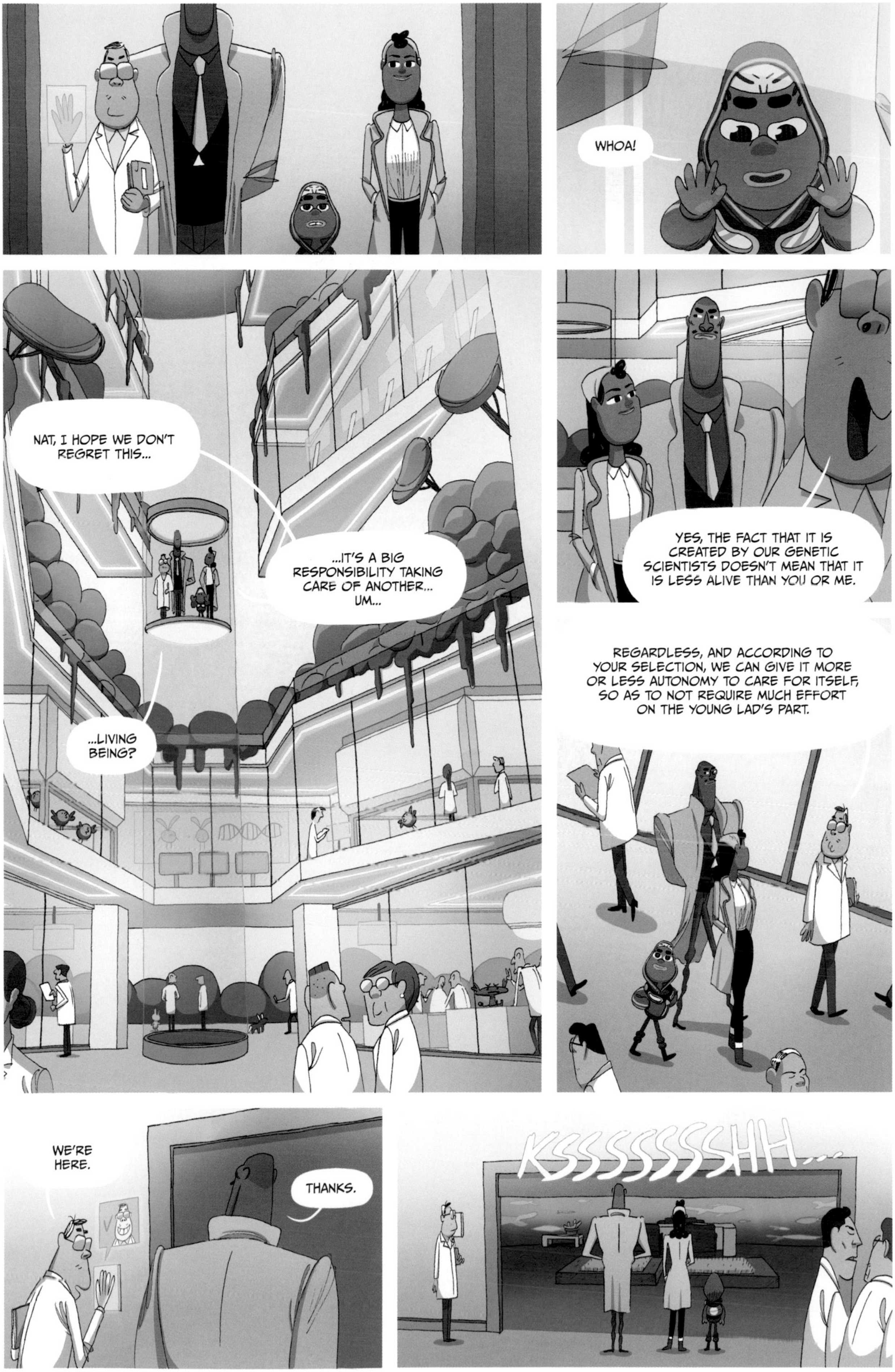

WHOA!
NAT, I HOPE WE DON'T REGRET THIS...
...IT'S A BIG RESPONSIBILITY TAKING CARE OF ANOTHER... UM...
...LIVING BEING?
YES, THE FACT THAT IT IS CREATED BY OUR GENETIC SCIENTISTS DOESN'T MEAN THAT IT IS LESS ALIVE THAN YOU OR ME.
REGARDLESS, AND ACCORDING TO YOUR SELECTION, WE CAN GIVE IT MORE OR LESS AUTONOMY TO CARE FOR ITSELF, SO AS TO NOT REQUIRE MUCH EFFORT ON THE YOUNG LAD'S PART.
WE'RE HERE.
THANKS.
KSSSSSSSHH...

WELCOME!

PLEASE, HAVE A SEAT.

TOO COOL!

AH! THAT'S MESI. TOTALLY HARMLESS BUT UNABLE TO STAND STILL.

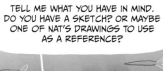

HE WAS ONE OF OUR FIRST TESTS, AND I MUST SAY THAT WE'VE MADE A LOT OF PROGRESS SINCE THEN.

NAT, FOR THE LAST TIME, COME SIT DOWN! YOU'LL HAVE PLENTY OF TIME TO PLAY WITH YOUR OWN GENPET.

IT'S FINE, MRS. KANAN. LET NAT HAVE FUN WHILE WE SETTLE THE LAST BIT OF FORMALITY.

TELL ME WHAT YOU HAVE IN MIND. DO YOU HAVE A SKETCH? OR MAYBE ONE OF NAT'S DRAWINGS TO USE AS A REFERENCE?

A DESIGN?!

YES, SOMETIMES CHILDREN BRING US DRAWINGS THAT OUR DESIGNERS CAN MODEL IN THREE DIMENSIONS.

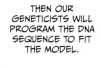

THEN OUR GENETICISTS WILL PROGRAM THE DNA SEQUENCE TO FIT THE MODEL.

WE CAN DO ALMOST ANYTHING HERE WITHOUT THE ABSURD RESTRICTIONS OF YOUR AMERICAN GOVERNMENT.

I IMAGINE THAT'S WHY YOU CAME HERE.

TO BE HONEST, YEAH. BUT WE DIDN'T THINK ABOUT A DESIGN...

YOU SEE, MY SITUATION IS A LITTLE... DELICATE. WE'D LIKE THE GENPET TO ALSO ACT LIKE A... HOW DO I PUT THIS...?

...LIKE A BODYGUARD. IS THAT A PROBLEM?

NATURALLY, OUR GENPETS ARE PROGRAMMED NOT TO HARM THEIR OWNERS.

THAT'S WHY WE'LL NEED A SAMPLE OF YOUR SON'S DNA, TO CREATE A BOND BETWEEN THEM.

YEAH, WE READ THAT IN THE BROCHURE.

WHAT WE'RE LOOKING FOR IS SOMETHING THAT CAN PROTECT HIM IN CASE OF AN... ATTACK.

HMM, THAT IS A BIT TRICKY...

IT WOULD REQUIRE CERTAIN PHYSICAL CHARACTERISTICS THAT COULD LEAD TO UNPREDICTABLE SCENARIOS...

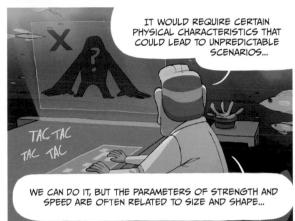

TAC-TAC TAC TAC

WE CAN DO IT, BUT THE PARAMETERS OF STRENGTH AND SPEED ARE OFTEN RELATED TO SIZE AND SHAPE...

THIS COULD RESTRICT HIS APPEARANCE OPTIONS. BUT WE CAN ALWAYS LOOK FOR INSPIRATION IN THE ANIMAL KINGDOM TO EQUIP OUR CREATION WITH THE CAPABILITIES YOU ARE LOOKING FOR.

AS FAR AS I'M CONCERNED, THE ONLY RULE IS: NO FUR!

PLEASE, SWEETIE.

WE DISCUSSED THIS. I THOUGHT WE WERE IN AGREEMENT ON THAT...

YOU CAN LEAVE THE DETAILS TO THE DESIGNERS IF YOU'D LIKE. I'LL TAKE YOU TO THE LABORATORY WHERE WE CAN COLLECT NAT'S DNA SAMPLE.

ONCE FINISHED, THEY'LL LET YOU KNOW WHAT DAY YOU CAN PICK UP YOUR NEW GENPET. HAVE YOU SELECTED A NAME YET?

WE'LL CALL HIM NIKO!

RIS RIS RIS

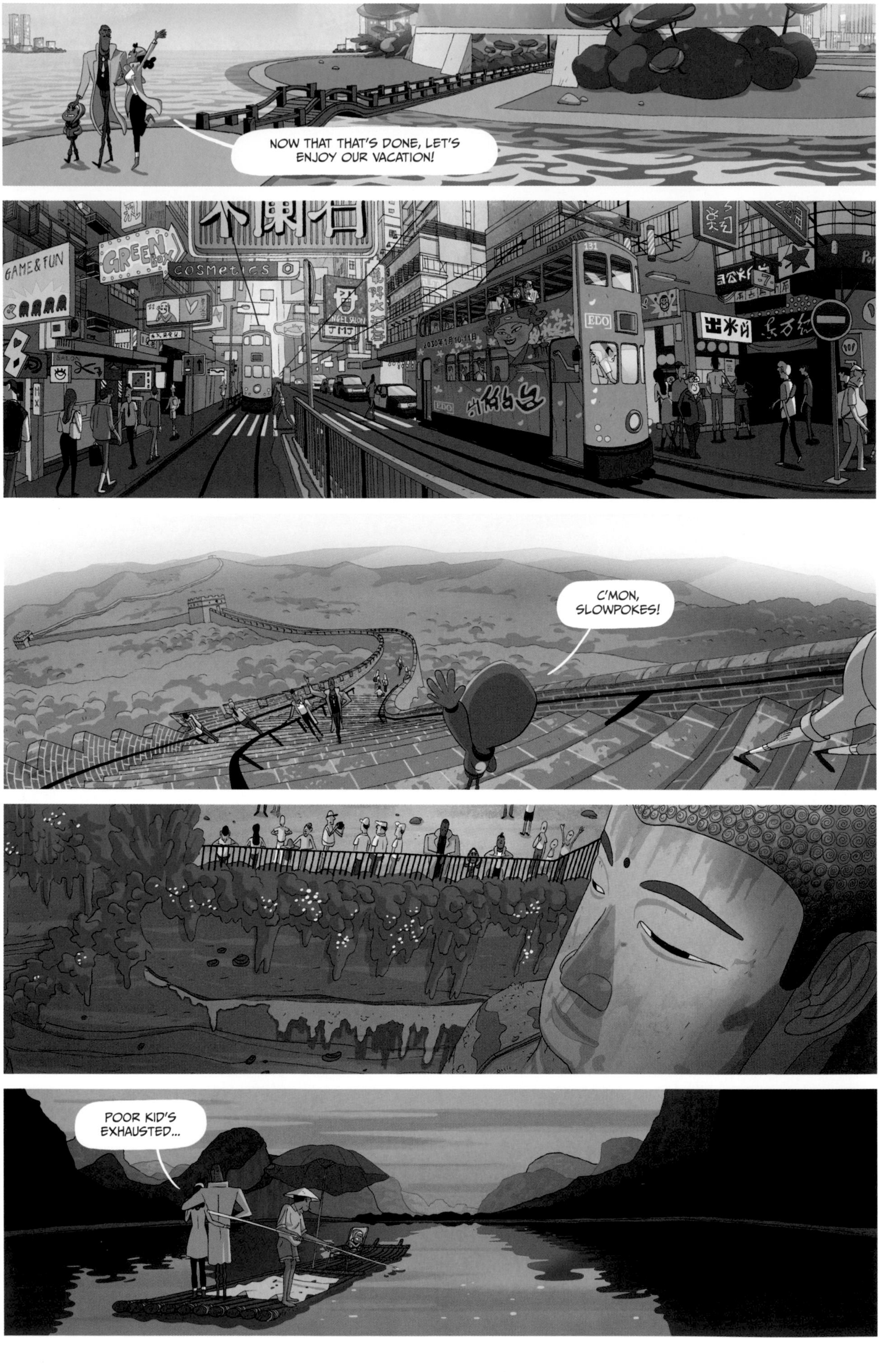
NOW THAT THAT'S DONE, LET'S ENJOY OUR VACATION!
GAME&FUN
GREEN BOX
COSMETICS
EDO
C'MON, SLOWPOKES!
POOR KID'S EXHAUSTED...

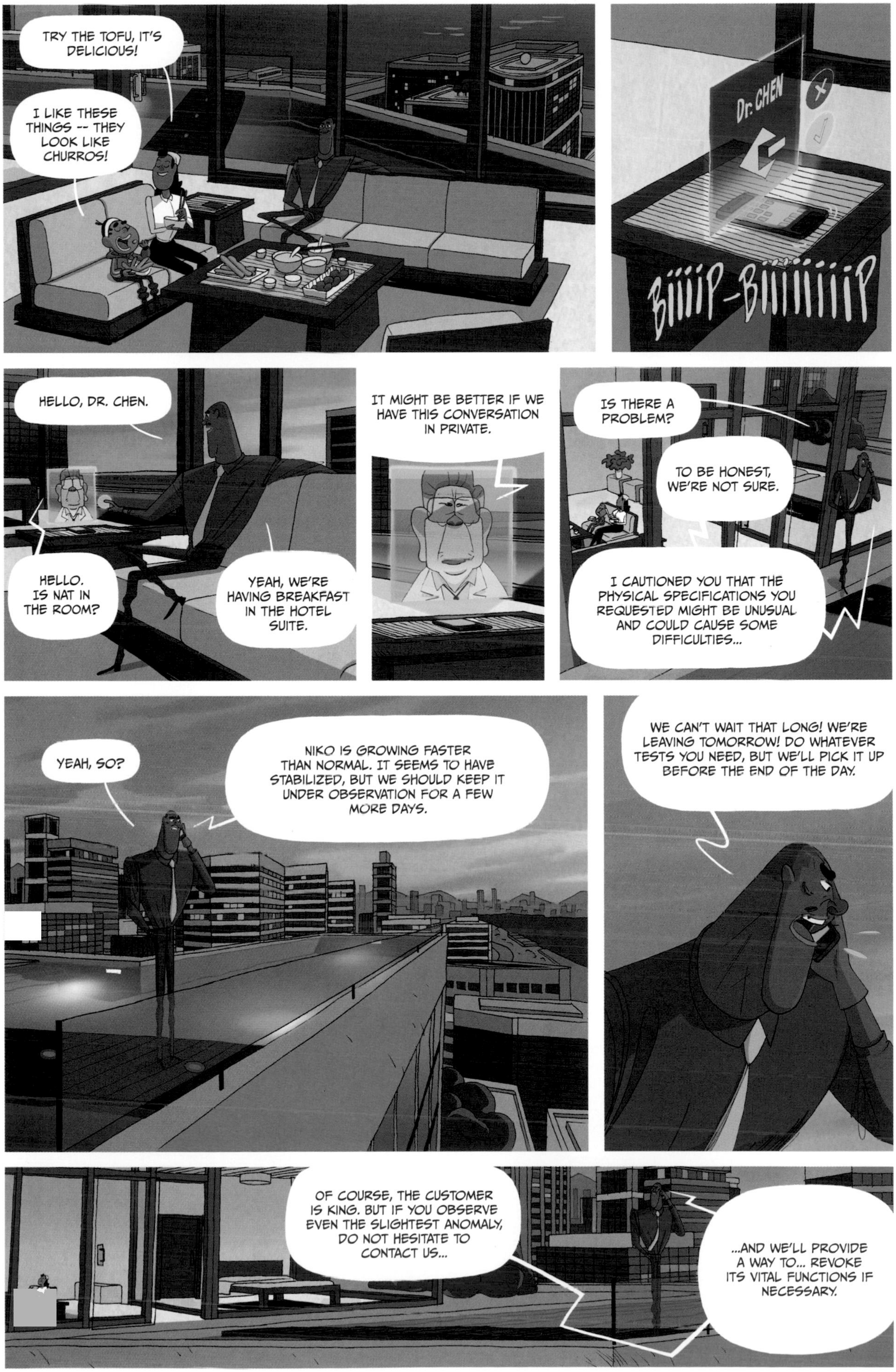
TRY THE TOFU, IT'S DELICIOUS!
I LIKE THESE THINGS -- THEY LOOK LIKE CHURROS!
Dr. CHEN
BiiiiP-BiiiiiiiiP
HELLO, DR. CHEN.
HELLO. IS NAT IN THE ROOM?
YEAH, WE'RE HAVING BREAKFAST IN THE HOTEL SUITE.
IT MIGHT BE BETTER IF WE HAVE THIS CONVERSATION IN PRIVATE.
IS THERE A PROBLEM?
TO BE HONEST, WE'RE NOT SURE.
I CAUTIONED YOU THAT THE PHYSICAL SPECIFICATIONS YOU REQUESTED MIGHT BE UNUSUAL AND COULD CAUSE SOME DIFFICULTIES...
YEAH, SO?
NIKO IS GROWING FASTER THAN NORMAL. IT SEEMS TO HAVE STABILIZED, BUT WE SHOULD KEEP IT UNDER OBSERVATION FOR A FEW MORE DAYS.
WE CAN'T WAIT THAT LONG! WE'RE LEAVING TOMORROW! DO WHATEVER TESTS YOU NEED, BUT WE'LL PICK IT UP BEFORE THE END OF THE DAY.
OF COURSE, THE CUSTOMER IS KING. BUT IF YOU OBSERVE EVEN THE SLIGHTEST ANOMALY, DO NOT HESITATE TO CONTACT US...
...AND WE'LL PROVIDE A WAY TO... REVOKE ITS VITAL FUNCTIONS IF NECESSARY.

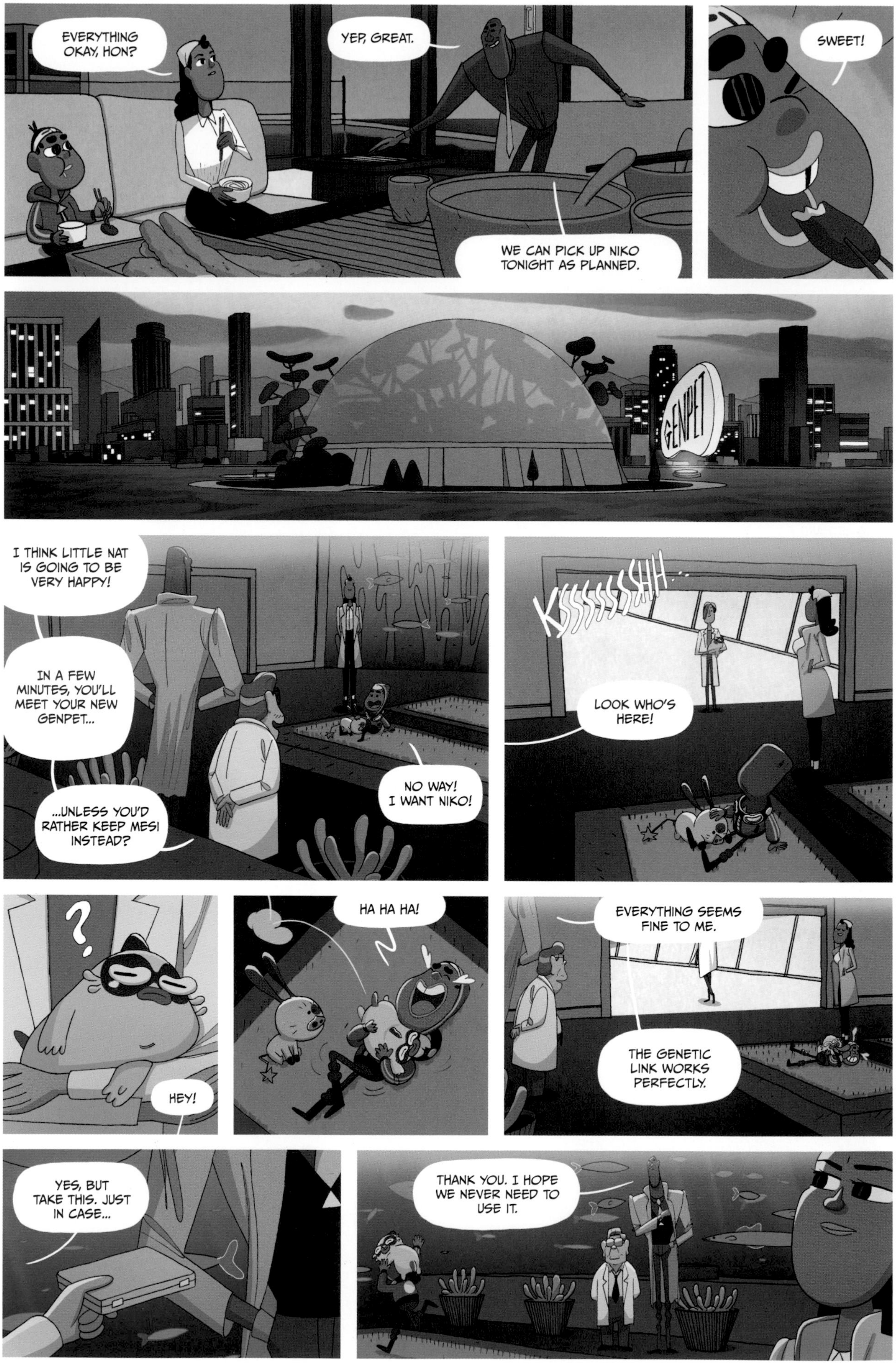
EVERYTHING OKAY, HON?
YEP, GREAT.
WE CAN PICK UP NIKO TONIGHT AS PLANNED.
SWEET!
GENPET
I THINK LITTLE NAT IS GOING TO BE VERY HAPPY!
IN A FEW MINUTES, YOU'LL MEET YOUR NEW GENPET...
...UNLESS YOU'D RATHER KEEP MESI INSTEAD?
NO WAY! I WANT NIKO!
KSSSSSSSHH...
LOOK WHO'S HERE!
?
HEY!
HA HA HA!
EVERYTHING SEEMS FINE TO ME.
THE GENETIC LINK WORKS PERFECTLY.
YES, BUT TAKE THIS. JUST IN CASE...
THANK YOU. I HOPE WE NEVER NEED TO USE IT.

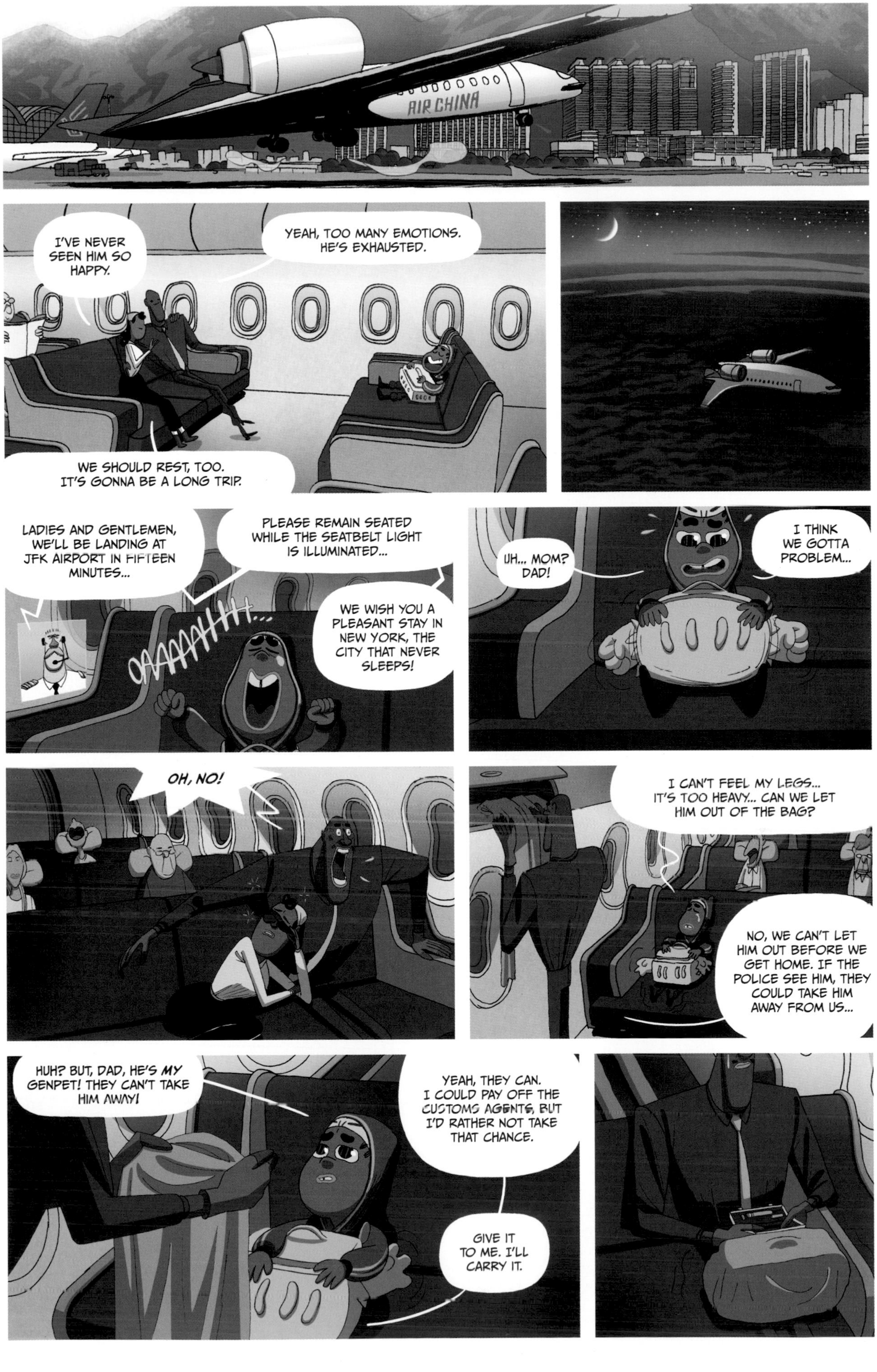
AIR CHINA
I'VE NEVER SEEN HIM SO HAPPY.
YEAH, TOO MANY EMOTIONS. HE'S EXHAUSTED.
WE SHOULD REST, TOO. IT'S GONNA BE A LONG TRIP.
LADIES AND GENTLEMEN, WE'LL BE LANDING AT JFK AIRPORT IN FIFTEEN MINUTES...
PLEASE REMAIN SEATED WHILE THE SEATBELT LIGHT IS ILLUMINATED...
WE WISH YOU A PLEASANT STAY IN NEW YORK, THE CITY THAT NEVER SLEEPS!
OAAAAAHHH...
UH... MOM? DAD!
I THINK WE GOTTA PROBLEM...
OH, NO!
I CAN'T FEEL MY LEGS... IT'S TOO HEAVY... CAN WE LET HIM OUT OF THE BAG?
NO, WE CAN'T LET HIM OUT BEFORE WE GET HOME. IF THE POLICE SEE HIM, THEY COULD TAKE HIM AWAY FROM US...
HUH? BUT, DAD, HE'S MY GENPET! THEY CAN'T TAKE HIM AWAY!
YEAH, THEY CAN. I COULD PAY OFF THE CUSTOMS AGENTS, BUT I'D RATHER NOT TAKE THAT CHANCE.
GIVE IT TO ME. I'LL CARRY IT.

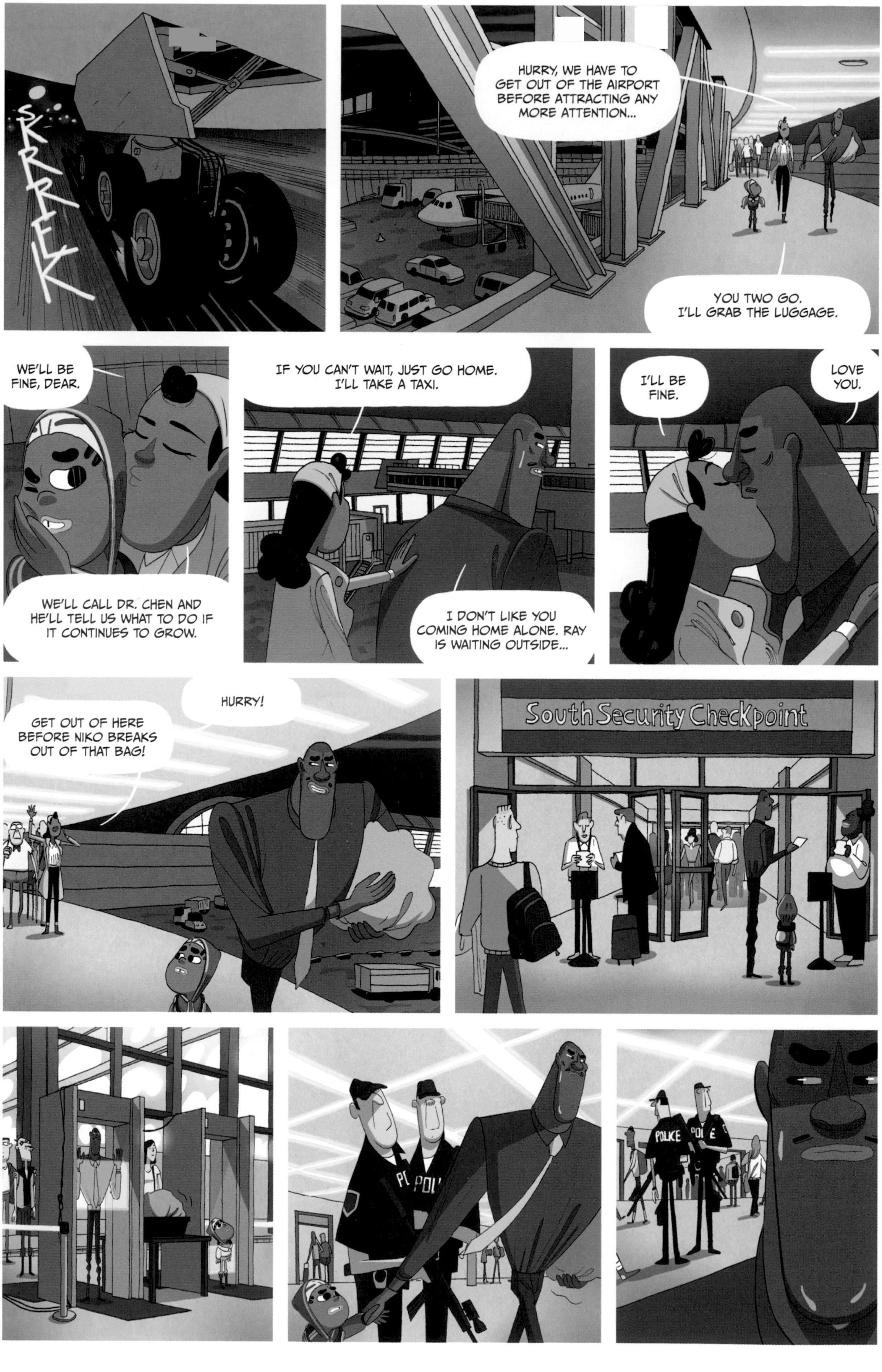
SKRREEK
HURRY, WE HAVE TO GET OUT OF THE AIRPORT BEFORE ATTRACTING ANY MORE ATTENTION...
YOU TWO GO. I'LL GRAB THE LUGGAGE.
WE'LL BE FINE, DEAR.
WE'LL CALL DR. CHEN AND HE'LL TELL US WHAT TO DO IF IT CONTINUES TO GROW.
IF YOU CAN'T WAIT, JUST GO HOME. I'LL TAKE A TAXI.
I DON'T LIKE YOU COMING HOME ALONE. RAY IS WAITING OUTSIDE...
I'LL BE FINE.
LOVE YOU.
GET OUT OF HERE BEFORE NIKO BREAKS OUT OF THAT BAG!
HURRY!
South Security Checkpoint
POLICE
POLICE

MADE IT. THERE'S RAY!

HURRY, OPEN THE DOOR! YOU DON'T KNOW WHAT KINDA TROUBLE THIS GENPET COULD BRING US...

THAT'S THE THING WIGGLING AROUND IN YOUR JACKET?!

I THOUGHT YOU WERE BRINGING BACK SOMETHING SMALLER...

THAT WAS THE IDEA.

NAT, GET IN THE CAR AND GET OUT OF HERE BEFORE HE GETS LOSE.

'KAY, DAD.

THEY WARNED ME THAT SOMETHING LIKE THIS COULD HAPPEN... SO THEY GAVE ME THIS, IN CASE IT GETS TOO BIG...

...BUT HE'LL PROBABLY STOP GROWING PRETTY SOON.

FINGERS CROSSED! I DON'T WANT HIM TEARING UP THE INSIDE OF MY CAR!

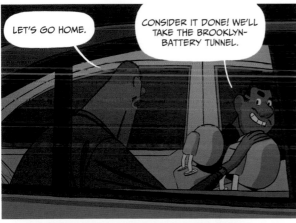

LET'S GO HOME.

CONSIDER IT DONE! WE'LL TAKE THE BROOKLYN-BATTERY TUNNEL.

IT'S THEM. MOVE IT.

NO, STOP! CUT IT OUT!

LET'S HOPE HE DOES MORE THAN SOME SLOBBERY DOG...

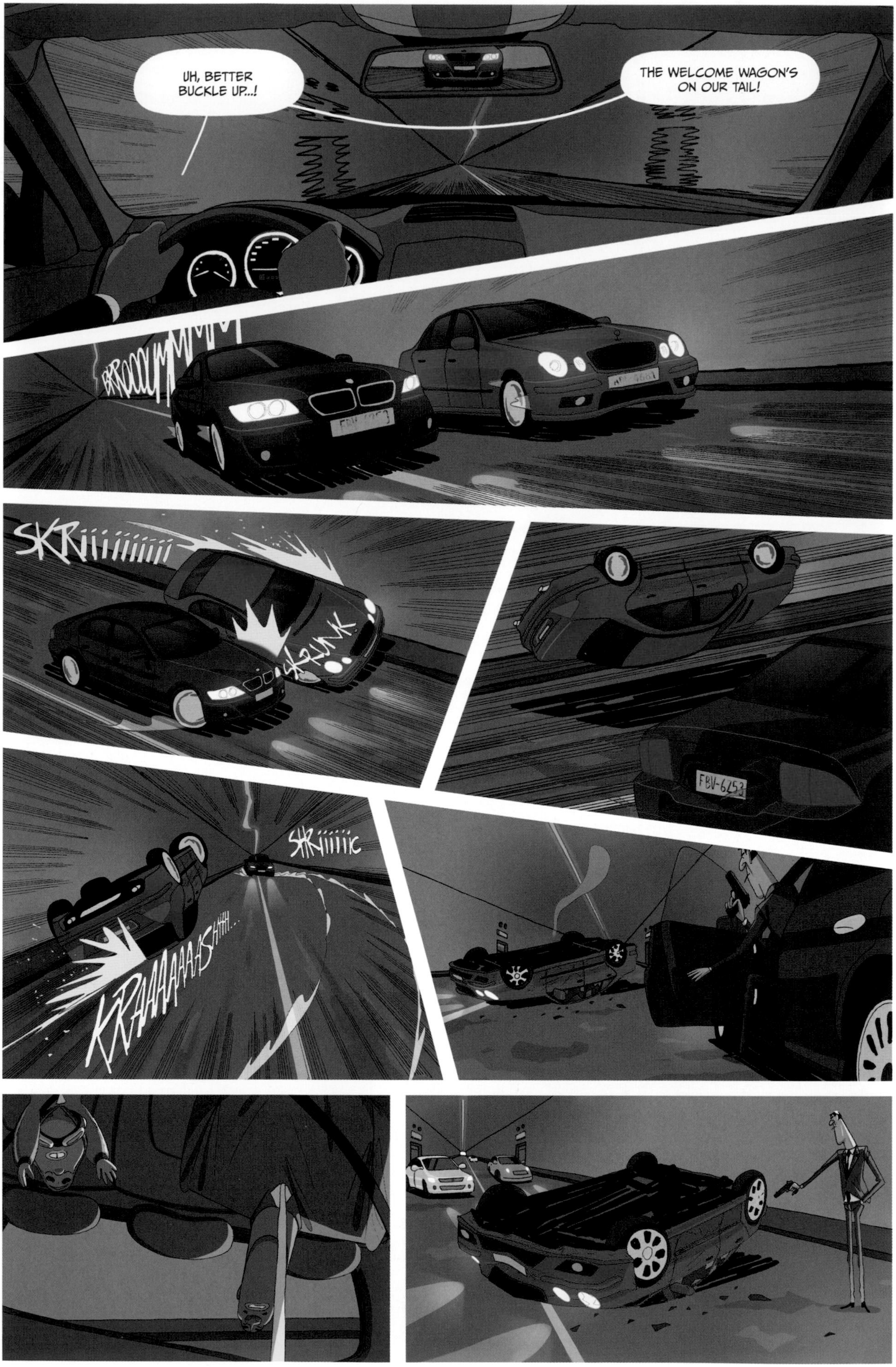
UH, BETTER BUCKLE UP...!
THE WELCOME WAGON'S ON OUR TAIL!

GROOARG
WHAT THE...?!
BLAM BLAM
AAAAAH!
WHAT HAPPENED?
THEY GOT GREG!
THIS JUST GOT MORE COMPLICATED...
NAT! RUN!
ROB... I'M STUCK! AND THERE'S TWO MORE GETTING OUT OF THE CAR!
NAT! TAKE THIS! IT'S FOR NIKO...
BLAM BLAM BLAM
RUN, NAT, RUN!
BLAM

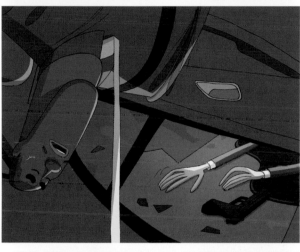

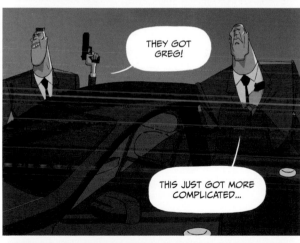

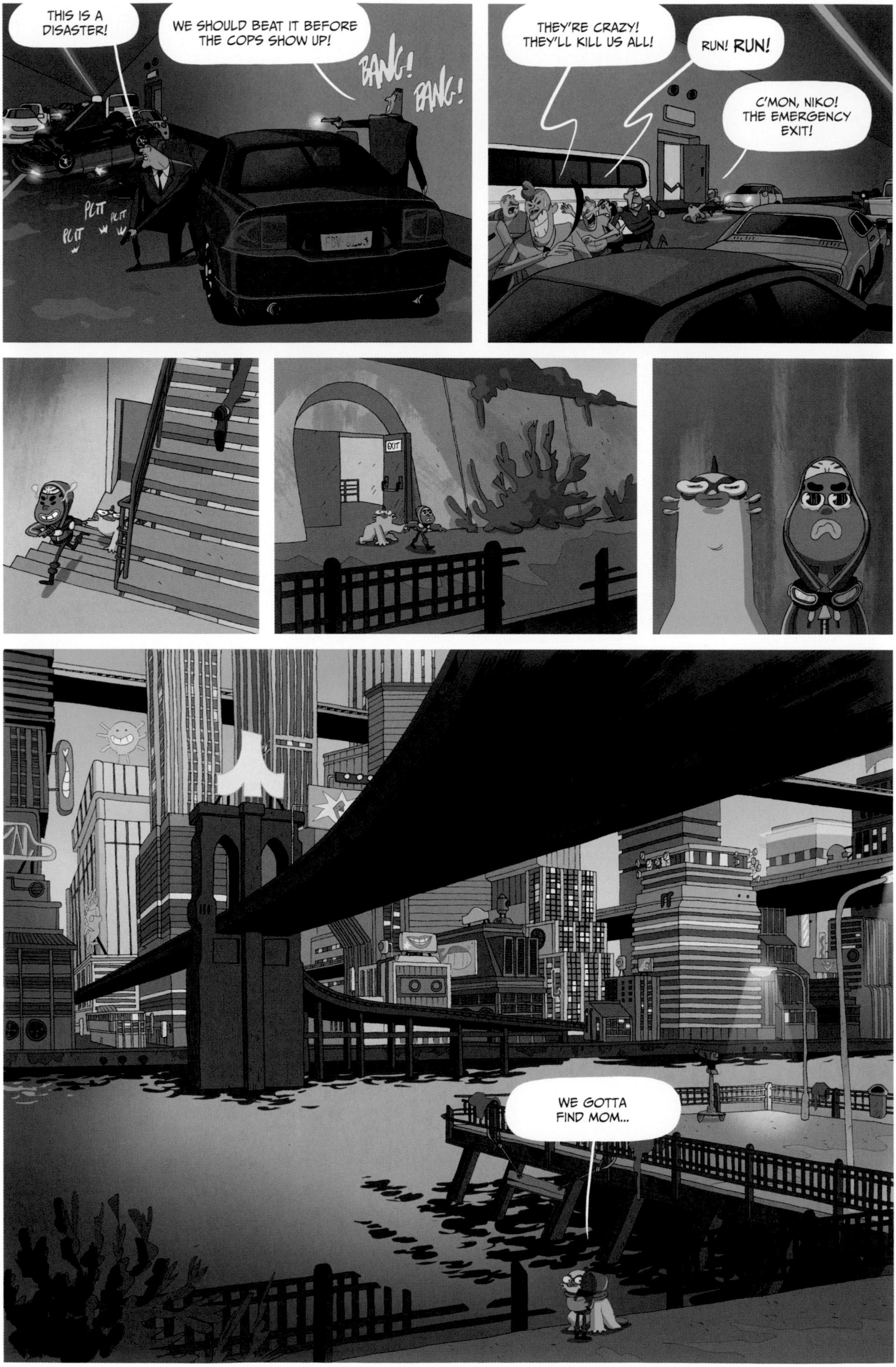
THIS IS A DISASTER!
WE SHOULD BEAT IT BEFORE THE COPS SHOW UP!
BANG!
BANG!
THEY'RE CRAZY! THEY'LL KILL US ALL!
RUN! RUN!
C'MON, NIKO! THE EMERGENCY EXIT!
EXIT
WE GOTTA FIND MOM...

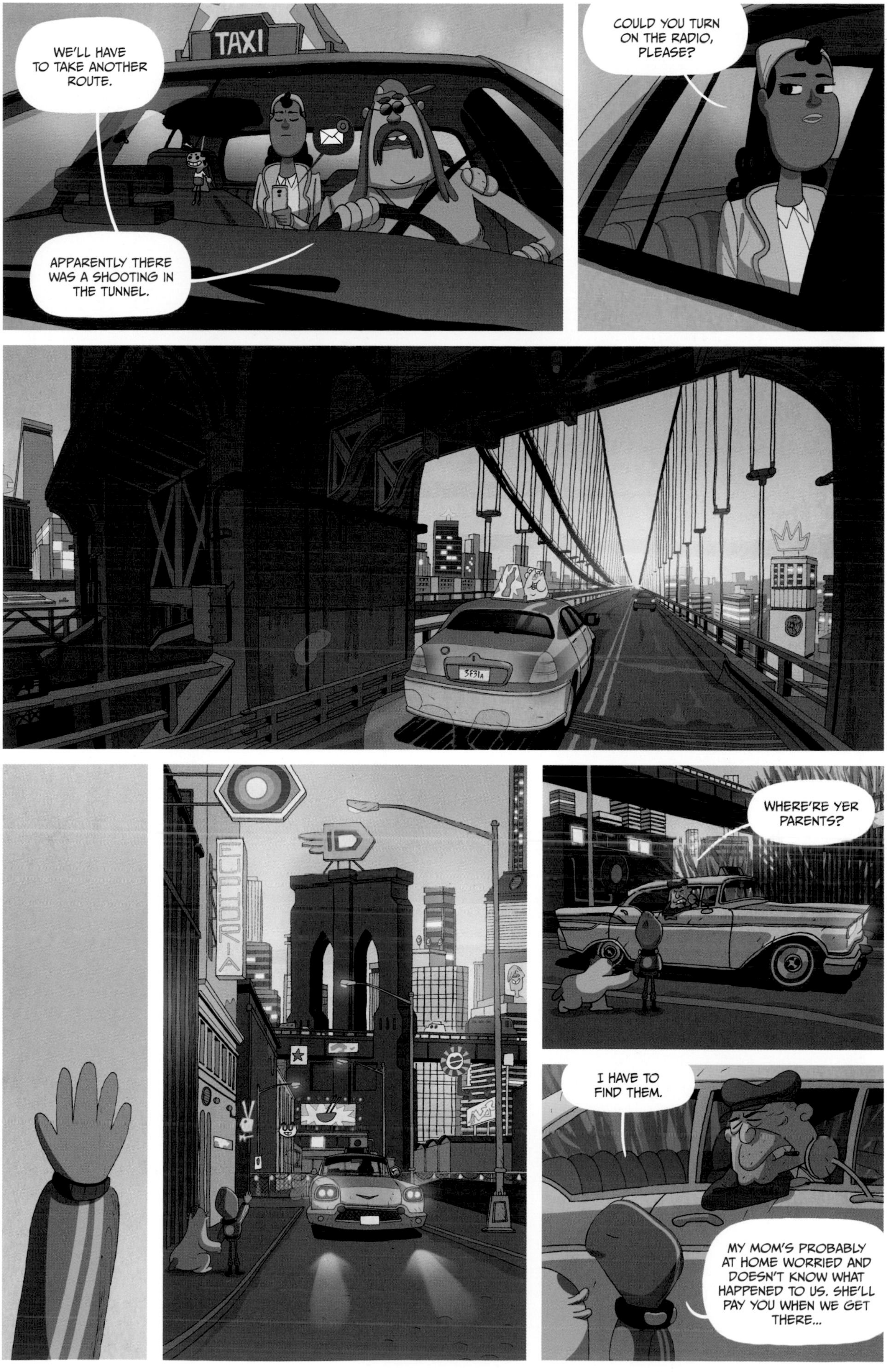
TAXI
WE'LL HAVE TO TAKE ANOTHER ROUTE.
APPARENTLY THERE WAS A SHOOTING IN THE TUNNEL.
COULD YOU TURN ON THE RADIO, PLEASE?
WHERE'RE YER PARENTS?
I HAVE TO FIND THEM.
MY MOM'S PROBABLY AT HOME WORRIED AND DOESN'T KNOW WHAT HAPPENED TO US. SHE'LL PAY YOU WHEN WE GET THERE...

YOU AIN'T GOT ANY MONEY?

NO... BUT YOU'LL SEE... MY DAD'S THE NEW PRESIDENT OF THE NEW YORK KNICKS.

WHEN WE GET HOME, HE'LL PAY YOU AND MAYBE EVEN GIVE YOU A REWARD FOR HELPING ME...

...OR COURTSIDE TICKETS...

YEAH, THAT AIN'T GONNA WORK ON ME.

YOU CAN TELL YOUR PALS OVER THERE I'M GONNA RADIO IN THAT YOU'RE CRUSIN' THIS BLOCK.

BUT... BUT...

YO, CUZ... A GIANT STUFFED ANIMAL!

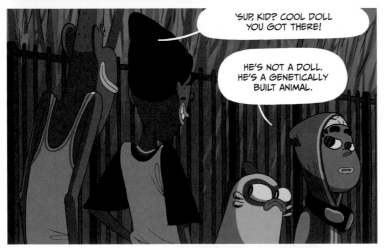

'SUP, KID? COOL DOLL YOU GOT THERE!

HE'S NOT A DOLL. HE'S A GENETICALLY BUILT ANIMAL.

WHOA! A GENETICALLY BUILT ANIMAL?!

WOW!

MUST BE EXPENSIVE, HUH? KIND OF A BIG DEAL?

I DUNNO. MY DAD BOUGHT HIM FOR ME IN CHINA.

AND AS SOON AS WE GOT BACK, WE WERE ATTACKED BY SOME GANGSTERS IN THE TUNNEL, AND OUR CAR ROLLED OVER, SO WE RAN, AND NOW I DON'T EVEN KNOW IF MY DAD'S OKAY...

SURE, KID. YOU GOT ANY PROOF? I'DA LIKED TO SEE THAT!

AH, GO EASY ON HIM.

MY NAME'S CHUCK, AND THIS HERE'S DRAYTON.

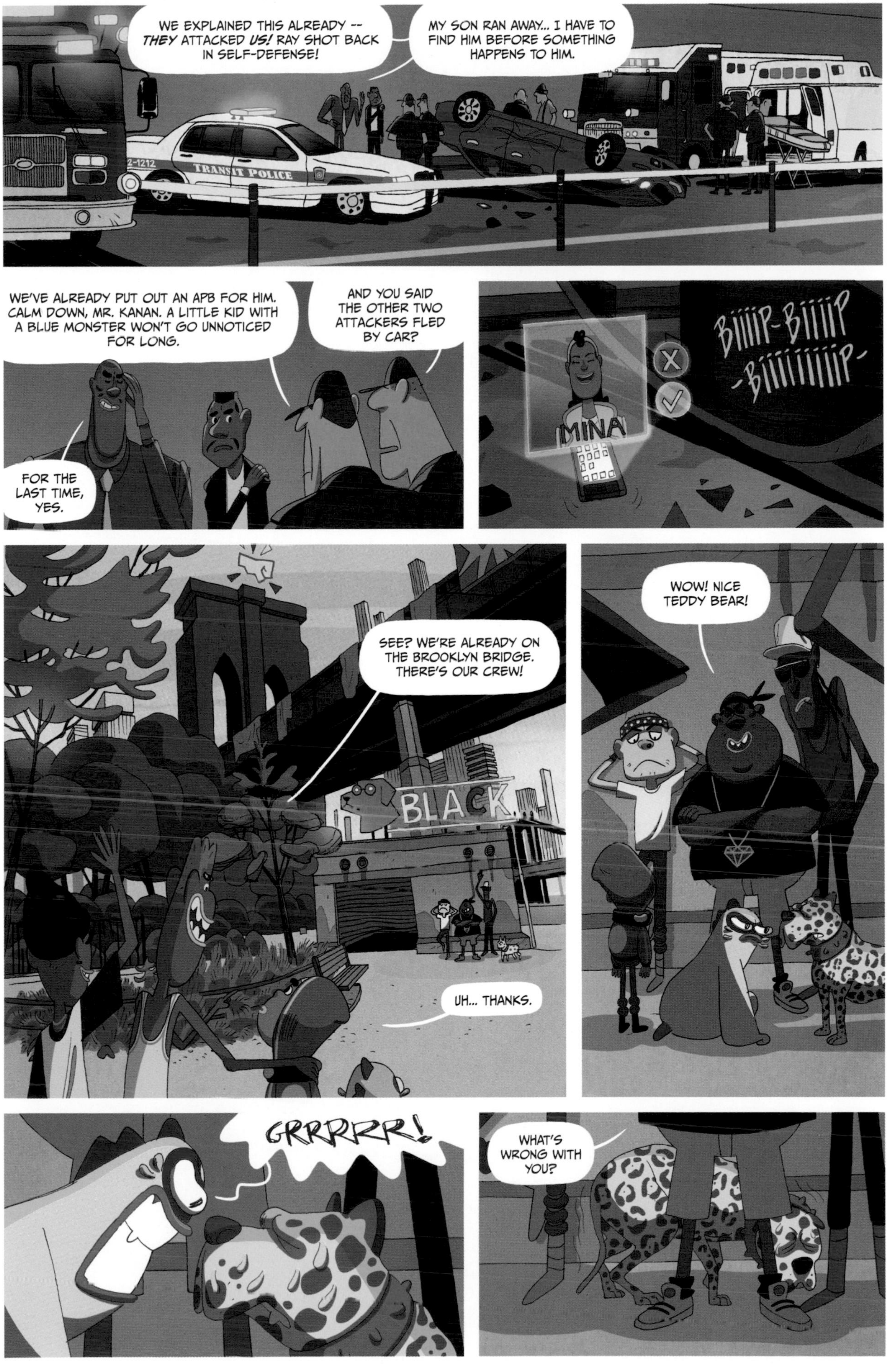
WE EXPLAINED THIS ALREADY -- *THEY* ATTACKED *US!* RAY SHOT BACK IN SELF-DEFENSE!
MY SON RAN AWAY... I HAVE TO FIND HIM BEFORE SOMETHING HAPPENS TO HIM.
TRANSIT POLICE
WE'VE ALREADY PUT OUT AN APB FOR HIM. CALM DOWN, MR. KANAN. A LITTLE KID WITH A BLUE MONSTER WON'T GO UNNOTICED FOR LONG.
AND YOU SAID THE OTHER TWO ATTACKERS FLED BY CAR?
FOR THE LAST TIME, YES.
BIIIIP-BIIIIP -BIIIIIIIIIP-
MINA
SEE? WE'RE ALREADY ON THE BROOKLYN BRIDGE. THERE'S OUR CREW!
BLACK
UH... THANKS.
WOW! NICE TEDDY BEAR!
GRRRRR!
WHAT'S WRONG WITH YOU?

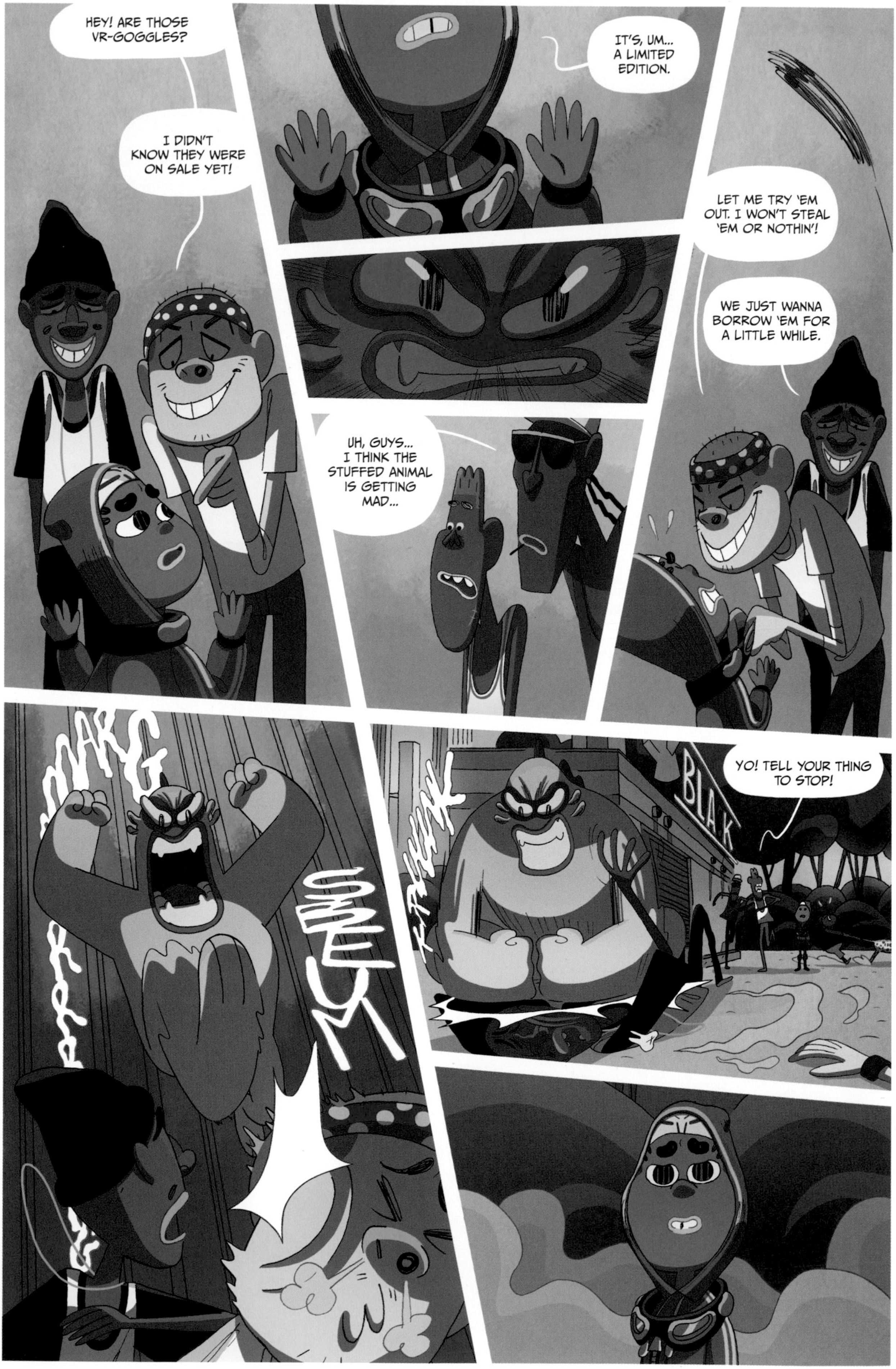
HEY! ARE THOSE VR-GOGGLES?
I DIDN'T KNOW THEY WERE ON SALE YET!
IT'S, UM... A LIMITED EDITION.
LET ME TRY 'EM OUT. I WON'T STEAL 'EM OR NOTHIN'!
WE JUST WANNA BORROW 'EM FOR A LITTLE WHILE.
UH, GUYS... I THINK THE STUFFED ANIMAL IS GETTING MAD...
YO! TELL YOUR THING TO STOP!

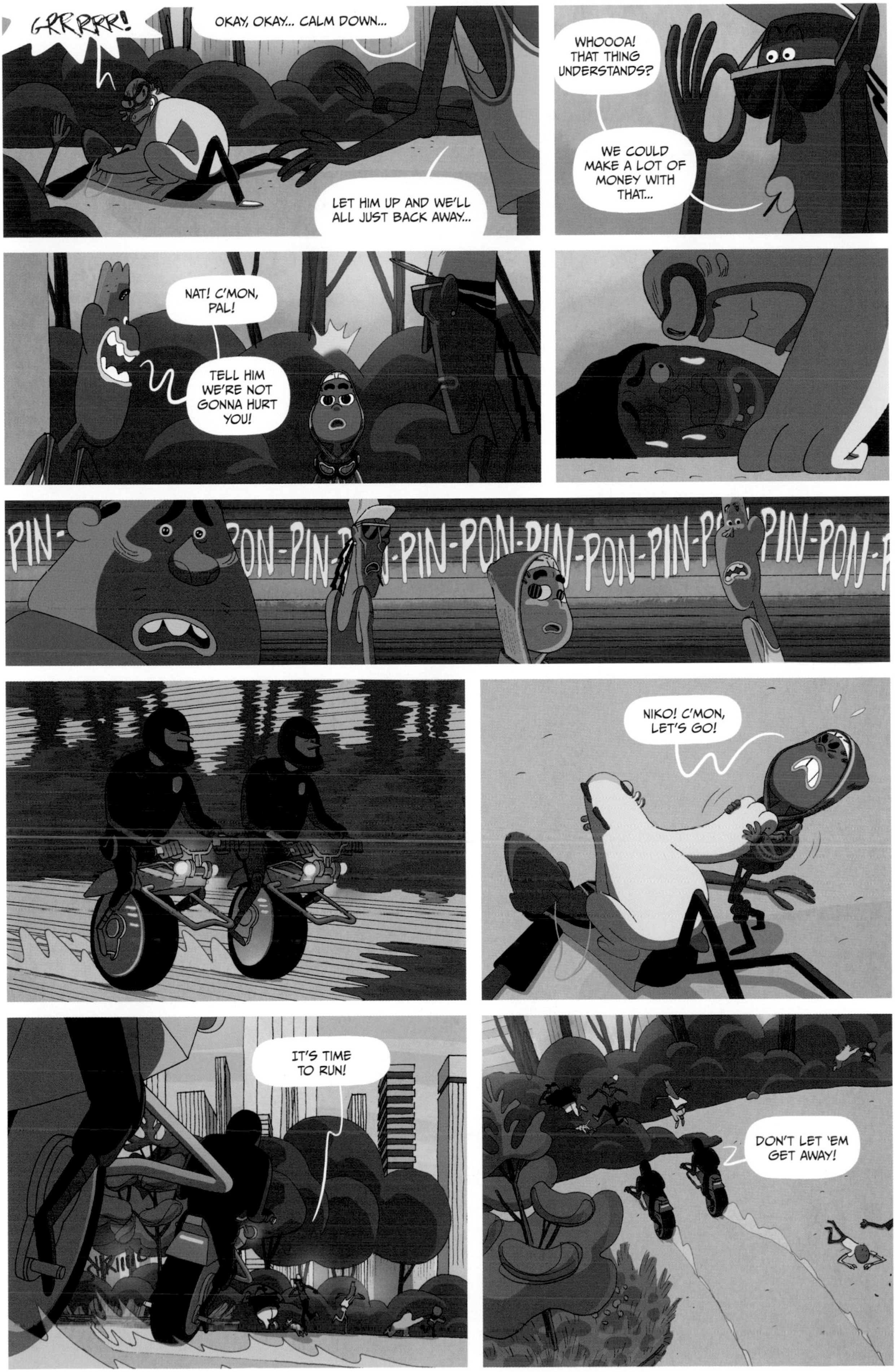
GRRRRR!
OKAY, OKAY... CALM DOWN...
LET HIM UP AND WE'LL ALL JUST BACK AWAY...
WHOOOA! THAT THING UNDERSTANDS?
WE COULD MAKE A LOT OF MONEY WITH THAT...
NAT! C'MON, PAL!
TELL HIM WE'RE NOT GONNA HURT YOU!
PIN-PON-PIN-PON-PIN-PON-PIN-PON-PIN-PON-PIN-PON
NIKO! C'MON, LET'S GO!
IT'S TIME TO RUN!
DON'T LET 'EM GET AWAY!

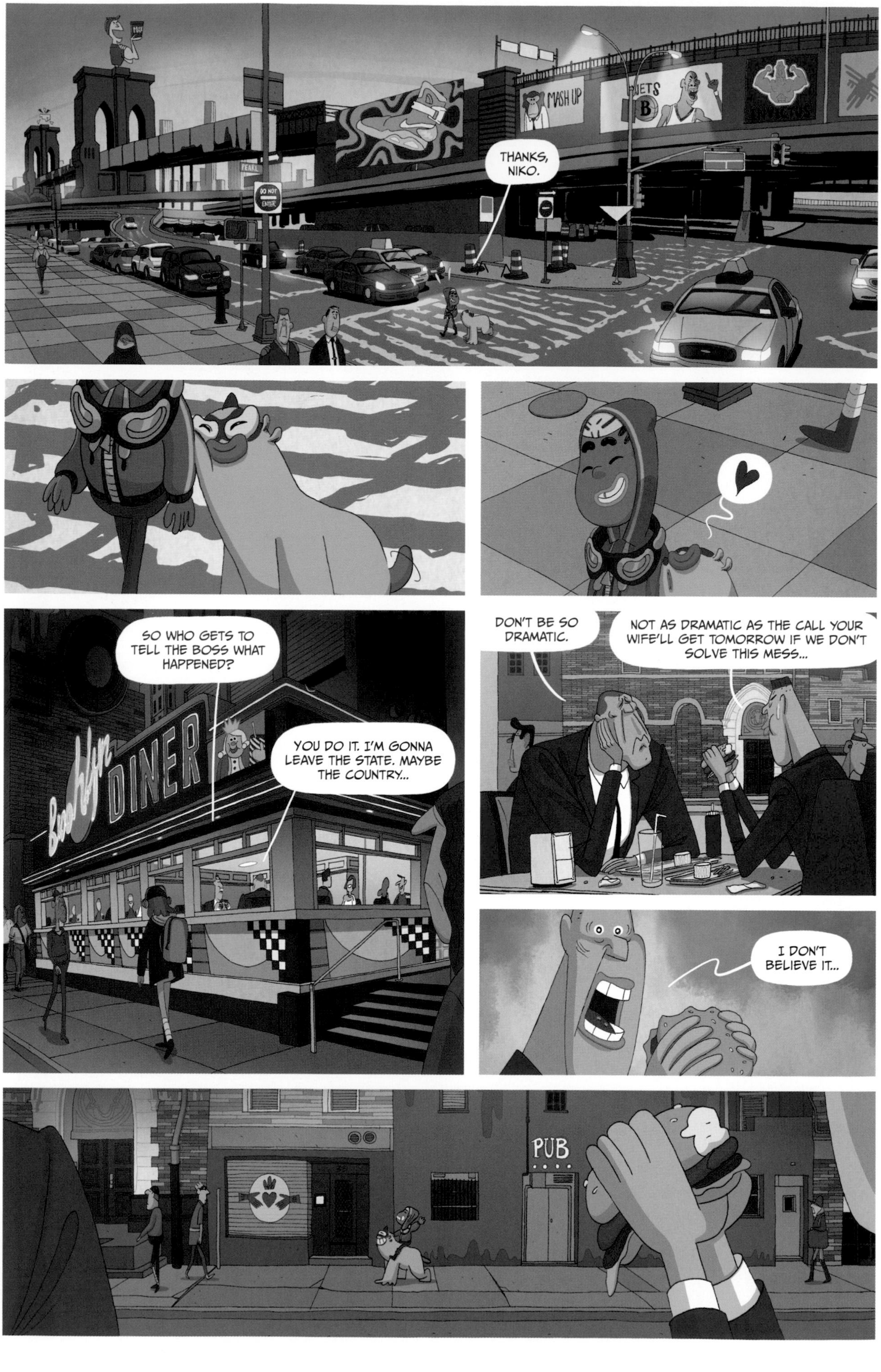
MASH UP
JETS
PEARL
DO NOT ENTER
THANKS, NIKO.
SO WHO GETS TO TELL THE BOSS WHAT HAPPENED?
YOU DO IT. I'M GONNA LEAVE THE STATE. MAYBE THE COUNTRY...
DINER
DON'T BE SO DRAMATIC.
NOT AS DRAMATIC AS THE CALL YOUR WIFE'LL GET TOMORROW IF WE DON'T SOLVE THIS MESS...
I DON'T BELIEVE IT...
PUB

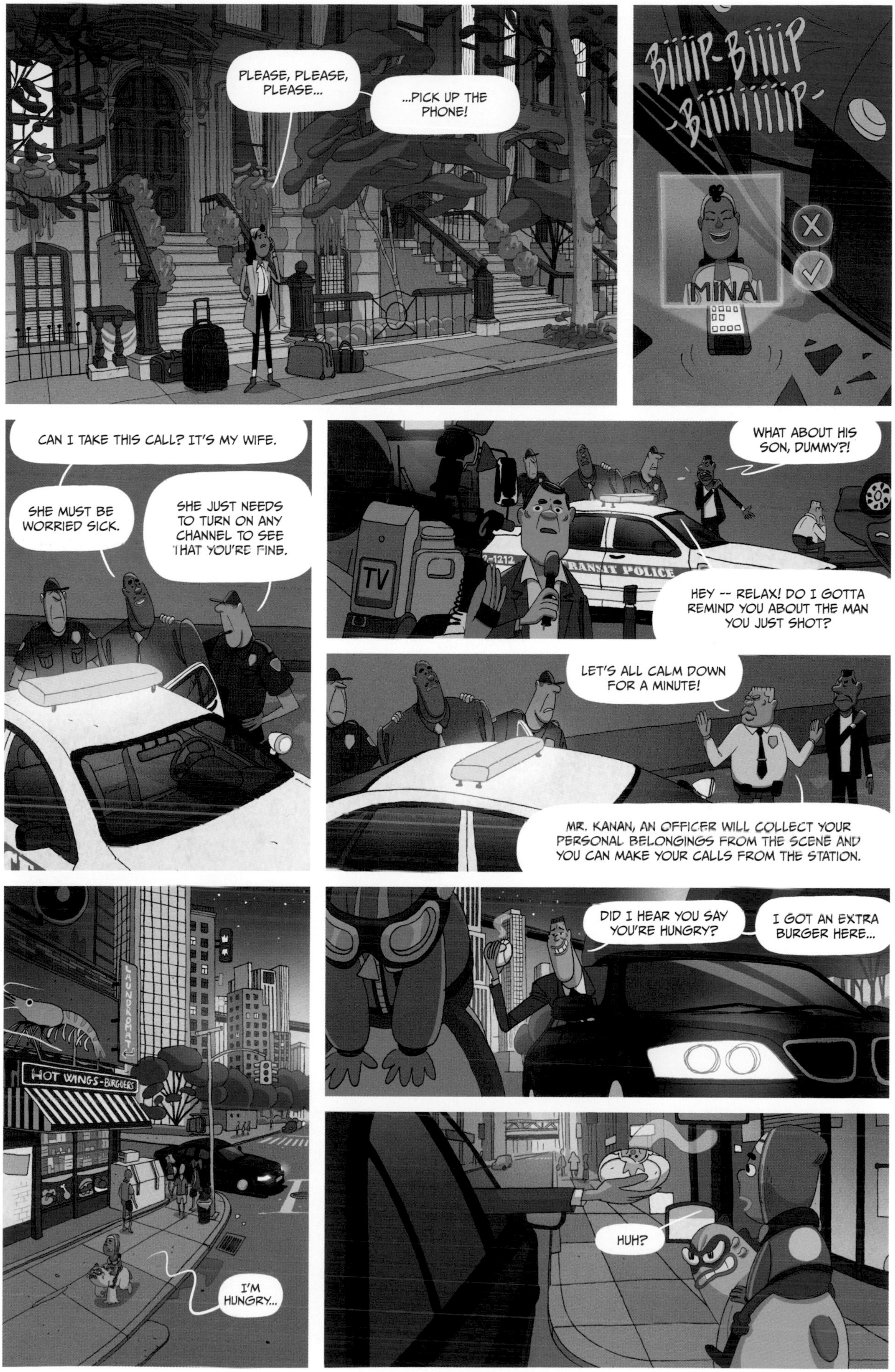
PLEASE, PLEASE, PLEASE...
...PICK UP THE PHONE!
BIIIIP-BIIIIP-BIIIIIIIP-
MINA
CAN I TAKE THIS CALL? IT'S MY WIFE.
SHE MUST BE WORRIED SICK.
SHE JUST NEEDS TO TURN ON ANY CHANNEL TO SEE THAT YOU'RE FINE.
TV
TRANSIT POLICE
WHAT ABOUT HIS SON, DUMMY?!
HEY -- RELAX! DO I GOTTA REMIND YOU ABOUT THE MAN YOU JUST SHOT?
LET'S ALL CALM DOWN FOR A MINUTE!
MR. KANAN, AN OFFICER WILL COLLECT YOUR PERSONAL BELONGINGS FROM THE SCENE AND YOU CAN MAKE YOUR CALLS FROM THE STATION.
LAUNDROMAT
HOT WINGS-BURGUERS
I'M HUNGRY...
DID I HEAR YOU SAY YOU'RE HUNGRY?
I GOT AN EXTRA BURGER HERE...
HUH?

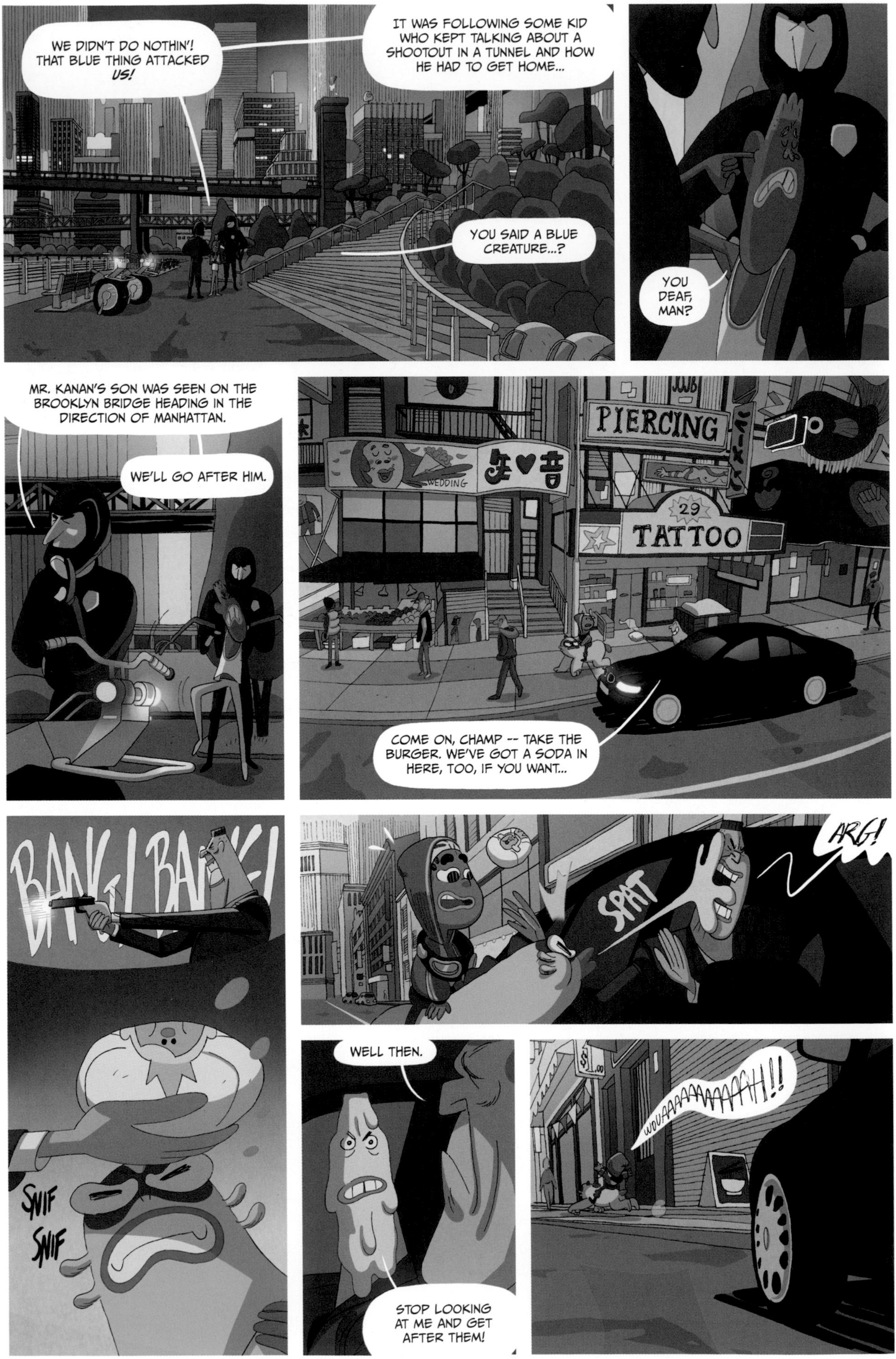
WE DIDN'T DO NOTHIN'! THAT BLUE THING ATTACKED US!
IT WAS FOLLOWING SOME KID WHO KEPT TALKING ABOUT A SHOOTOUT IN A TUNNEL AND HOW HE HAD TO GET HOME...
YOU SAID A BLUE CREATURE...?
YOU DEAF, MAN?
MR. KANAN'S SON WAS SEEN ON THE BROOKLYN BRIDGE HEADING IN THE DIRECTION OF MANHATTAN.
WE'LL GO AFTER HIM.
PIERCING
WEDDING
29
TATTOO
COME ON, CHAMP -- TAKE THE BURGER. WE'VE GOT A SODA IN HERE, TOO, IF YOU WANT...
SPAT
ARG!
SNIF
SNIF
WELL THEN.
STOP LOOKING AT ME AND GET AFTER THEM!
WOUAAAAAAAAAAAH!!

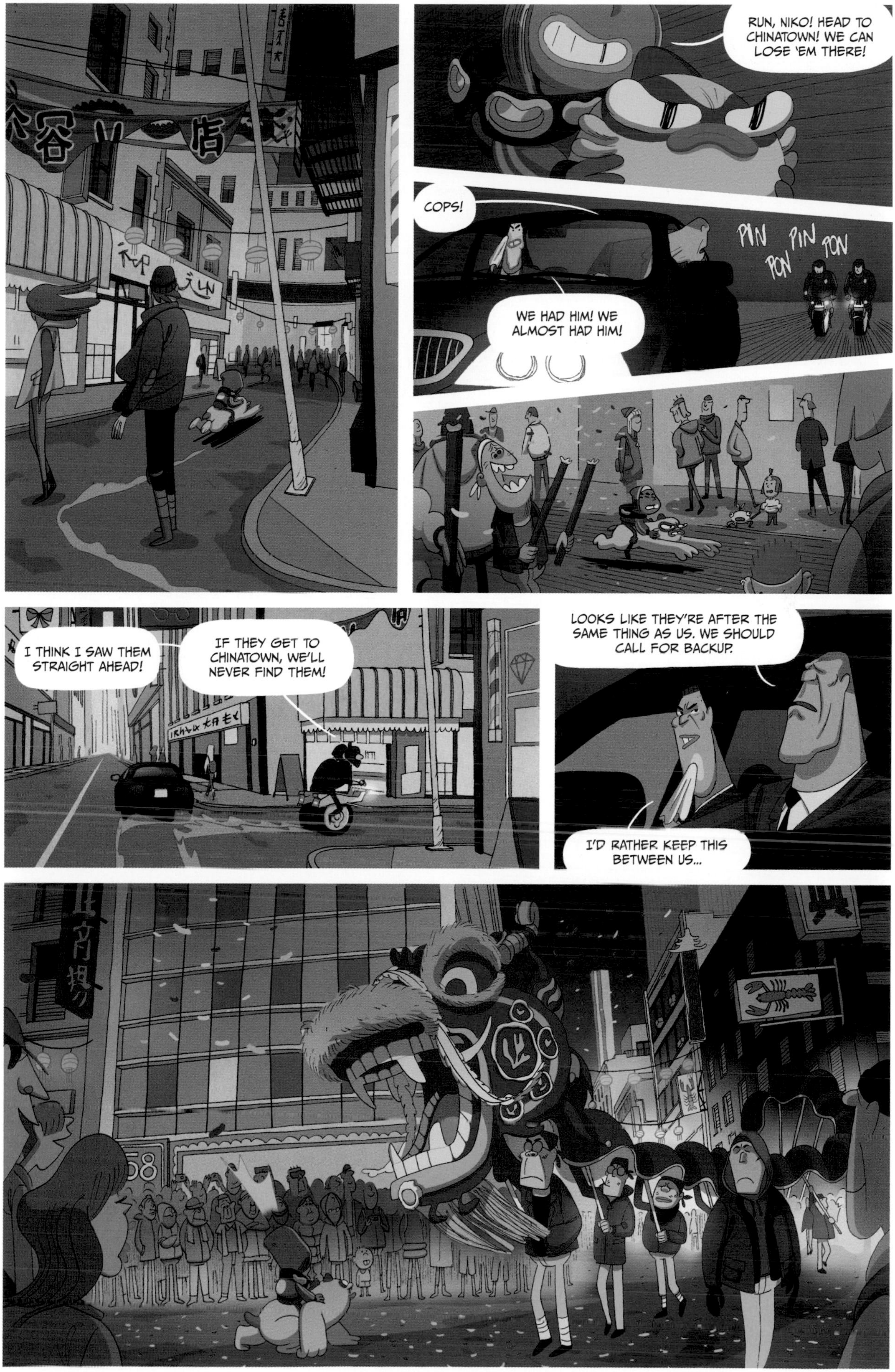
RUN, NIKO! HEAD TO CHINATOWN! WE CAN LOSE 'EM THERE!
COPS!
WE HAD HIM! WE ALMOST HAD HIM!
PIN PON PIN PON
I THINK I SAW THEM STRAIGHT AHEAD!
IF THEY GET TO CHINATOWN, WE'LL NEVER FIND THEM!
LOOKS LIKE THEY'RE AFTER THE SAME THING AS US. WE SHOULD CALL FOR BACKUP.
I'D RATHER KEEP THIS BETWEEN US...

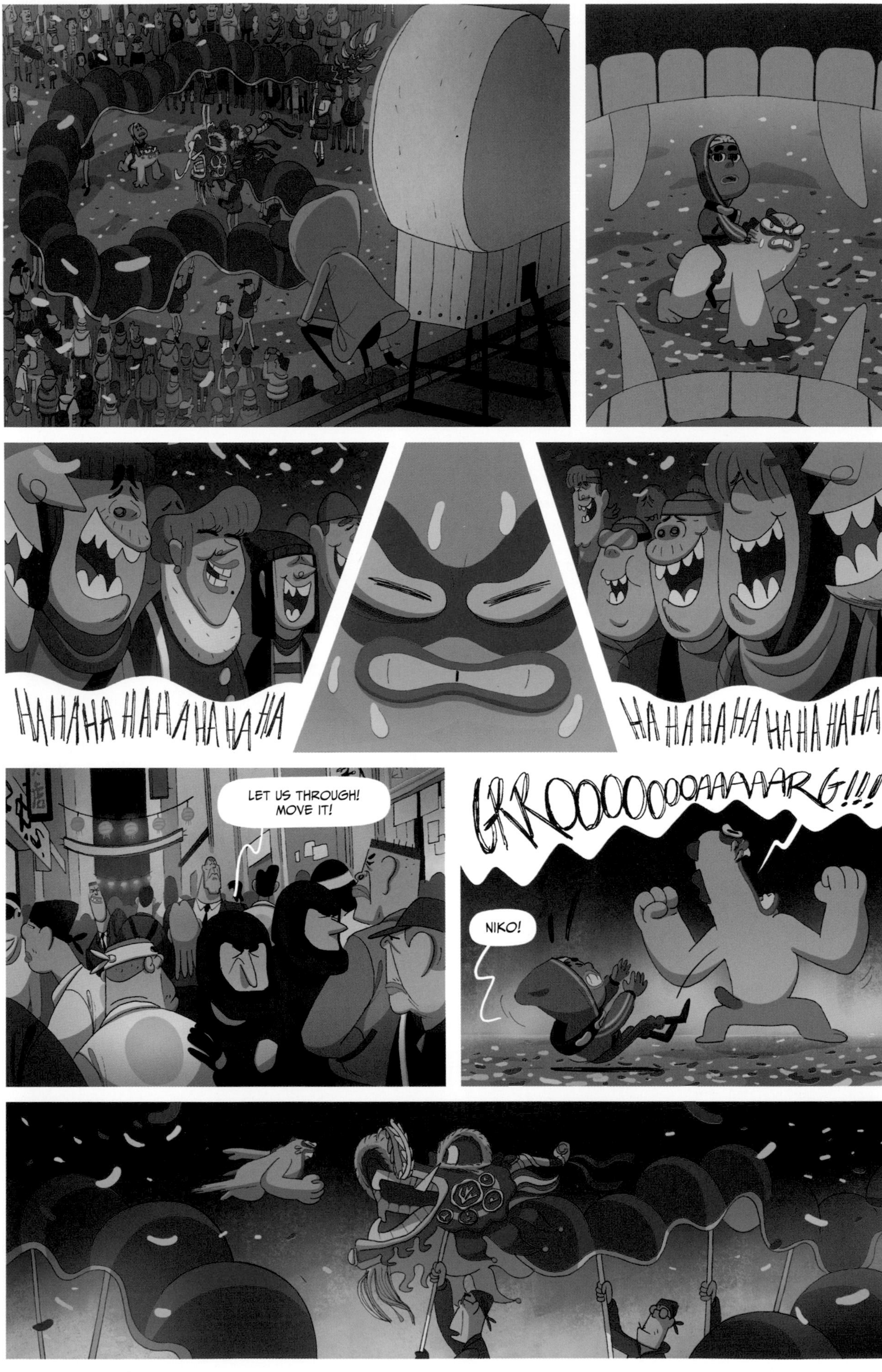
HAHAHA HAHAHAHAHA HA
HA HA HA HA HA HA HA HA HA HA
LET US THROUGH! MOVE IT!
GRROOOOOOOOAAAAARG!!!
NIKO!

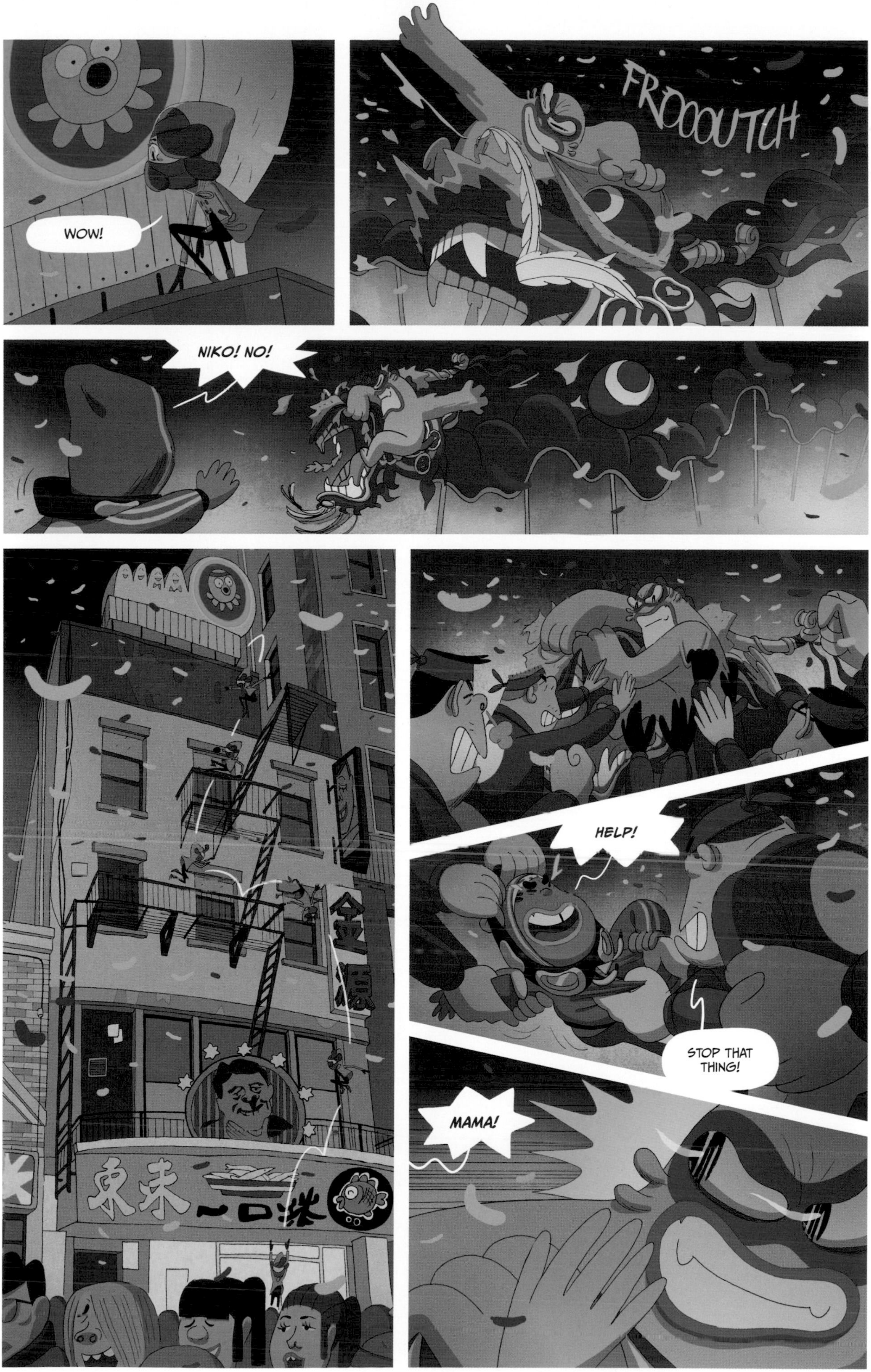
WOW!
FROOOUTCH
NIKO! NO!
HELP!
STOP THAT THING!
MAMA!

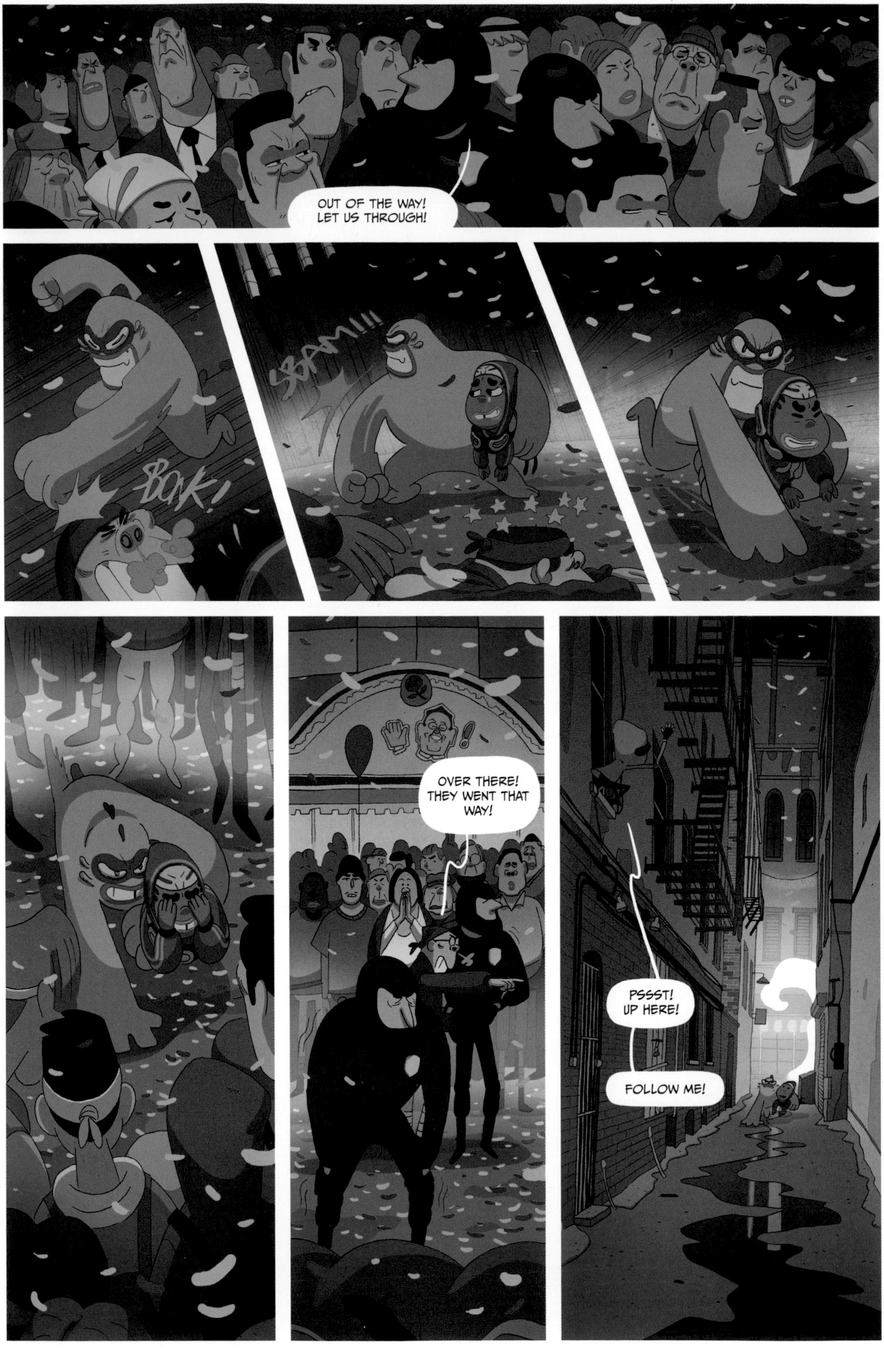
OUT OF THE WAY!
LET US THROUGH!
BONK!
SBAM!!!
OVER THERE! THEY WENT THAT WAY!
PSSST! UP HERE!
FOLLOW ME!

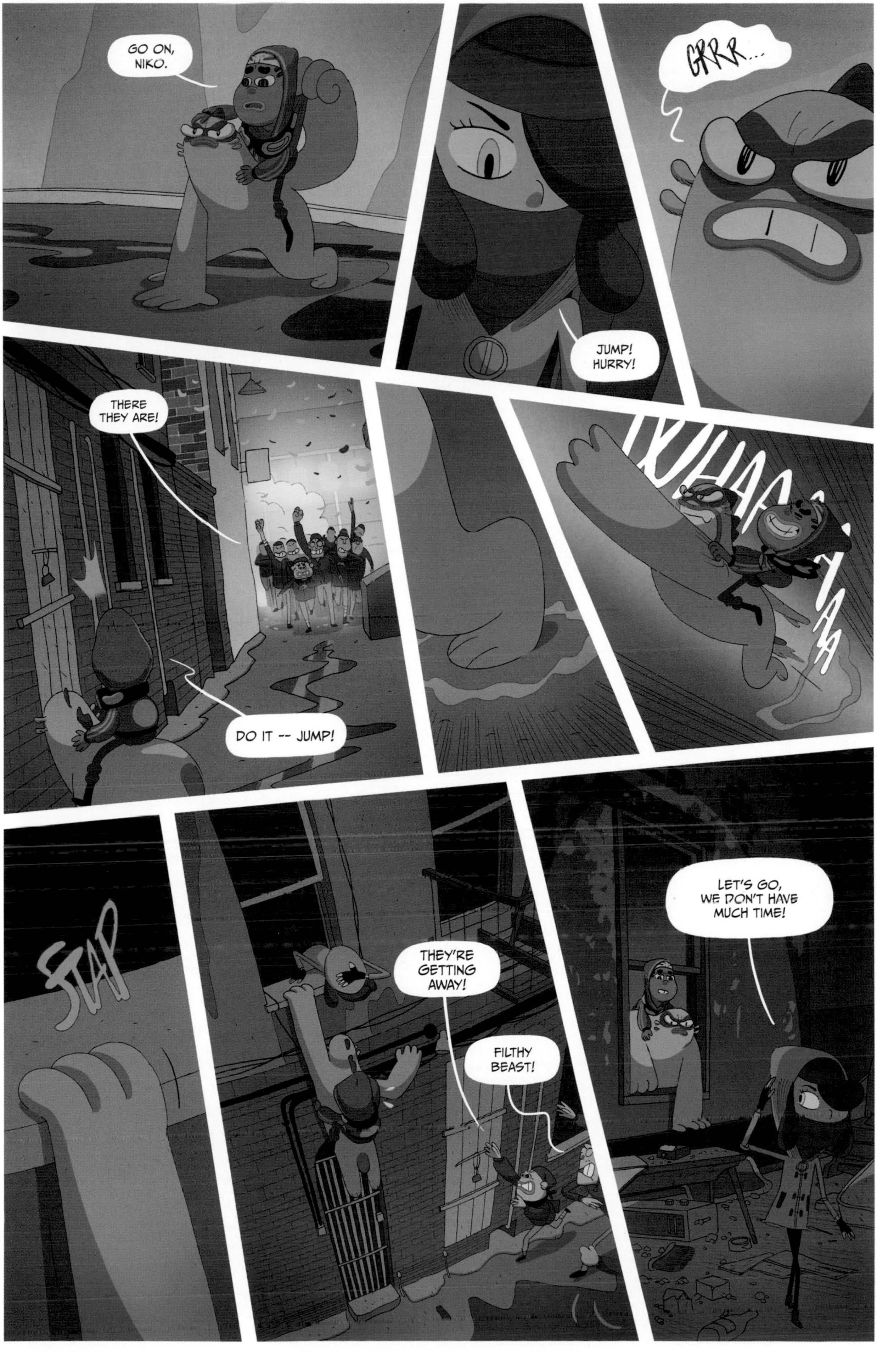
GO ON, NIKO.
GRRR...
JUMP! HURRY!
THERE THEY ARE!
DO IT -- JUMP!
STAP
THEY'RE GETTING AWAY!
FILTHY BEAST!
LET'S GO, WE DON'T HAVE MUCH TIME!

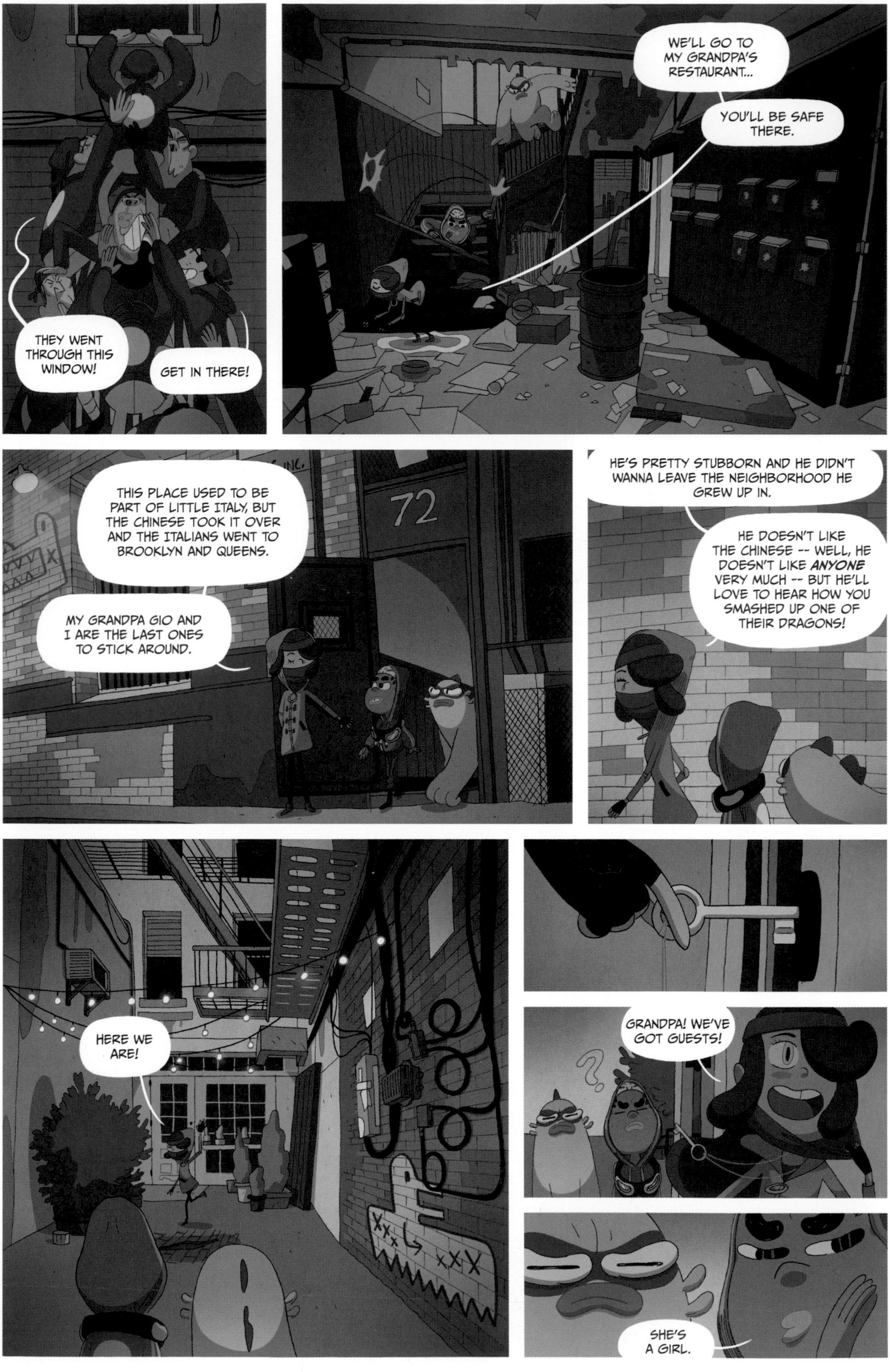
THEY WENT THROUGH THIS WINDOW!
GET IN THERE!
WE'LL GO TO MY GRANDPA'S RESTAURANT...
YOU'LL BE SAFE THERE.
72
THIS PLACE USED TO BE PART OF LITTLE ITALY, BUT THE CHINESE TOOK IT OVER AND THE ITALIANS WENT TO BROOKLYN AND QUEENS.
MY GRANDPA GIO AND I ARE THE LAST ONES TO STICK AROUND.
HE'S PRETTY STUBBORN AND HE DIDN'T WANNA LEAVE THE NEIGHBORHOOD HE GREW UP IN.
HE DOESN'T LIKE THE CHINESE -- WELL, HE DOESN'T LIKE ***ANYONE*** VERY MUCH -- BUT HE'LL LOVE TO HEAR HOW YOU SMASHED UP ONE OF THEIR DRAGONS!
HERE WE ARE!
GRANDPA! WE'VE GOT GUESTS!
SHE'S A GIRL.

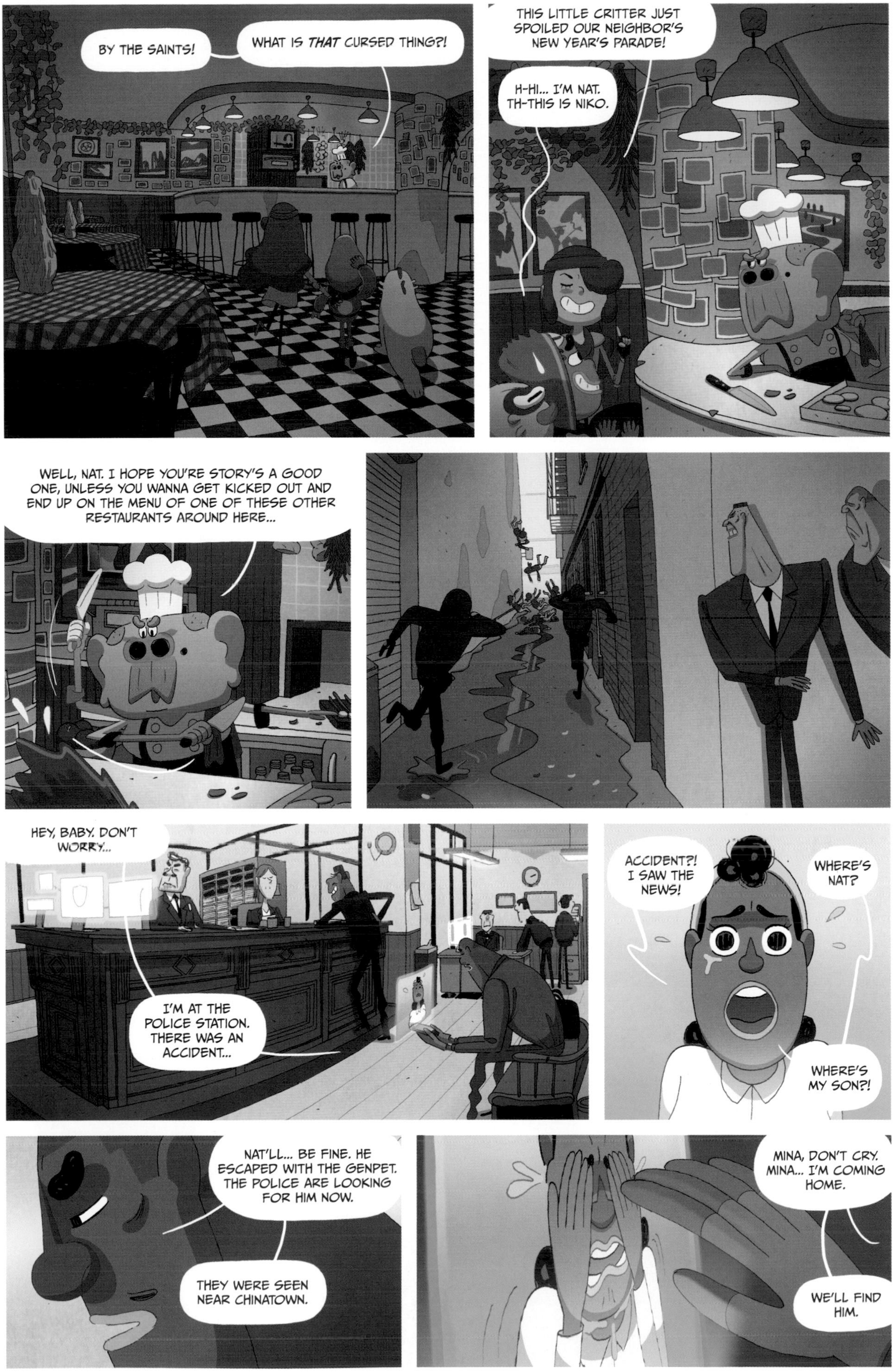
BY THE SAINTS!
WHAT IS *THAT* CURSED THING?!
THIS LITTLE CRITTER JUST SPOILED OUR NEIGHBOR'S NEW YEAR'S PARADE!
H-HI... I'M NAT. TH-THIS IS NIKO.
WELL, NAT. I HOPE YOU'RE STORY'S A GOOD ONE, UNLESS YOU WANNA GET KICKED OUT AND END UP ON THE MENU OF ONE OF THESE OTHER RESTAURANTS AROUND HERE...
HEY, BABY. DON'T WORRY...
I'M AT THE POLICE STATION. THERE WAS AN ACCIDENT...
ACCIDENT?! I SAW THE NEWS!
WHERE'S NAT?
WHERE'S MY SON?!
NAT'LL... BE FINE. HE ESCAPED WITH THE GENPET. THE POLICE ARE LOOKING FOR HIM NOW.
THEY WERE SEEN NEAR CHINATOWN.
MINA, DON'T CRY. MINA... I'M COMING HOME.
WE'LL FIND HIM.

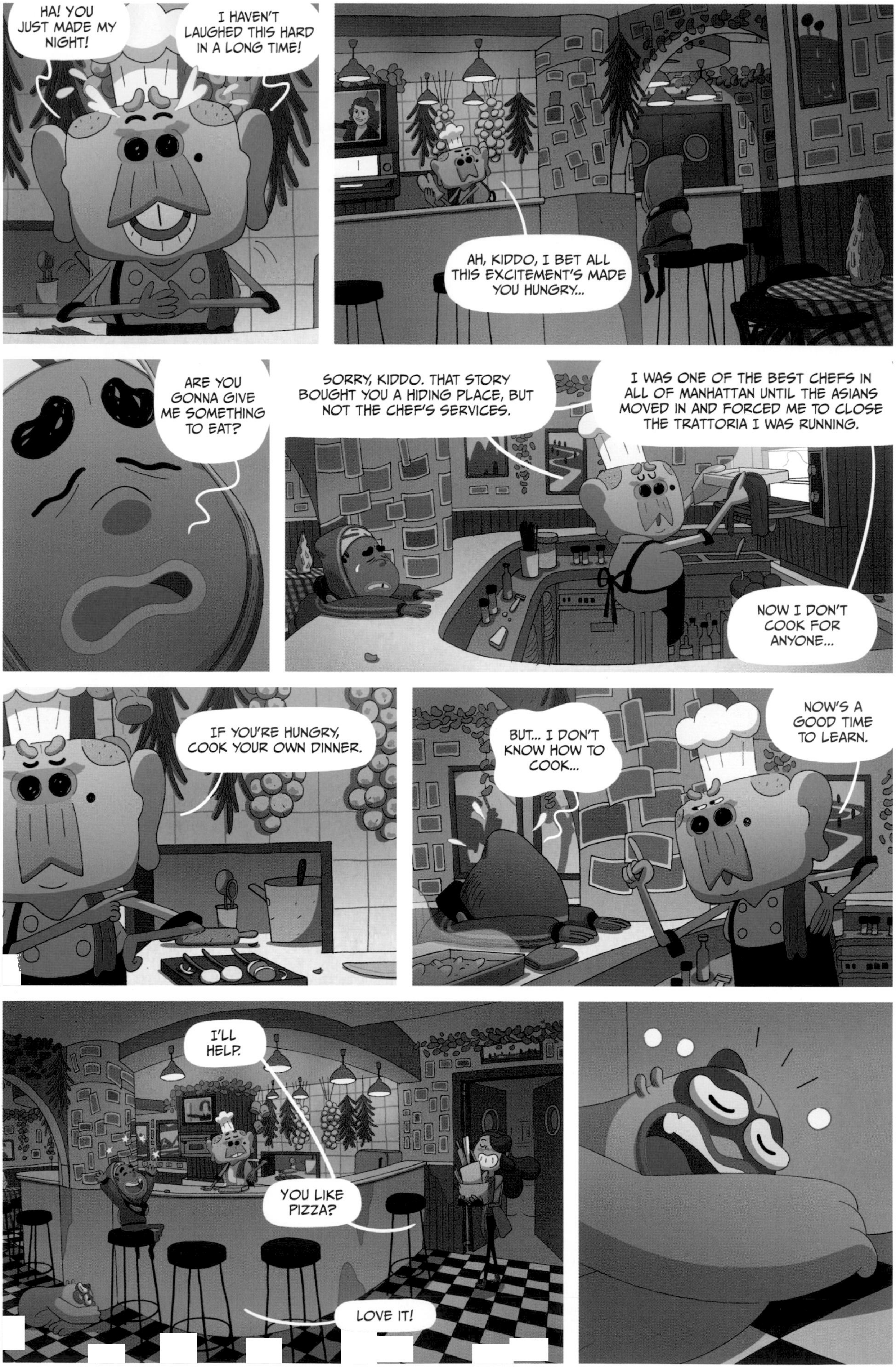
HA! YOU JUST MADE MY NIGHT!
I HAVEN'T LAUGHED THIS HARD IN A LONG TIME!
AH, KIDDO, I BET ALL THIS EXCITEMENT'S MADE YOU HUNGRY...
ARE YOU GONNA GIVE ME SOMETHING TO EAT?
SORRY, KIDDO. THAT STORY BOUGHT YOU A HIDING PLACE, BUT NOT THE CHEF'S SERVICES.
I WAS ONE OF THE BEST CHEFS IN ALL OF MANHATTAN UNTIL THE ASIANS MOVED IN AND FORCED ME TO CLOSE THE TRATTORIA I WAS RUNNING.
NOW I DON'T COOK FOR ANYONE...
IF YOU'RE HUNGRY, COOK YOUR OWN DINNER.
BUT... I DON'T KNOW HOW TO COOK...
NOW'S A GOOD TIME TO LEARN.
I'LL HELP.
YOU LIKE PIZZA?
LOVE IT!

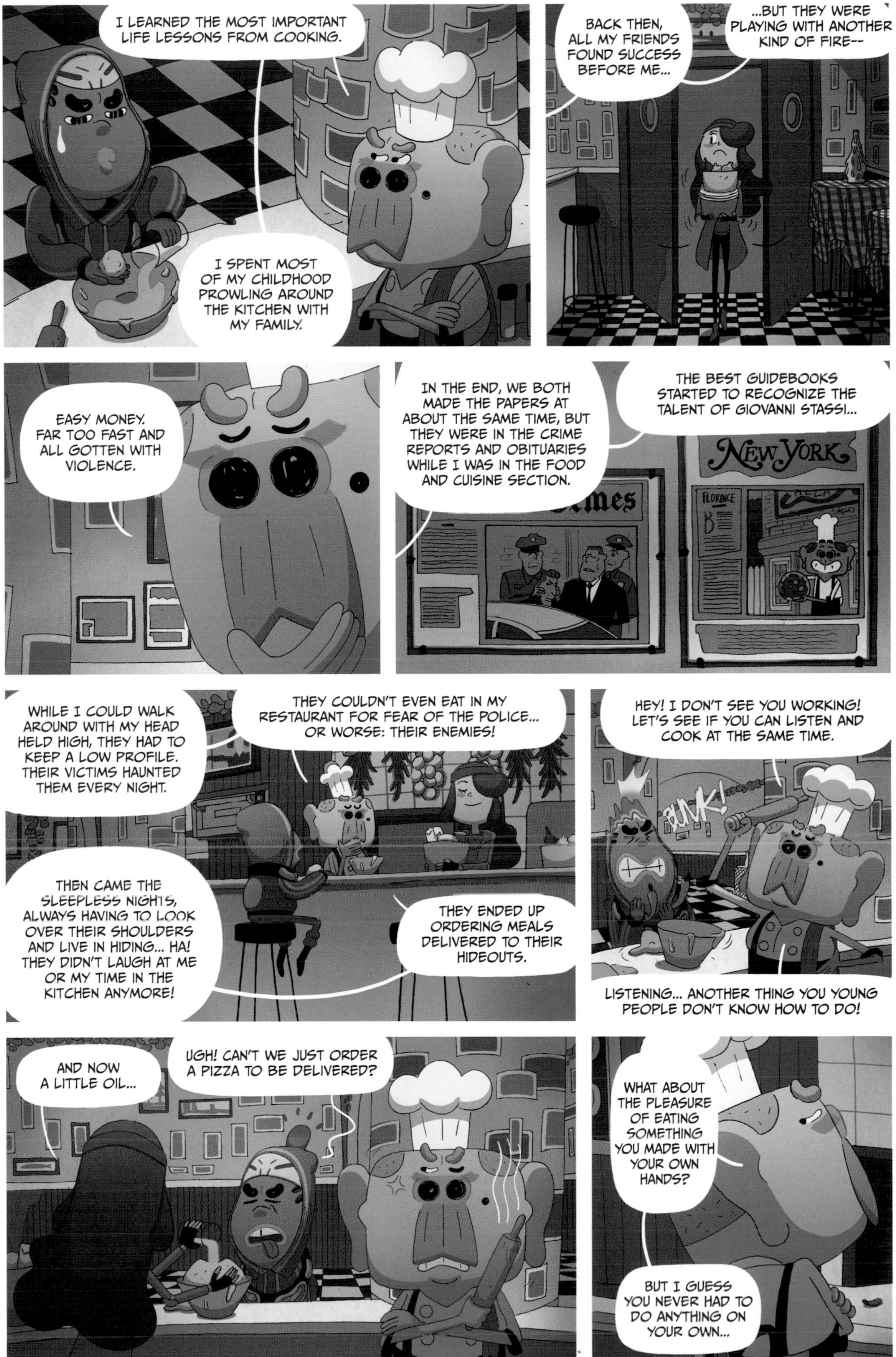

I LEARNED THE MOST IMPORTANT LIFE LESSONS FROM COOKING.
I SPENT MOST OF MY CHILDHOOD PROWLING AROUND THE KITCHEN WITH MY FAMILY.
BACK THEN, ALL MY FRIENDS FOUND SUCCESS BEFORE ME...
...BUT THEY WERE PLAYING WITH ANOTHER KIND OF FIRE--
EASY MONEY. FAR TOO FAST AND ALL GOTTEN WITH VIOLENCE.
IN THE END, WE BOTH MADE THE PAPERS AT ABOUT THE SAME TIME, BUT THEY WERE IN THE CRIME REPORTS AND OBITUARIES WHILE I WAS IN THE FOOD AND CUISINE SECTION.
THE BEST GUIDEBOOKS STARTED TO RECOGNIZE THE TALENT OF GIOVANNI STASSI...
NEW YORK
WHILE I COULD WALK AROUND WITH MY HEAD HELD HIGH, THEY HAD TO KEEP A LOW PROFILE. THEIR VICTIMS HAUNTED THEM EVERY NIGHT.
THEY COULDN'T EVEN EAT IN MY RESTAURANT FOR FEAR OF THE POLICE... OR WORSE: THEIR ENEMIES!
THEN CAME THE SLEEPLESS NIGHTS, ALWAYS HAVING TO LOOK OVER THEIR SHOULDERS AND LIVE IN HIDING... HA! THEY DIDN'T LAUGH AT ME OR MY TIME IN THE KITCHEN ANYMORE!
THEY ENDED UP ORDERING MEALS DELIVERED TO THEIR HIDEOUTS.
HEY! I DON'T SEE YOU WORKING! LET'S SEE IF YOU CAN LISTEN AND COOK AT THE SAME TIME.
BUNK!
LISTENING... ANOTHER THING YOU YOUNG PEOPLE DON'T KNOW HOW TO DO!
AND NOW A LITTLE OIL...
UGH! CAN'T WE JUST ORDER A PIZZA TO BE DELIVERED?
WHAT ABOUT THE PLEASURE OF EATING SOMETHING YOU MADE WITH YOUR OWN HANDS?
BUT I GUESS YOU NEVER HAD TO DO ANYTHING ON YOUR OWN...

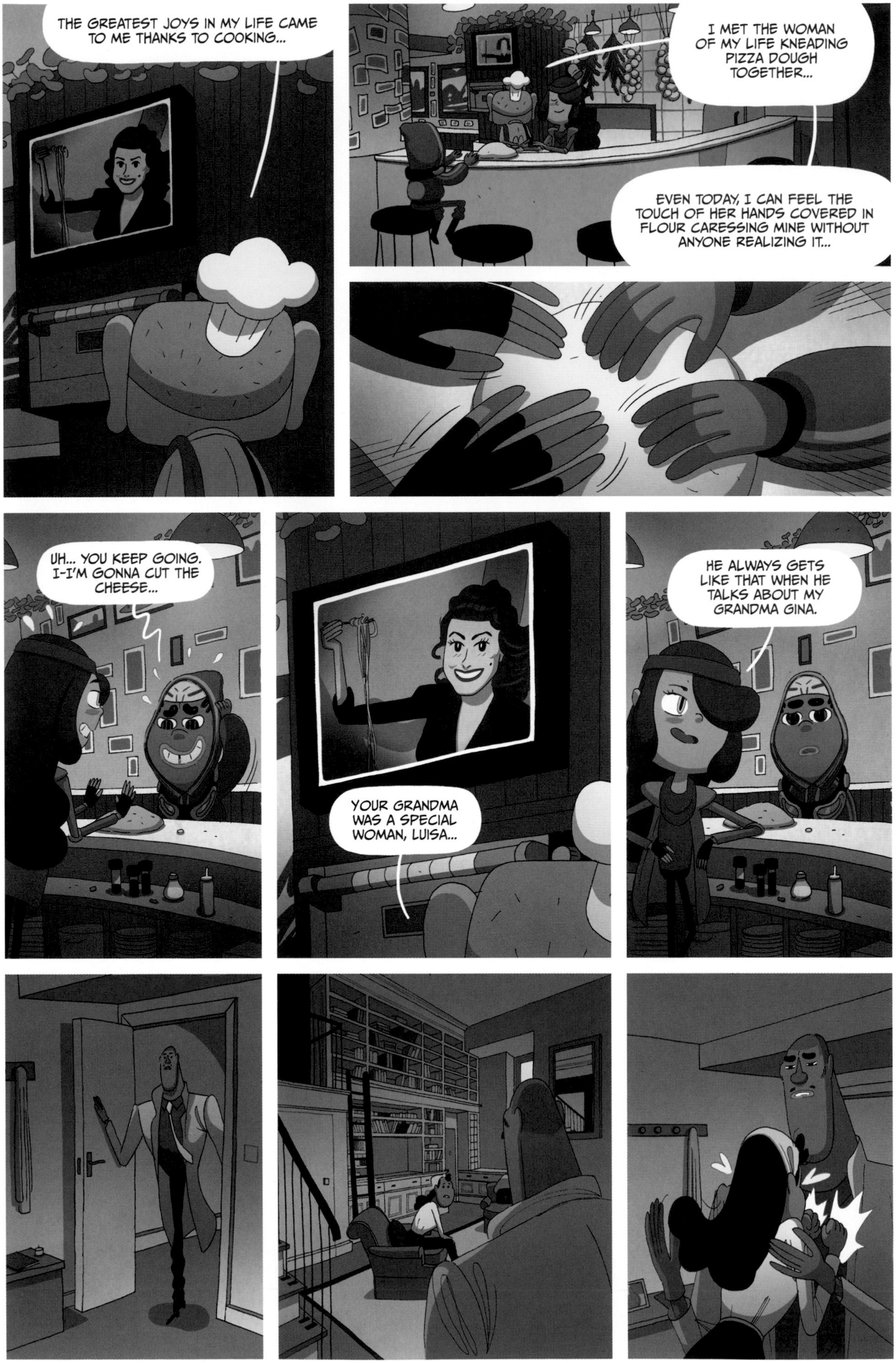

THE GREATEST JOYS IN MY LIFE CAME TO ME THANKS TO COOKING...
I MET THE WOMAN OF MY LIFE KNEADING PIZZA DOUGH TOGETHER...
EVEN TODAY, I CAN FEEL THE TOUCH OF HER HANDS COVERED IN FLOUR CARESSING MINE WITHOUT ANYONE REALIZING IT...
UH... YOU KEEP GOING. I-I'M GONNA CUT THE CHEESE...
YOUR GRANDMA WAS A SPECIAL WOMAN, LUISA...
HE ALWAYS GETS LIKE THAT WHEN HE TALKS ABOUT MY GRANDMA GINA.

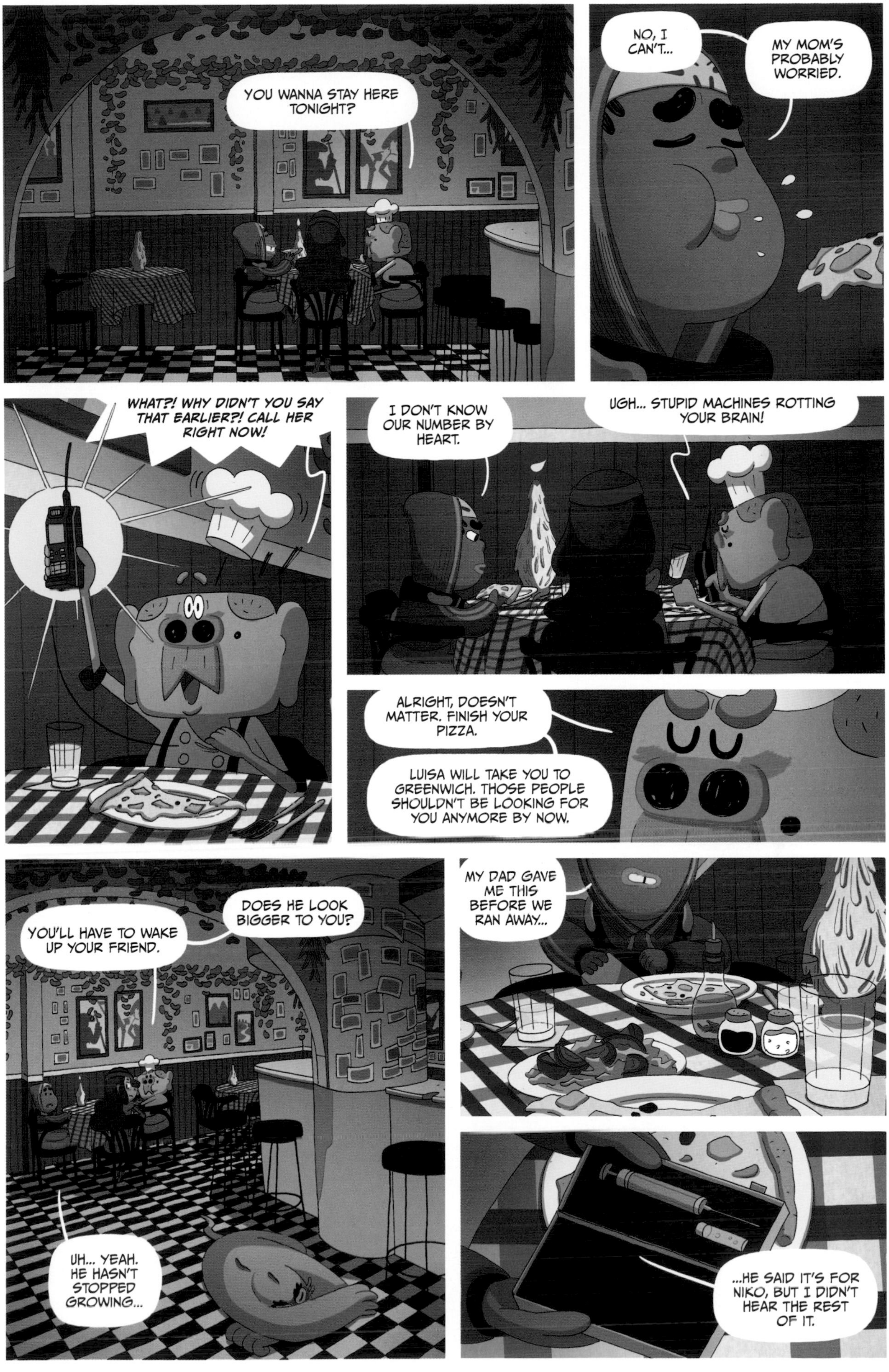
YOU WANNA STAY HERE TONIGHT?
NO, I CAN'T...
MY MOM'S PROBABLY WORRIED.
WHAT?! WHY DIDN'T YOU SAY THAT EARLIER?! CALL HER RIGHT NOW!
I DON'T KNOW OUR NUMBER BY HEART.
UGH... STUPID MACHINES ROTTING YOUR BRAIN!
ALRIGHT, DOESN'T MATTER. FINISH YOUR PIZZA.
LUISA WILL TAKE YOU TO GREENWICH. THOSE PEOPLE SHOULDN'T BE LOOKING FOR YOU ANYMORE BY NOW.
YOU'LL HAVE TO WAKE UP YOUR FRIEND.
DOES HE LOOK BIGGER TO YOU?
UH... YEAH. HE HASN'T STOPPED GROWING...
MY DAD GAVE ME THIS BEFORE WE RAN AWAY...
...HE SAID IT'S FOR NIKO, BUT I DIDN'T HEAR THE REST OF IT.

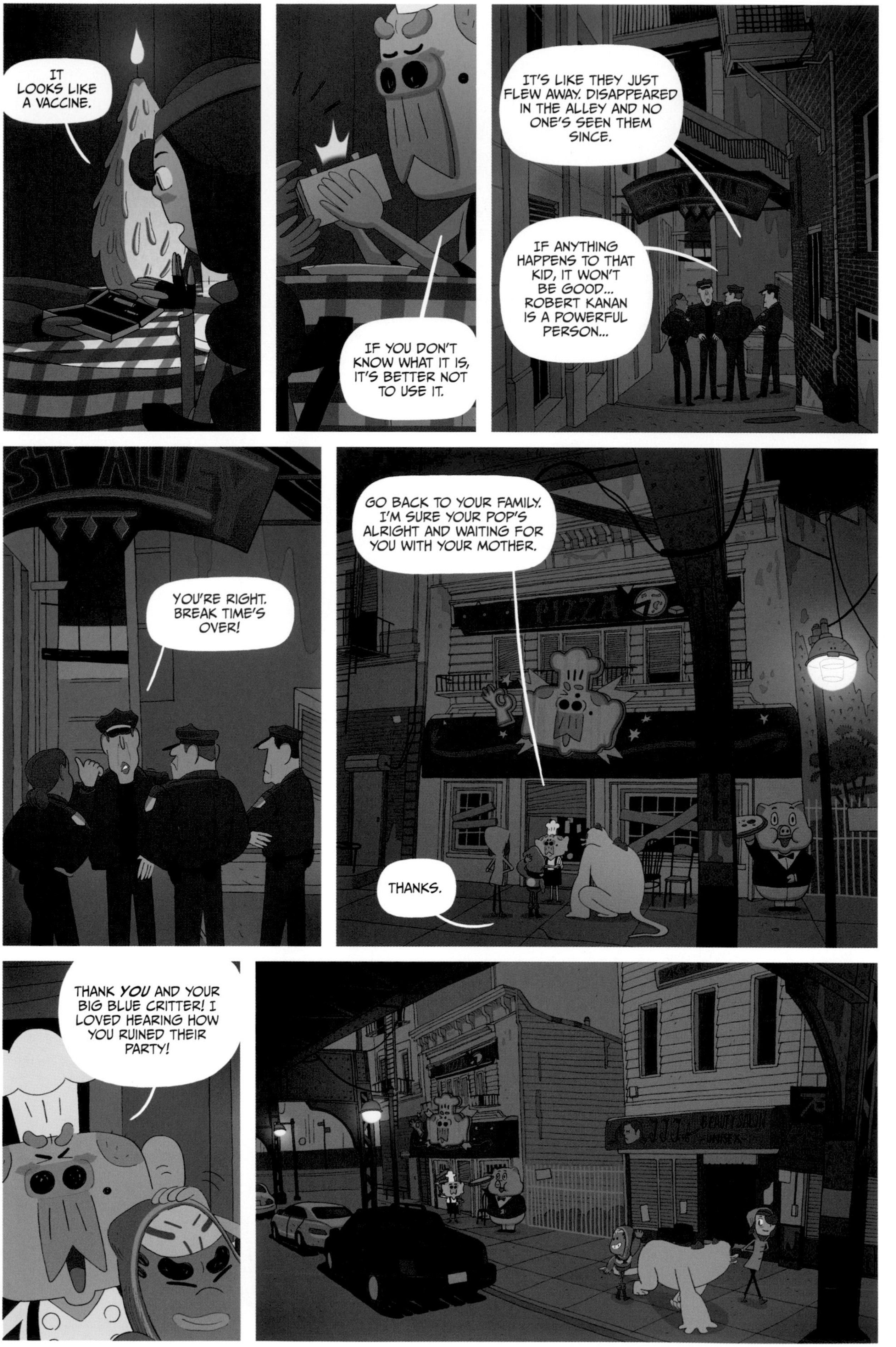

IT LOOKS LIKE A VACCINE.
IF YOU DON'T KNOW WHAT IT IS, IT'S BETTER NOT TO USE IT.
IT'S LIKE THEY JUST FLEW AWAY. DISAPPEARED IN THE ALLEY AND NO ONE'S SEEN THEM SINCE.
IF ANYTHING HAPPENS TO THAT KID, IT WON'T BE GOOD... ROBERT KANAN IS A POWERFUL PERSON...
YOU'RE RIGHT. BREAK TIME'S OVER!
GO BACK TO YOUR FAMILY. I'M SURE YOUR POP'S ALRIGHT AND WAITING FOR YOU WITH YOUR MOTHER.
PIZZA
THANKS.
THANK *YOU* AND YOUR BIG BLUE CRITTER! I LOVED HEARING HOW YOU RUINED THEIR PARTY!

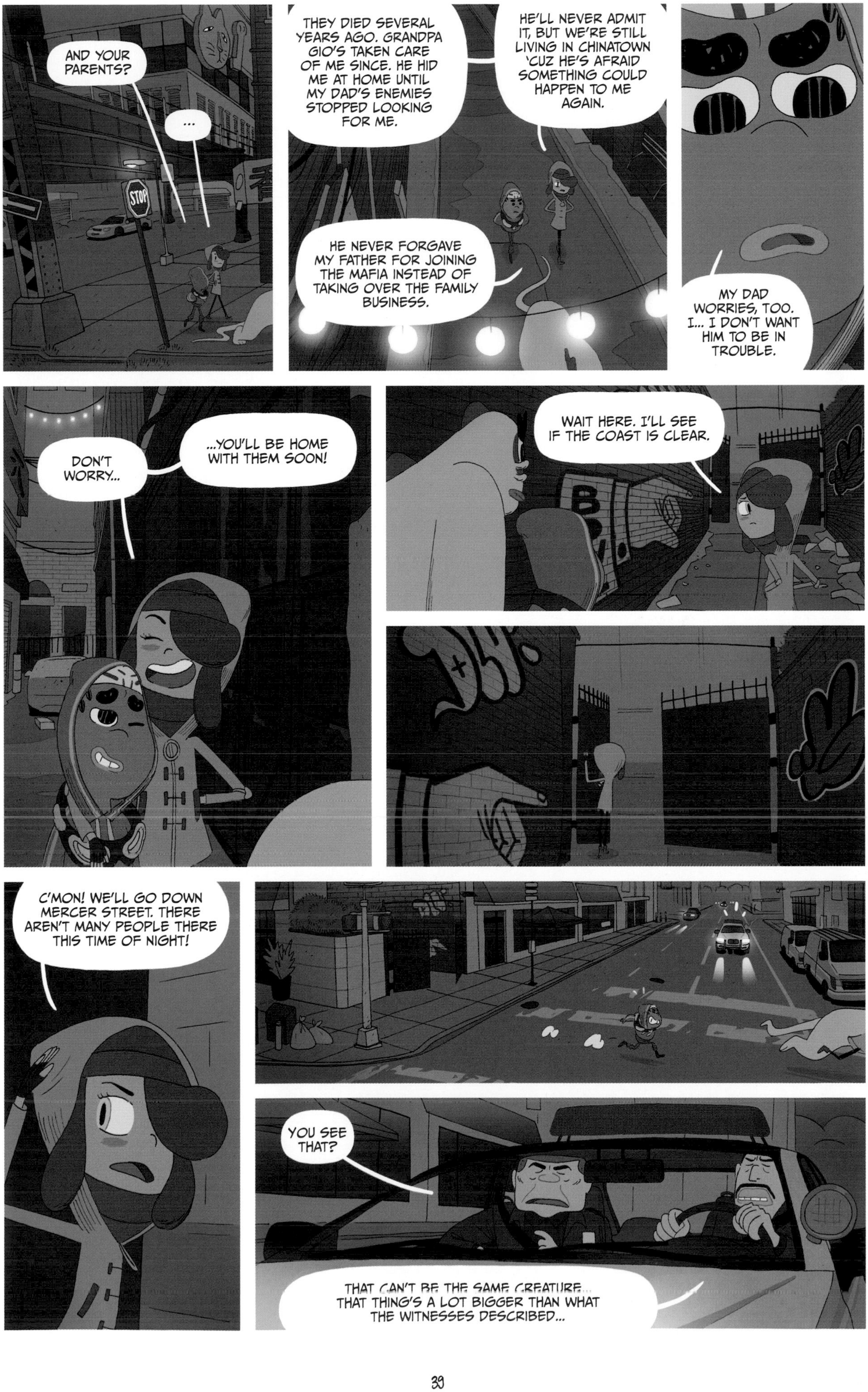

AND YOUR PARENTS?
...
THEY DIED SEVERAL YEARS AGO. GRANDPA GIO'S TAKEN CARE OF ME SINCE. HE HID ME AT HOME UNTIL MY DAD'S ENEMIES STOPPED LOOKING FOR ME.
HE NEVER FORGAVE MY FATHER FOR JOINING THE MAFIA INSTEAD OF TAKING OVER THE FAMILY BUSINESS.
HE'LL NEVER ADMIT IT, BUT WE'RE STILL LIVING IN CHINATOWN 'CUZ HE'S AFRAID SOMETHING COULD HAPPEN TO ME AGAIN.
MY DAD WORRIES, TOO. I... I DON'T WANT HIM TO BE IN TROUBLE.
DON'T WORRY...
...YOU'LL BE HOME WITH THEM SOON!
WAIT HERE. I'LL SEE IF THE COAST IS CLEAR.
C'MON! WE'LL GO DOWN MERCER STREET. THERE AREN'T MANY PEOPLE THERE THIS TIME OF NIGHT!
YOU SEE THAT?
THAT CAN'T BE THE SAME CREATURE... THAT THING'S A LOT BIGGER THAN WHAT THE WITNESSES DESCRIBED...

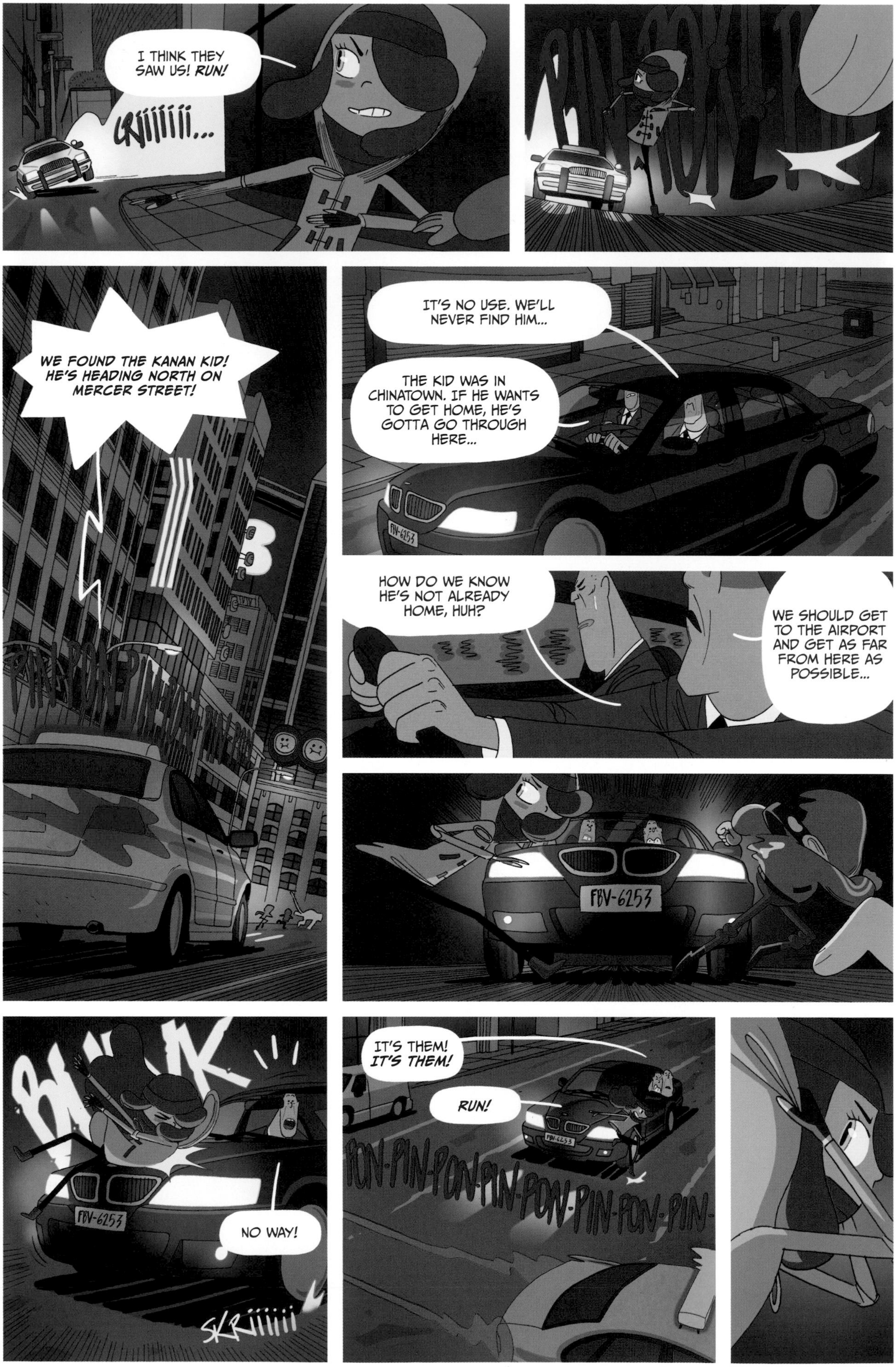

I THINK THEY SAW US! *RUN!*
CRIIIIII...
WE FOUND THE KANAN KID! HE'S HEADING NORTH ON MERCER STREET!
IT'S NO USE. WE'LL NEVER FIND HIM...
THE KID WAS IN CHINATOWN. IF HE WANTS TO GET HOME, HE'S GOTTA GO THROUGH HERE...
HOW DO WE KNOW HE'S NOT ALREADY HOME, HUH?
WE SHOULD GET TO THE AIRPORT AND GET AS FAR FROM HERE AS POSSIBLE...
FBV-6253
FBV-6253
NO WAY!
SKRIIIII
IT'S THEM! *IT'S THEM!*
RUN!
PON-PIN-PON-PIN-PON-PIN-PON-PIN-

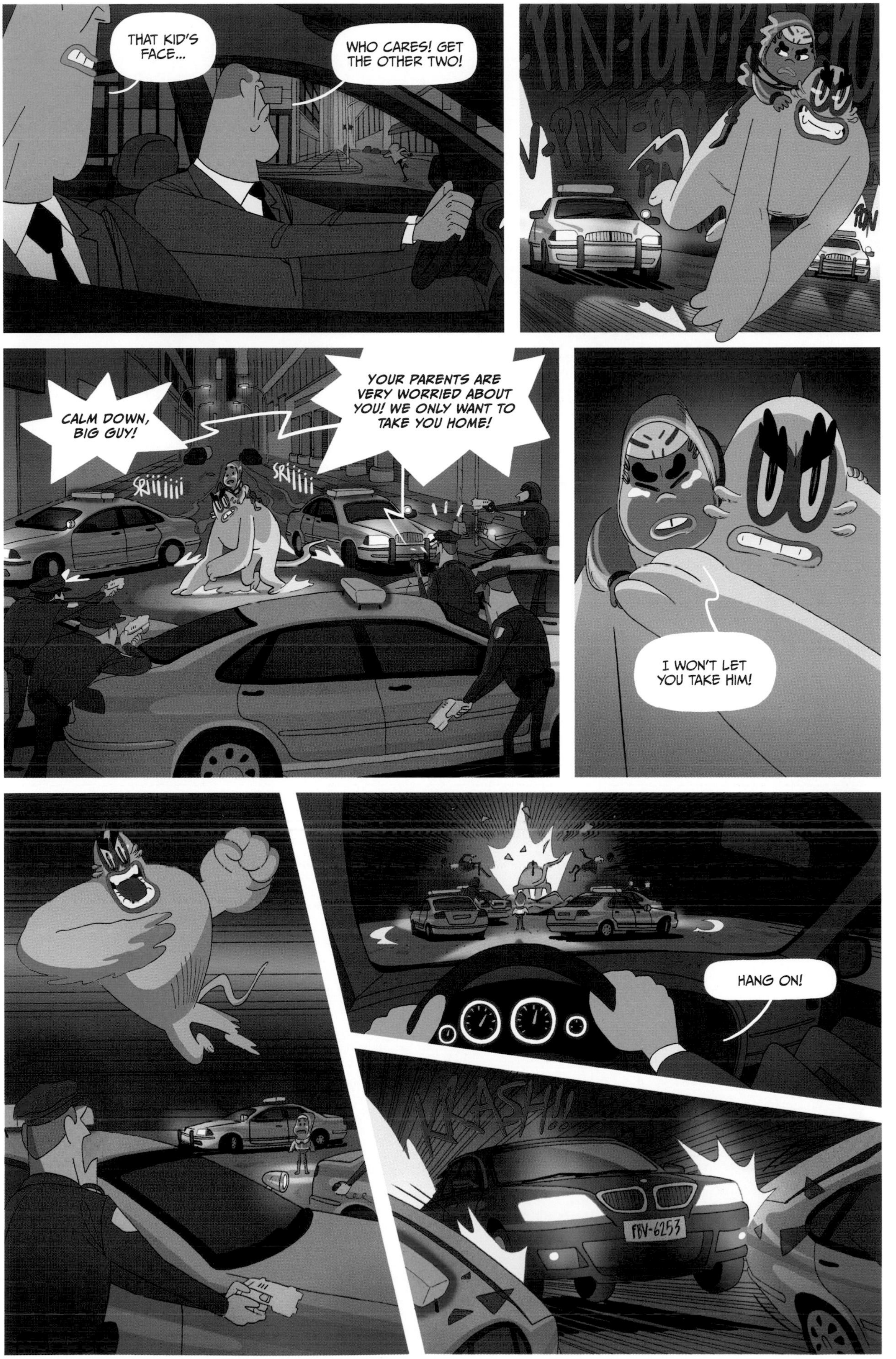
THAT KID'S FACE...
WHO CARES! GET THE OTHER TWO!
CALM DOWN, BIG GUY!
YOUR PARENTS ARE VERY WORRIED ABOUT YOU! WE ONLY WANT TO TAKE YOU HOME!
I WON'T LET YOU TAKE HIM!
HANG ON!
KLASH!!
FBV-6253

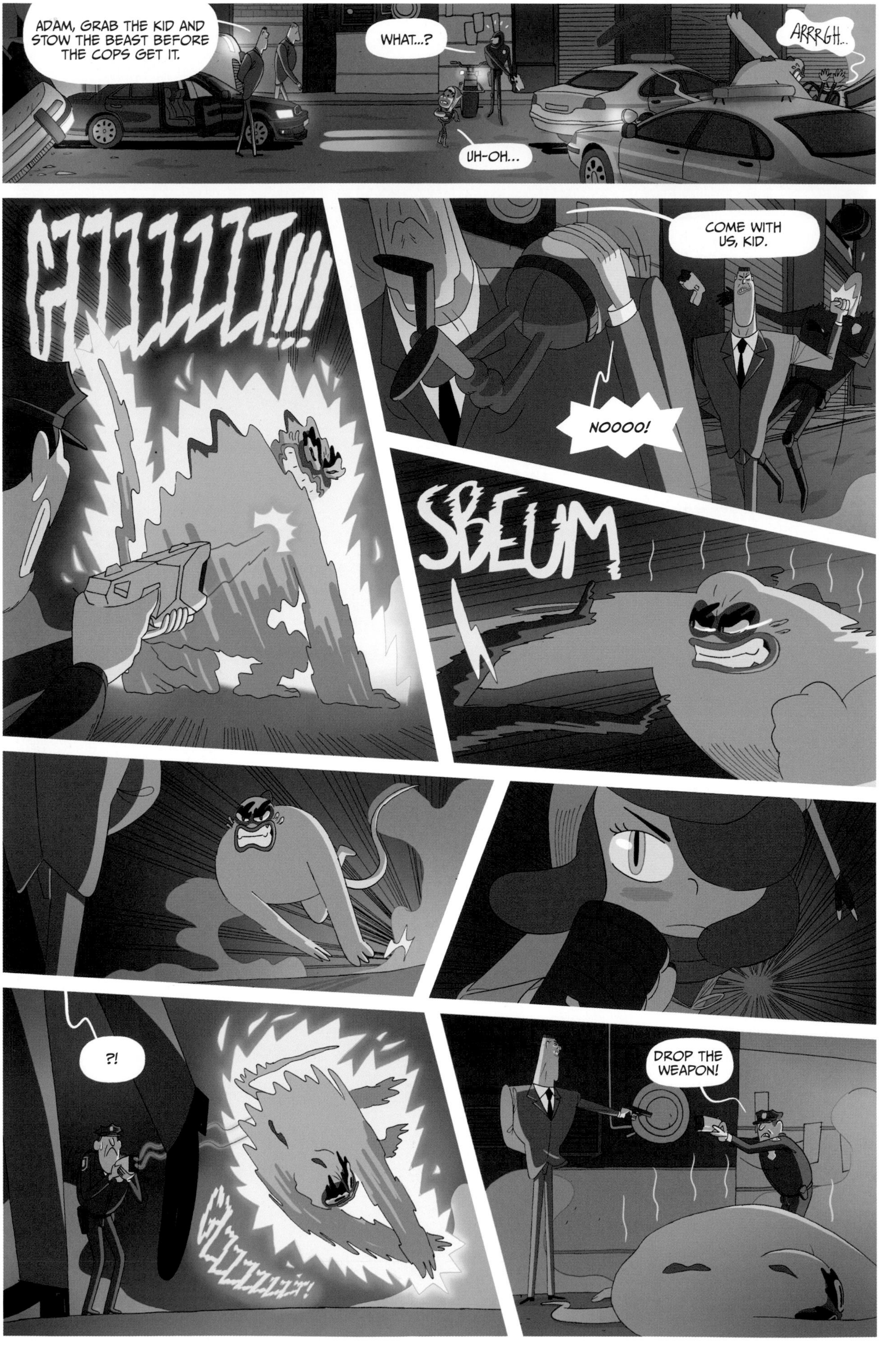
ADAM, GRAB THE KID AND STOW THE BEAST BEFORE THE COPS GET IT.
WHAT...?
UH-OH...
ARRRGH..
GZZZZZZT!!!
COME WITH US, KID.
NOOOO!
SBEUM
?!
DROP THE WEAPON!

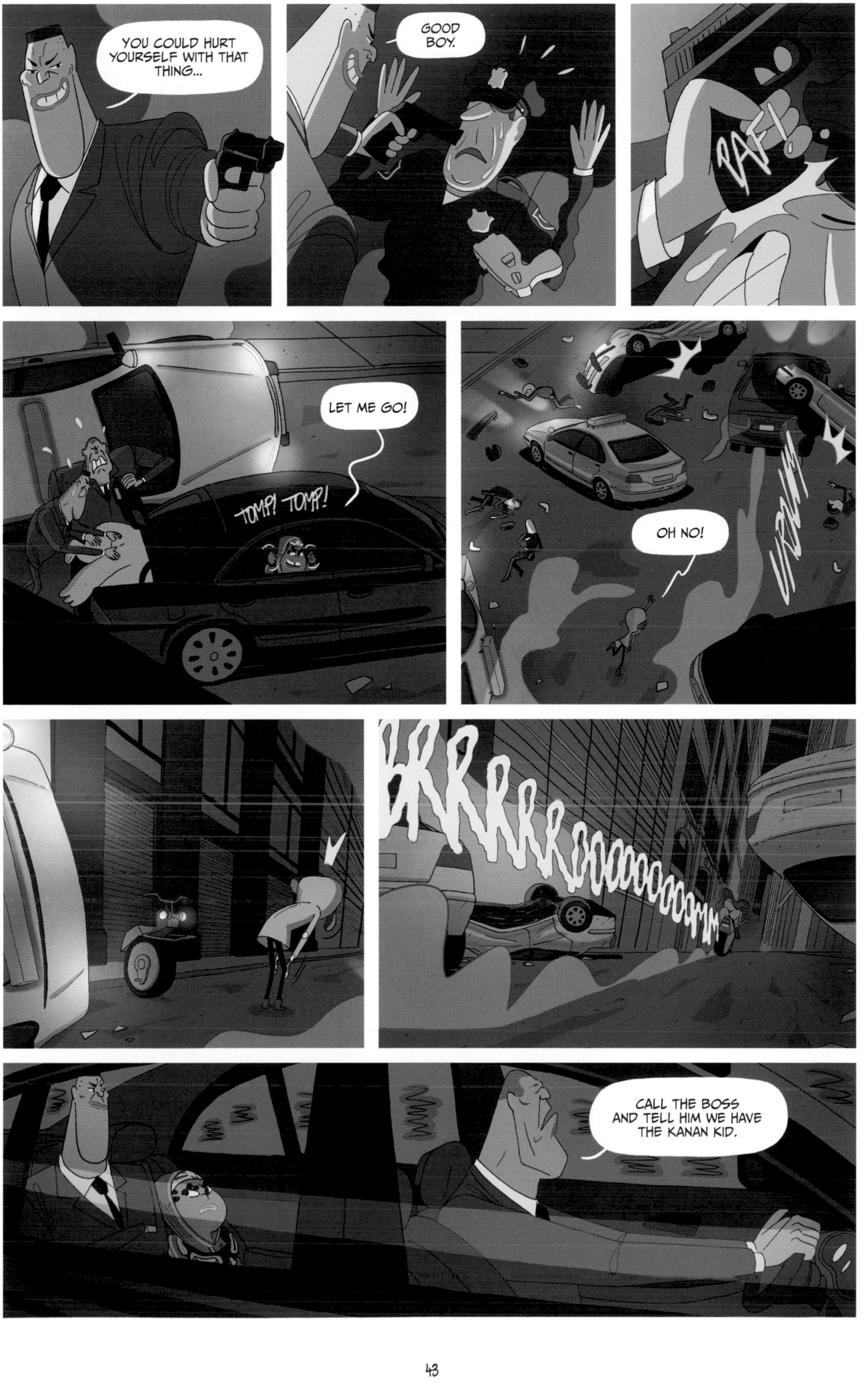
YOU COULD HURT YOURSELF WITH THAT THING...
GOOD BOY.
PAF!
LET ME GO!
TOMP! TOMP!
OH NO!
VRUUM
BRRRRRROOOOOOOOOOMM
CALL THE BOSS AND TELL HIM WE HAVE THE KANAN KID.

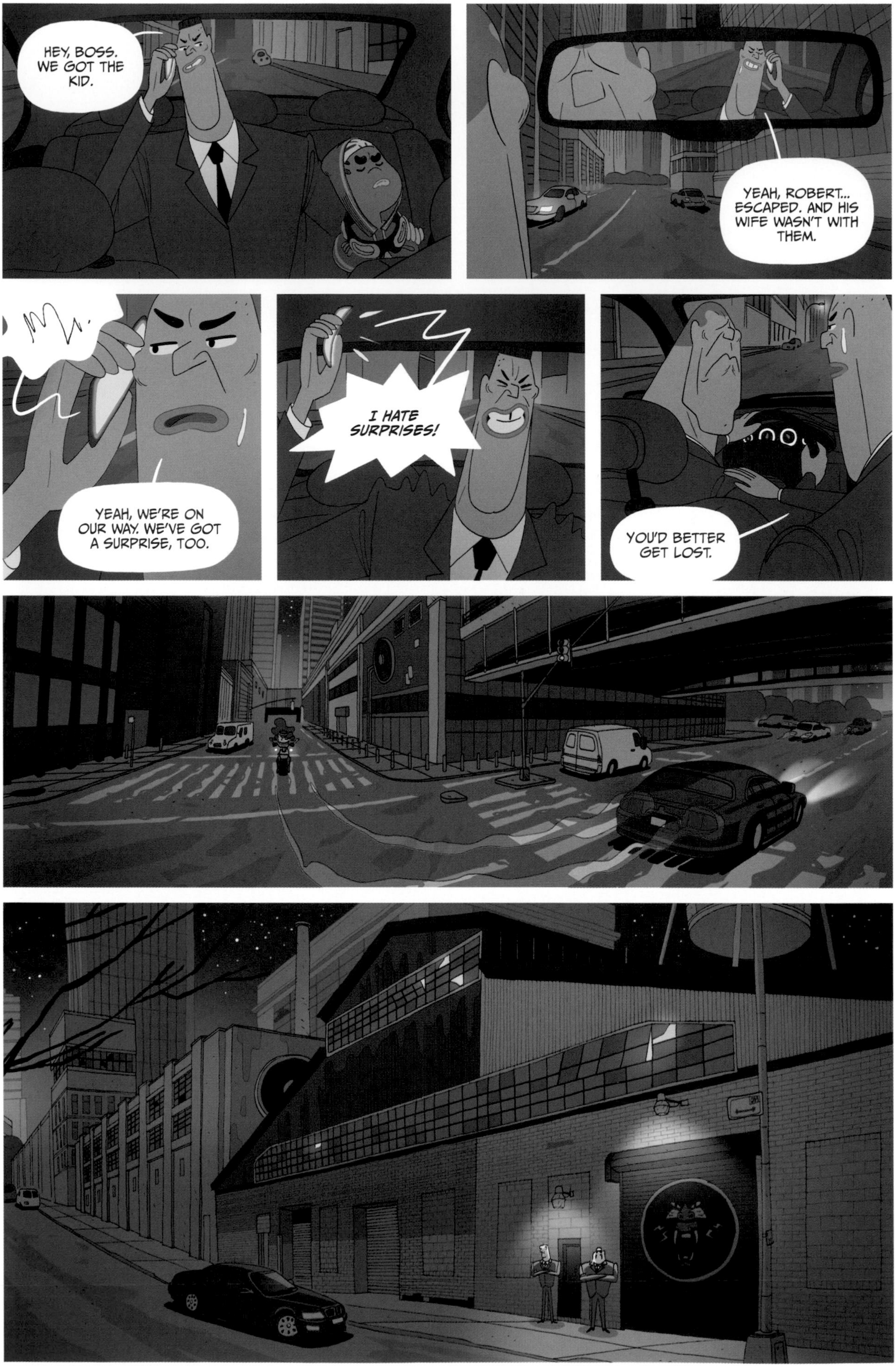
HEY, BOSS. WE GOT THE KID.
YEAH, ROBERT... ESCAPED. AND HIS WIFE WASN'T WITH THEM.
YEAH, WE'RE ON OUR WAY. WE'VE GOT A SURPRISE, TOO.
I HATE SURPRISES!
YOU'D BETTER GET LOST.

LET GO OF ME! WHEN NIKO WAKES UP, HE'LL KNOCK YOU GUYS OUT!

SHUT UP AND MOVE!

JASON! C'MERE AND GIMME A HAND WITH THIS.

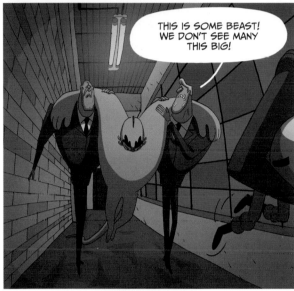

THIS IS SOME BEAST! WE DON'T SEE MANY THIS BIG!

AT LAST, THE USELESS DUO...

I NEVER THOUGHT SUCH A SIMPLE TASK WOULD TAKE SO LONG...

BUT WE WOUND UP WITH A CONSOLATION PRIZE...

BAIT TO LURE THE BIGGER FISH TO US.

WHAT DO YOU SAY, KID?

YOU LIKE GAMES?

YEAH, LOVE 'EM.

I HOPE YOU'RE A GOOD LOSER.

YOU GOT GUTS.

GOOD, LET'S NOT WASTE ANY MORE TIME.

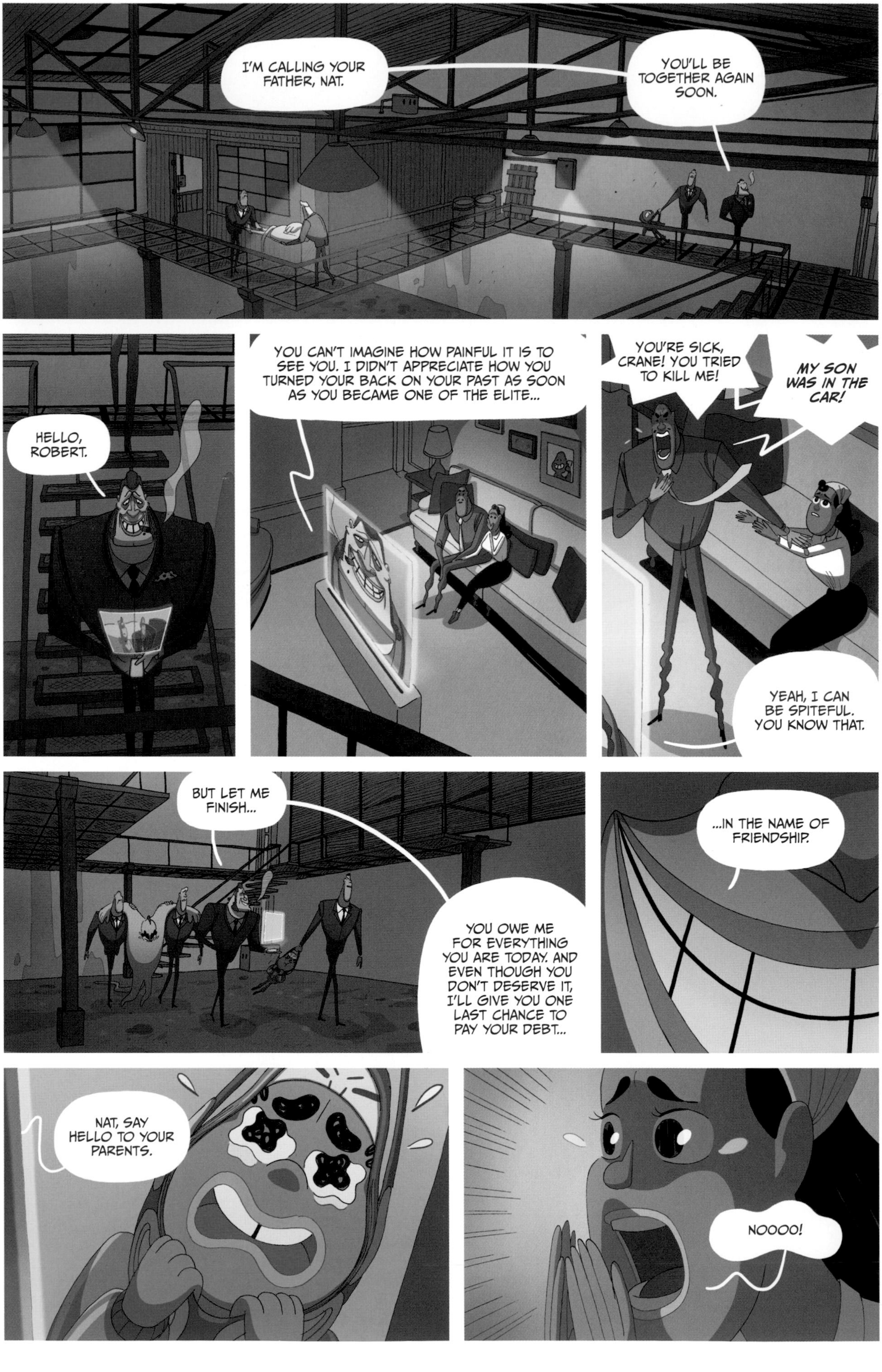
I'M CALLING YOUR FATHER, NAT.
YOU'LL BE TOGETHER AGAIN SOON.
HELLO, ROBERT.
YOU CAN'T IMAGINE HOW PAINFUL IT IS TO SEE YOU. I DIDN'T APPRECIATE HOW YOU TURNED YOUR BACK ON YOUR PAST AS SOON AS YOU BECAME ONE OF THE ELITE...
YOU'RE SICK, CRANE! YOU TRIED TO KILL ME!
MY SON WAS IN THE CAR!
YEAH, I CAN BE SPITEFUL. YOU KNOW THAT.
BUT LET ME FINISH...
YOU OWE ME FOR EVERYTHING YOU ARE TODAY. AND EVEN THOUGH YOU DON'T DESERVE IT, I'LL GIVE YOU ONE LAST CHANCE TO PAY YOUR DEBT...
...IN THE NAME OF FRIENDSHIP.
NAT, SAY HELLO TO YOUR PARENTS.
NOOOO!

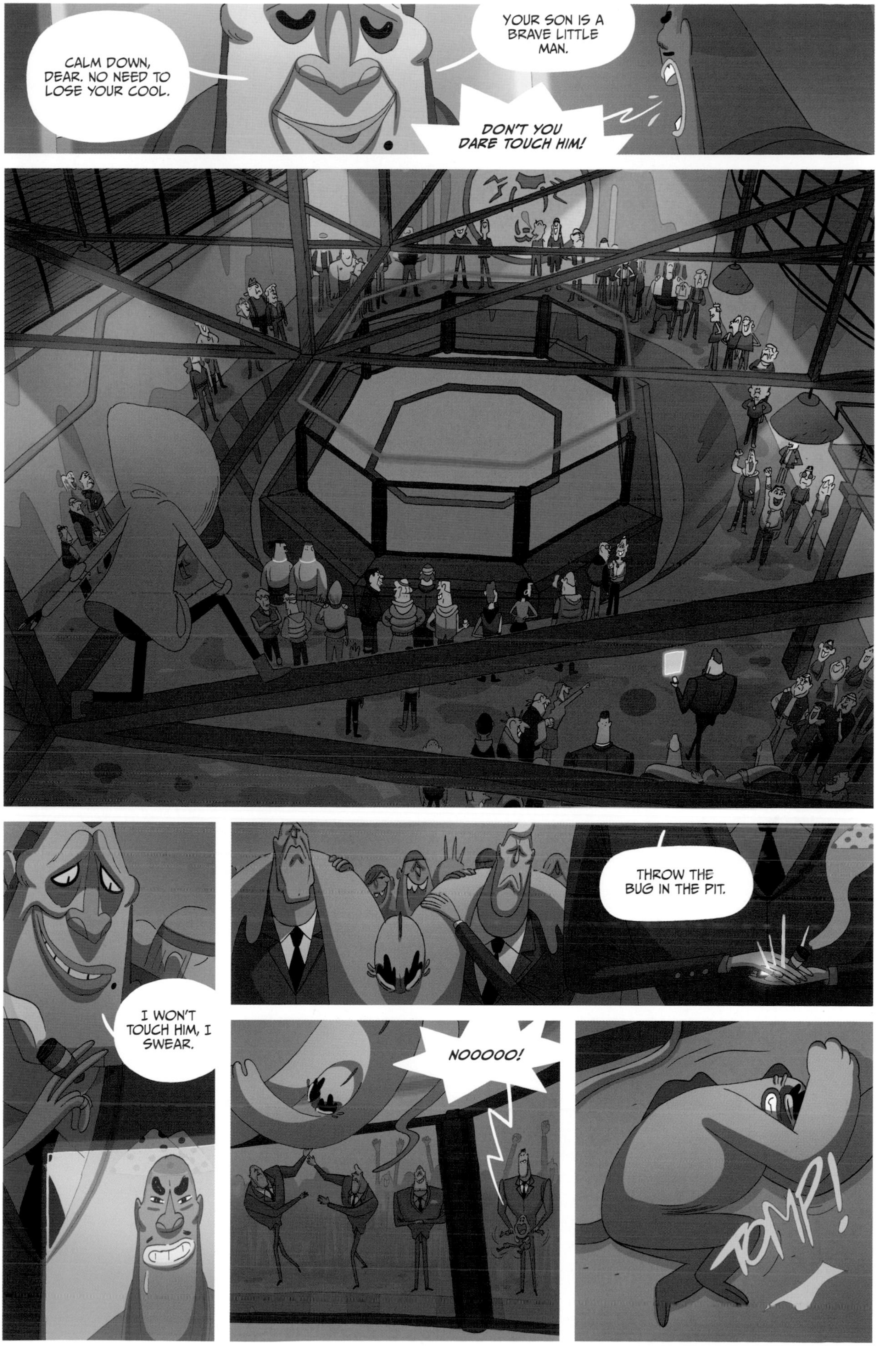

CALM DOWN, DEAR. NO NEED TO LOSE YOUR COOL.
YOUR SON IS A BRAVE LITTLE MAN.
DON'T YOU DARE TOUCH HIM!
THROW THE BUG IN THE PIT.
I WON'T TOUCH HIM, I SWEAR.
NOOOOO!
TOMP!

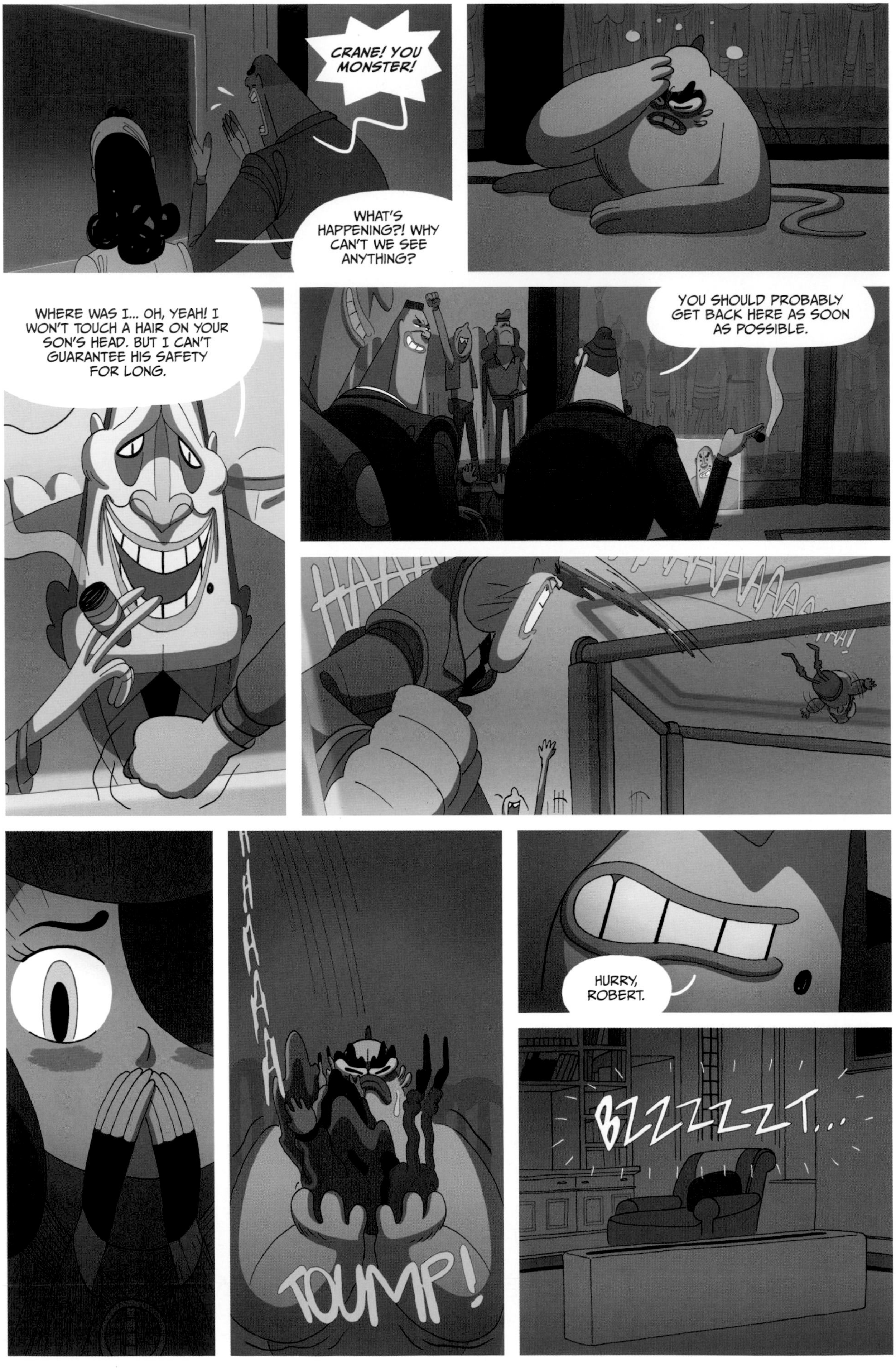
CRANE! YOU MONSTER!
WHAT'S HAPPENING?! WHY CAN'T WE SEE ANYTHING?
WHERE WAS I... OH, YEAH! I WON'T TOUCH A HAIR ON YOUR SON'S HEAD. BUT I CAN'T GUARANTEE HIS SAFETY FOR LONG.
YOU SHOULD PROBABLY GET BACK HERE AS SOON AS POSSIBLE.
TOUMP!
HURRY, ROBERT.
BZZZZZT...

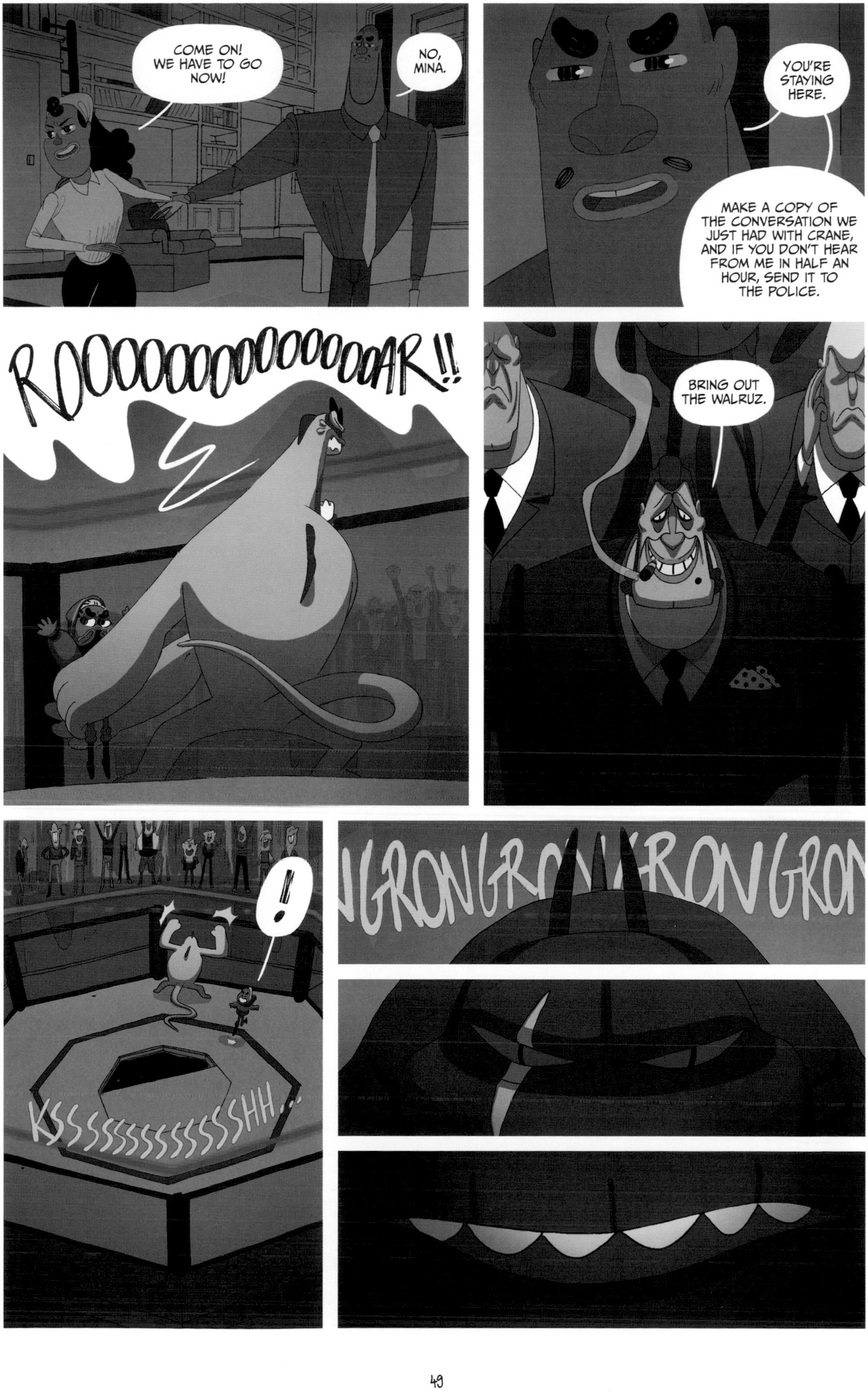
COME ON! WE HAVE TO GO NOW!
NO, MINA.
YOU'RE STAYING HERE.
MAKE A COPY OF THE CONVERSATION WE JUST HAD WITH CRANE, AND IF YOU DON'T HEAR FROM ME IN HALF AN HOUR, SEND IT TO THE POLICE.
ROOOOOOOOOOOOOAR!!
BRING OUT THE WALRUZ.
!!
KSSSSSSSSSSSSSHH...
GRONGRONGRONGRON

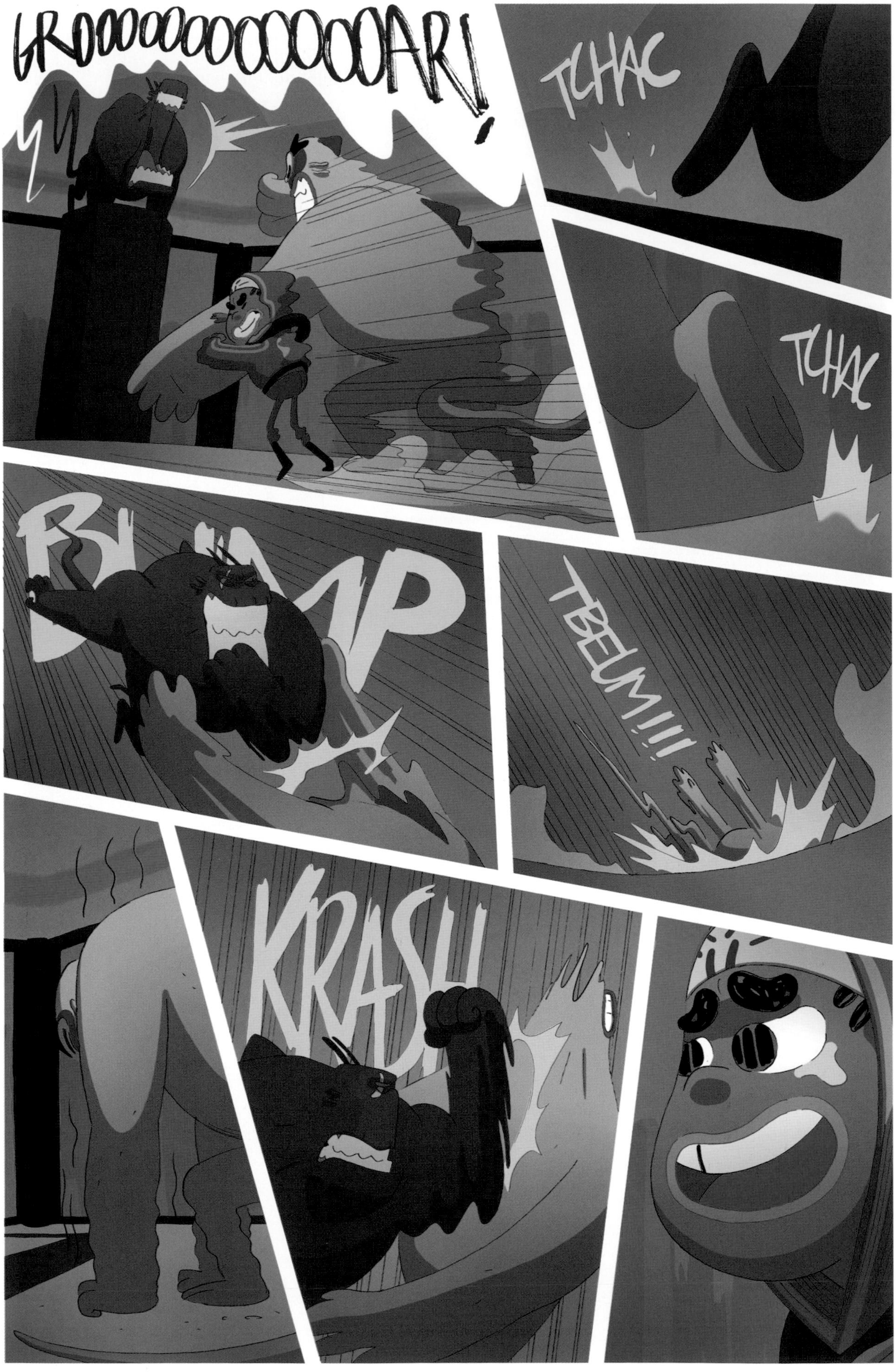
GROOOOOOOOOOOOOAR!!
TCHAC
TCHAC
BUMP
TBEUM!!!!!
KRASH

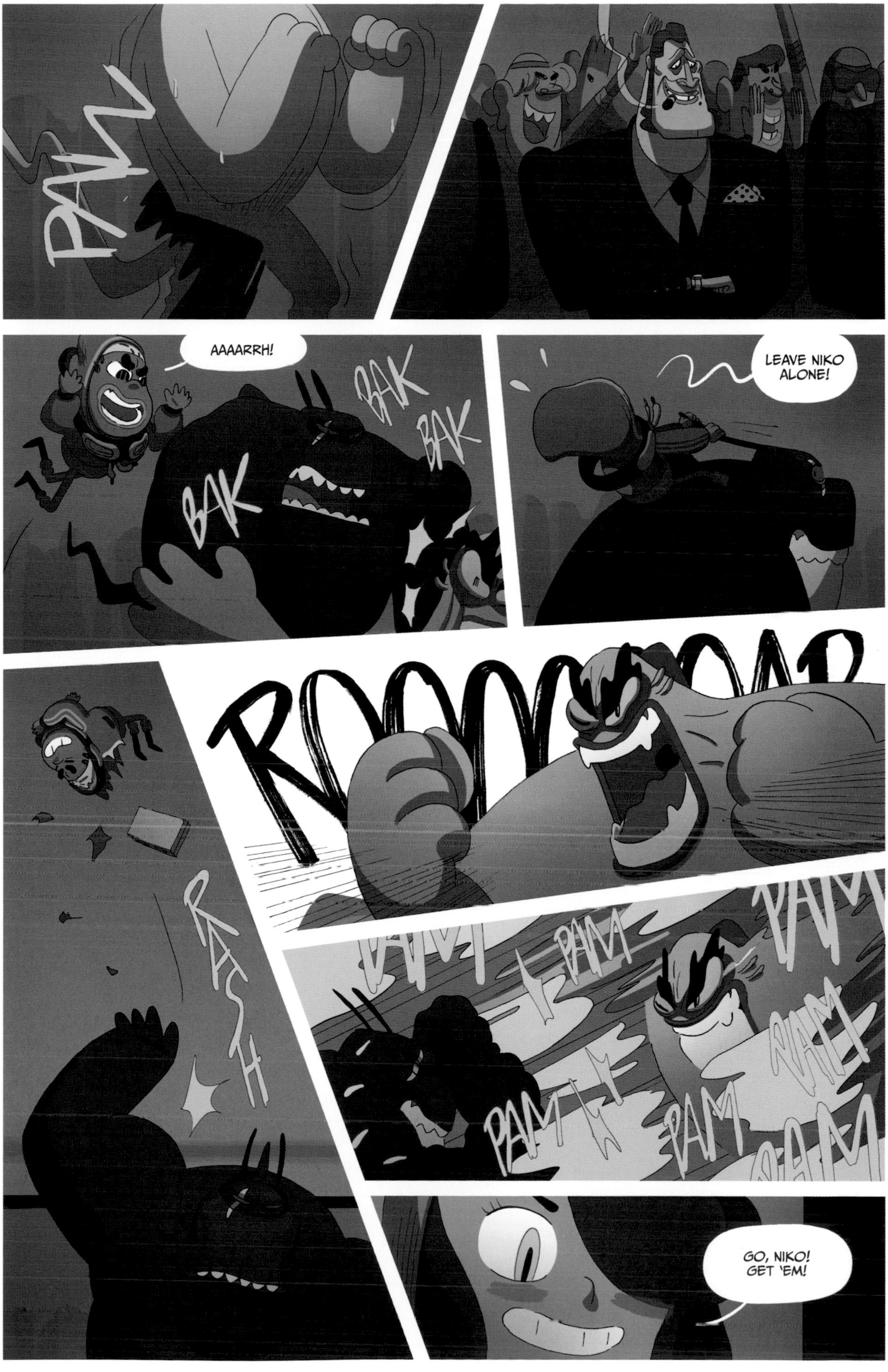
PAW
AAAARRH!
BAK
BAK
BAK
LEAVE NIKO ALONE!
ROOOOOOAR
RASH
PAM PAM PAM PAM PAM PAM PAM PAM PAM
GO, NIKO! GET 'EM!

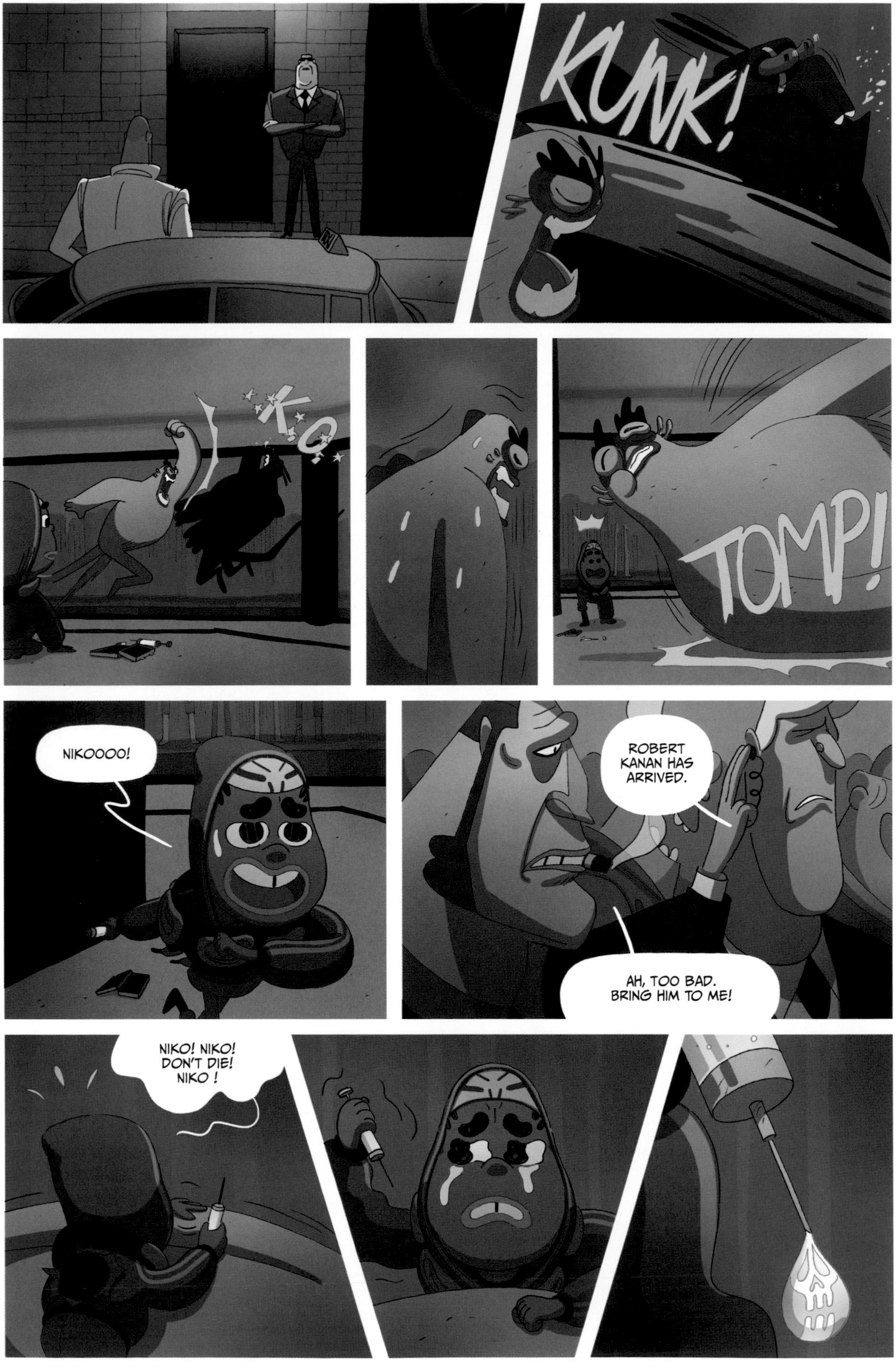
KUNK!
K.O.
TOMP!
NIKOOOO!
ROBERT KANAN HAS ARRIVED.
AH, TOO BAD. BRING HIM TO ME!
NIKO! NIKO! DON'T DIE! NIKO !

Chapter 2. The New Heroes

WHERE'S MY SON?!

NIKO... WAKE UP...

NAT! NAT!

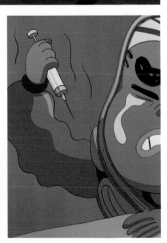

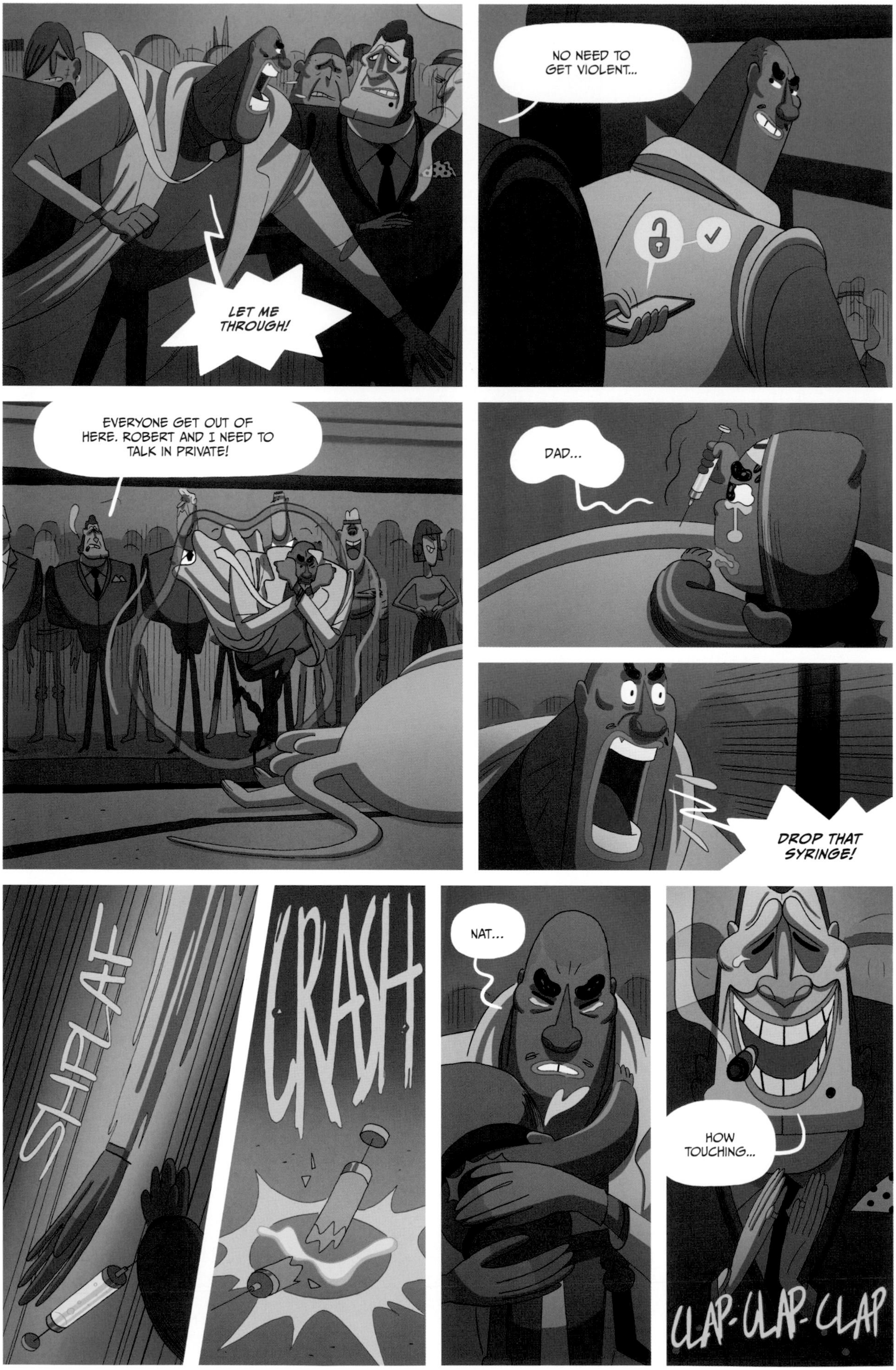
LET ME THROUGH!
NO NEED TO GET VIOLENT...
EVERYONE GET OUT OF HERE. ROBERT AND I NEED TO TALK IN PRIVATE!
DAD...
DROP THAT SYRINGE!
SHPLAF
CRASH
NAT...
HOW TOUCHING...
CLAP-CLAP-CLAP

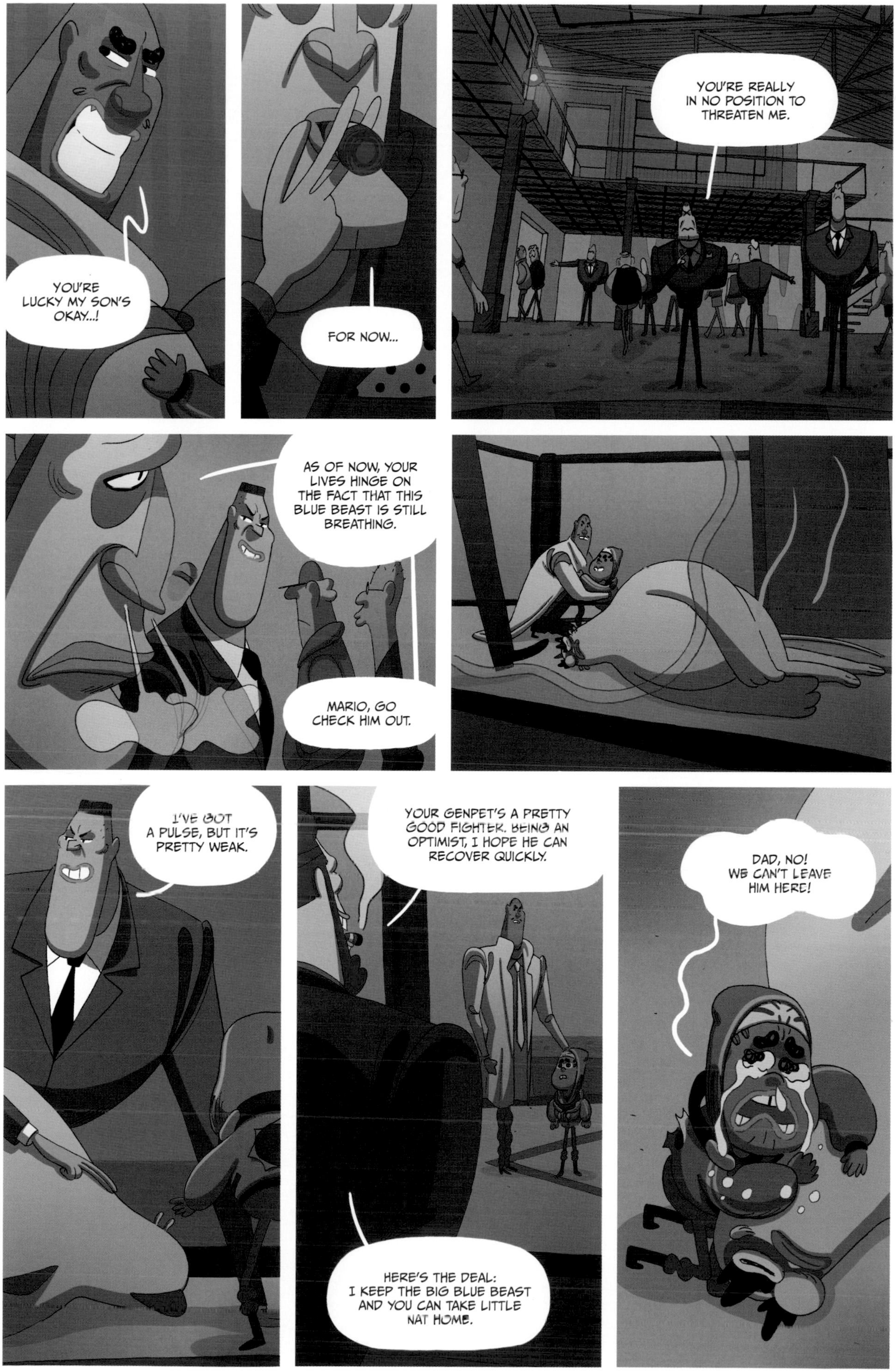
YOU'RE LUCKY MY SON'S OKAY...!
FOR NOW...
YOU'RE REALLY IN NO POSITION TO THREATEN ME.
AS OF NOW, YOUR LIVES HINGE ON THE FACT THAT THIS BLUE BEAST IS STILL BREATHING.
MARIO, GO CHECK HIM OUT.
I'VE GOT A PULSE, BUT IT'S PRETTY WEAK.
YOUR GENPET'S A PRETTY GOOD FIGHTER. BEING AN OPTIMIST, I HOPE HE CAN RECOVER QUICKLY.
HERE'S THE DEAL: I KEEP THE BIG BLUE BEAST AND YOU CAN TAKE LITTLE NAT HOME.
DAD, NO! WE CAN'T LEAVE HIM HERE!

NAT, I NEVER SHOULD HAVE PUT YOU IN DANGER.

IT'S ALL MY FAULT AND I'M SORRY. BUT... I DON'T KNOW WHAT ELSE TO DO...

THIS MAN IS CRAZY. HE TRIED TO KILL US ONCE AND HE CAN DO IT AGAIN.

WE HAVE TO BRING HIM BACK WITH US!

THEY'LL HURT HIM...

SO?

YOU CAN KEEP NIKO...

⇒SNIF⇐ ⇒SOB⇐

NO! LET ME GO!

LET ME GO! NIKO!

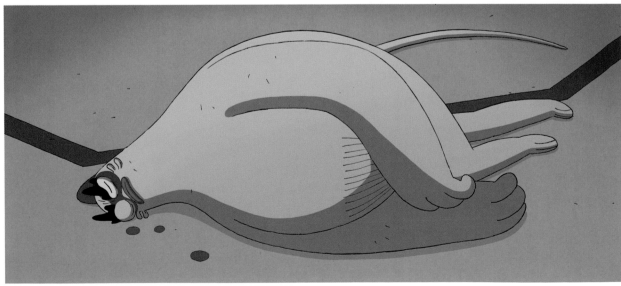

NIKO...

WE'RE NOT
FINISHED.

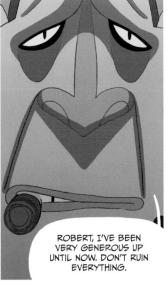
ROBERT, I'VE BEEN
VERY GENEROUS UP
UNTIL NOW. DON'T RUIN
EVERYTHING.

IF THAT BLUE THING
EARNS ME ENOUGH MONEY IN
THE RING, I'LL CONSIDER YOUR
DEBT SETTLED.

IT'S BEEN A LONG NIGHT
FOR ALL OF US. YOU SHOULD
GET YOUR KID HOME.

I HAVE TO
GET OUT OF THIS
RAT HOLE.

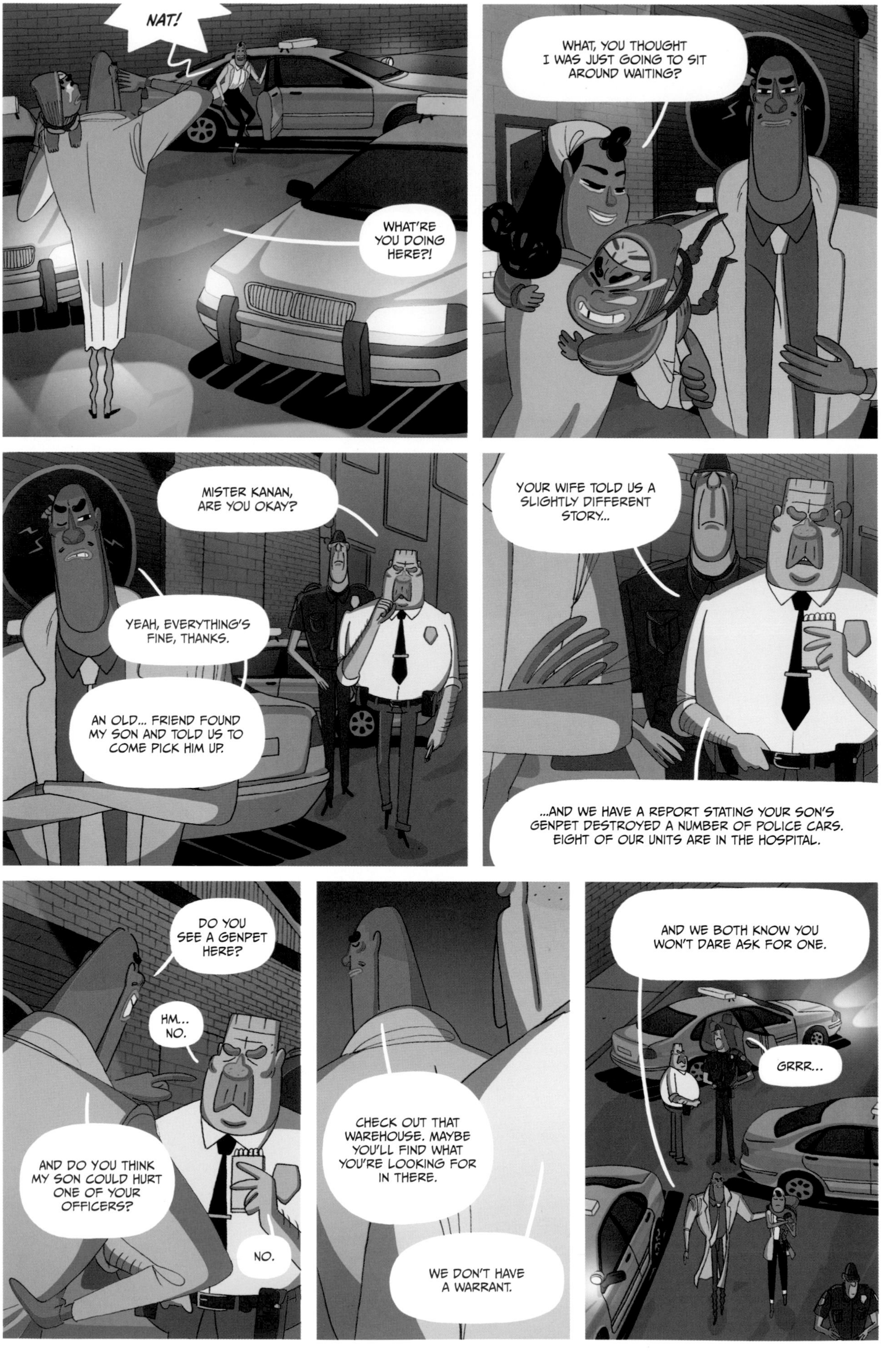
NAT!
WHAT'RE YOU DOING HERE?!
WHAT, YOU THOUGHT I WAS JUST GOING TO SIT AROUND WAITING?
MISTER KANAN, ARE YOU OKAY?
YEAH, EVERYTHING'S FINE, THANKS.
AN OLD... FRIEND FOUND MY SON AND TOLD US TO COME PICK HIM UP.
YOUR WIFE TOLD US A SLIGHTLY DIFFERENT STORY...
...AND WE HAVE A REPORT STATING YOUR SON'S GENPET DESTROYED A NUMBER OF POLICE CARS. EIGHT OF OUR UNITS ARE IN THE HOSPITAL.
DO YOU SEE A GENPET HERE?
HM... NO.
AND DO YOU THINK MY SON COULD HURT ONE OF YOUR OFFICERS?
NO.
CHECK OUT THAT WAREHOUSE. MAYBE YOU'LL FIND WHAT YOU'RE LOOKING FOR IN THERE.
WE DON'T HAVE A WARRANT.
AND WE BOTH KNOW YOU WON'T DARE ASK FOR ONE.
GRRR...

FALSE ALARM, PEOPLE! NOTHING LEFT TO DO HERE...

WE'RE GOING!

NAT...

LUISA?!

WHERE WERE YOU?

I FOLLOWED YOU. I SAW EVERYTHING!

WHO'S THIS?

THIS IS MY FRIEND... SHE HID ME FROM THE CHINESE WHEN NIKO DESTROYED THEIR DRAGON, AND HER GRANDPA GIO TAUGHT ME HOW TO MAKE PIZZA...

SHE WAS TAKING ME HOME WHEN THOSE MOBSTERS GRABBED US AND BROUGHT US HERE...

AND NOW THEY HAVE NIKO...

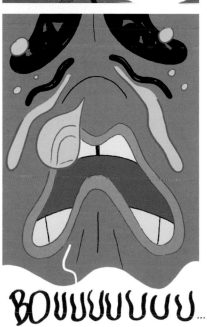

BOUUUUUUU...

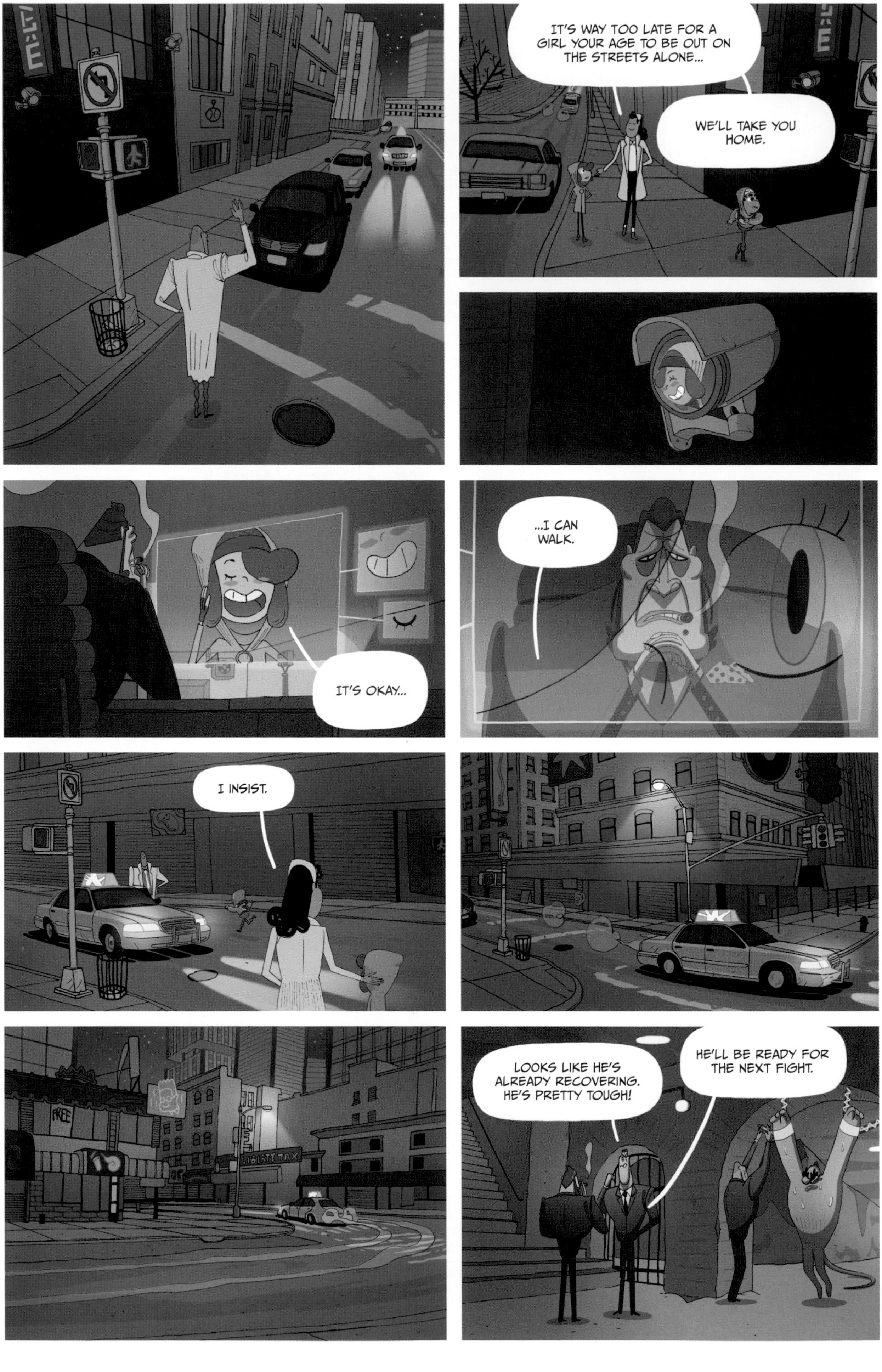
IT'S WAY TOO LATE FOR A GIRL YOUR AGE TO BE OUT ON THE STREETS ALONE...
WE'LL TAKE YOU HOME.
IT'S OKAY...
...I CAN WALK.
I INSIST.
LIBERTY TAX
LOOKS LIKE HE'S ALREADY RECOVERING. HE'S PRETTY TOUGH!
HE'LL BE READY FOR THE NEXT FIGHT.

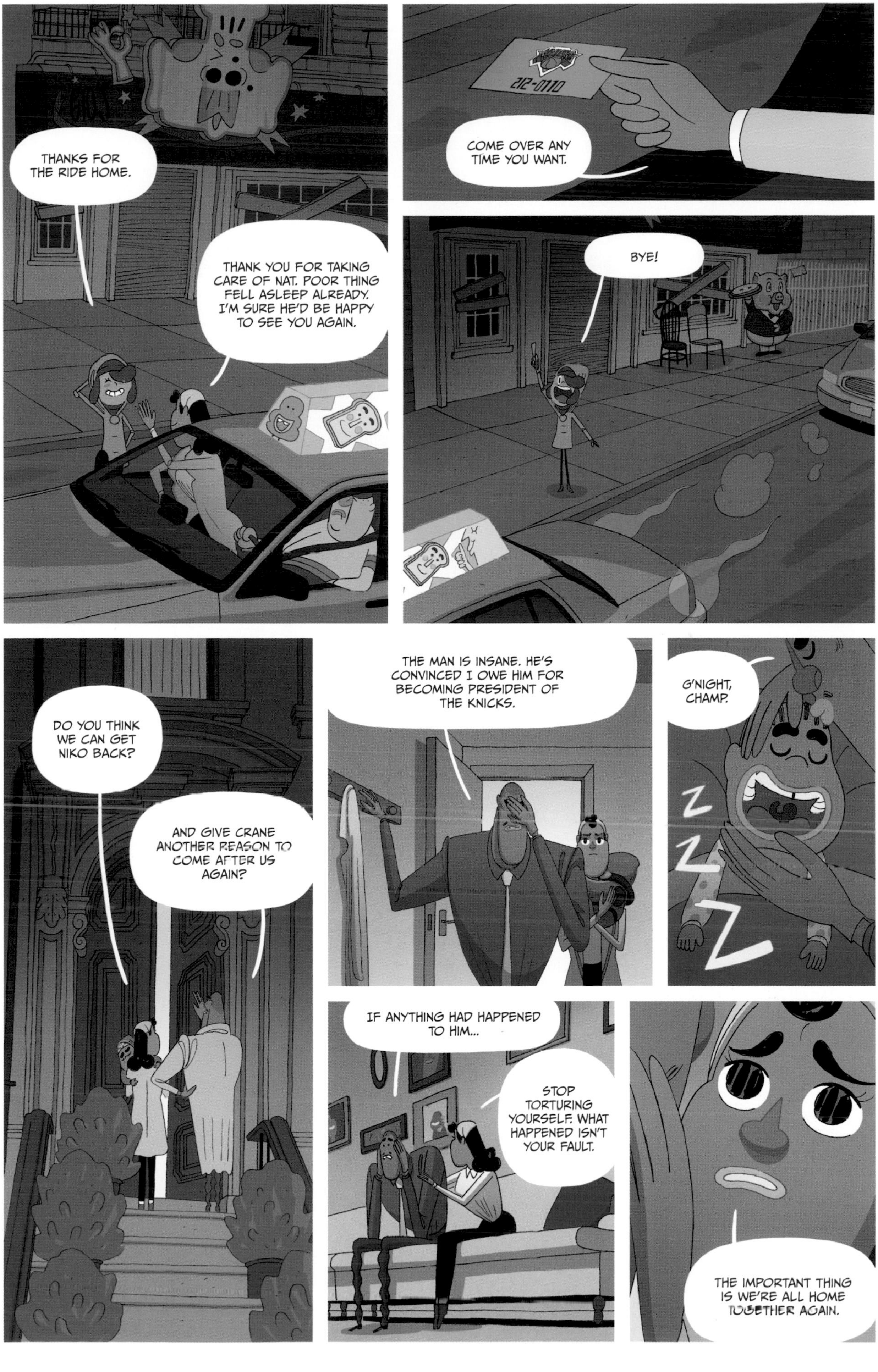
THANKS FOR THE RIDE HOME.
THANK YOU FOR TAKING CARE OF NAT. POOR THING FELL ASLEEP ALREADY. I'M SURE HE'D BE HAPPY TO SEE YOU AGAIN.
212-0110
COME OVER ANY TIME YOU WANT.
BYE!
DO YOU THINK WE CAN GET NIKO BACK?
AND GIVE CRANE ANOTHER REASON TO COME AFTER US AGAIN?
THE MAN IS INSANE. HE'S CONVINCED I OWE HIM FOR BECOMING PRESIDENT OF THE KNICKS.
G'NIGHT, CHAMP.
Z
Z
Z
IF ANYTHING HAD HAPPENED TO HIM...
STOP TORTURING YOURSELF. WHAT HAPPENED ISN'T YOUR FAULT.
THE IMPORTANT THING IS WE'RE ALL HOME TOGETHER AGAIN.

NAT, SWEETIE, ARE YOU GONNA STAY IN BED ALL DAY...?

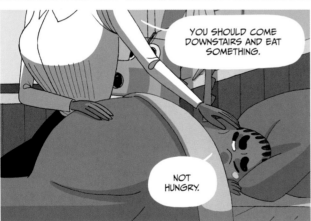

YOU SHOULD COME DOWNSTAIRS AND EAT SOMETHING.

NOT HUNGRY.

I UNDERSTAND YOU'RE ANGRY, BUT YOU CAN'T STAY IN YOUR ROOM FOREVER.

WE'LL GO GET YOU ANOTHER GENPET.

I DON'T WANT ANOTHER GENPET! I WANT NIKO!

THAT'S NOT POSSIBLE, NAT. I'M SORRY.

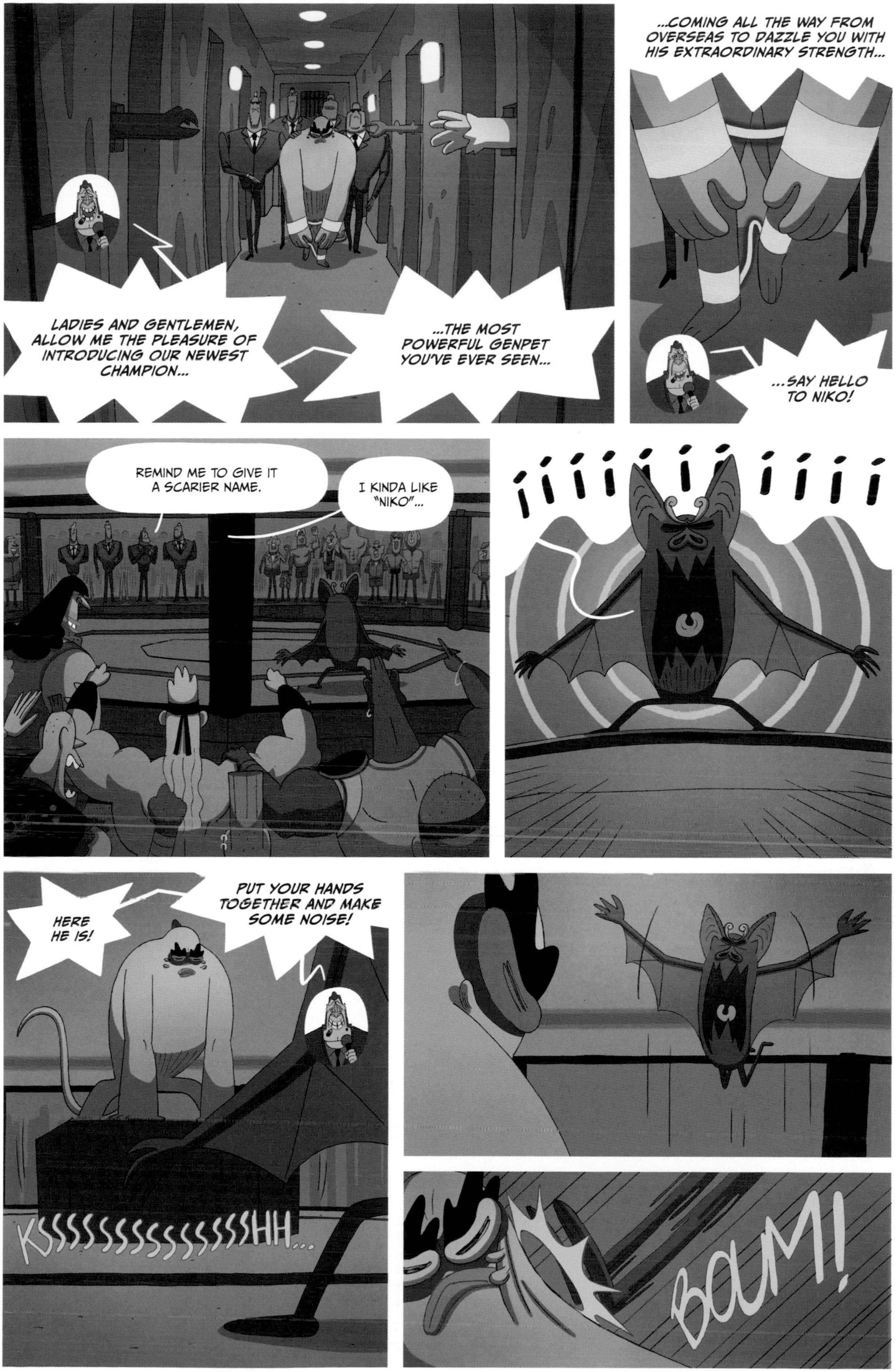
LADIES AND GENTLEMEN, ALLOW ME THE PLEASURE OF INTRODUCING OUR NEWEST CHAMPION...
...THE MOST POWERFUL GENPET YOU'VE EVER SEEN...
...COMING ALL THE WAY FROM OVERSEAS TO DAZZLE YOU WITH HIS EXTRAORDINARY STRENGTH...
...SAY HELLO TO NIKO!
REMIND ME TO GIVE IT A SCARIER NAME.
I KINDA LIKE "NIKO"...
¡¡¡¡¡¡¡¡¡¡
HERE HE IS!
PUT YOUR HANDS TOGETHER AND MAKE SOME NOISE!
KSSSSSSSSSSSSSSSHH...
BOUM!

WH... WHAT'S HE DOING? WHY DOESN'T HE DEFEND HIMSELF?
I THINK HE'S SAD.
DUMB ANIMAL!
HE CAN'T BE SAD!
TOMP TOMP TOMP TOMP
TOMP TOMP TOMP TOMP
YEAH, HE CAN.
OUR FAMILY DOG DIED OF SADNESS A FEW DAYS AFTER MY GRANDFATHER PASSED AWAY...
STOP, ADAM, YOU'RE GONNA MAKE ME CRY...
C'MON! FIGHT, DUMMY!
TOUMP!!
KRAK !!
BOUM
WH... WHAT'D HE JUST DO?
HE, UH... HE CAN'T JUMP OUT OF THE PIT, CAN HE?
PROBABLY.
I'VE SEEN HIM JUMP A LOT HIGHER.

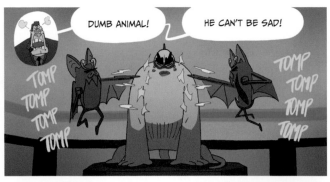

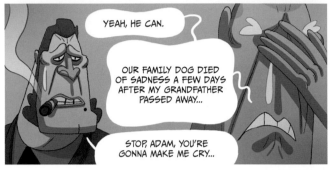

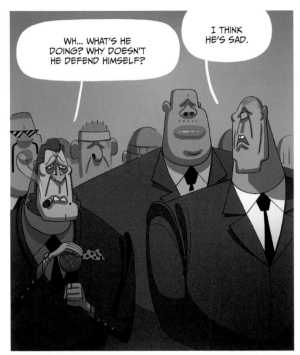

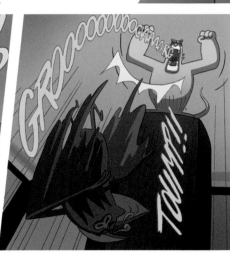

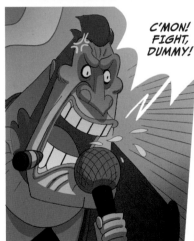

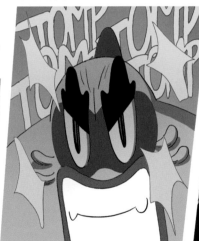

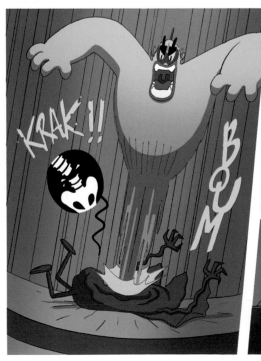

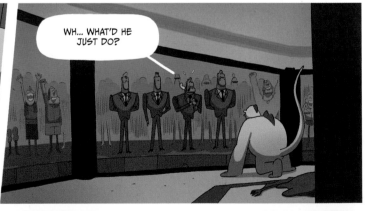

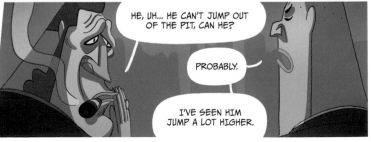

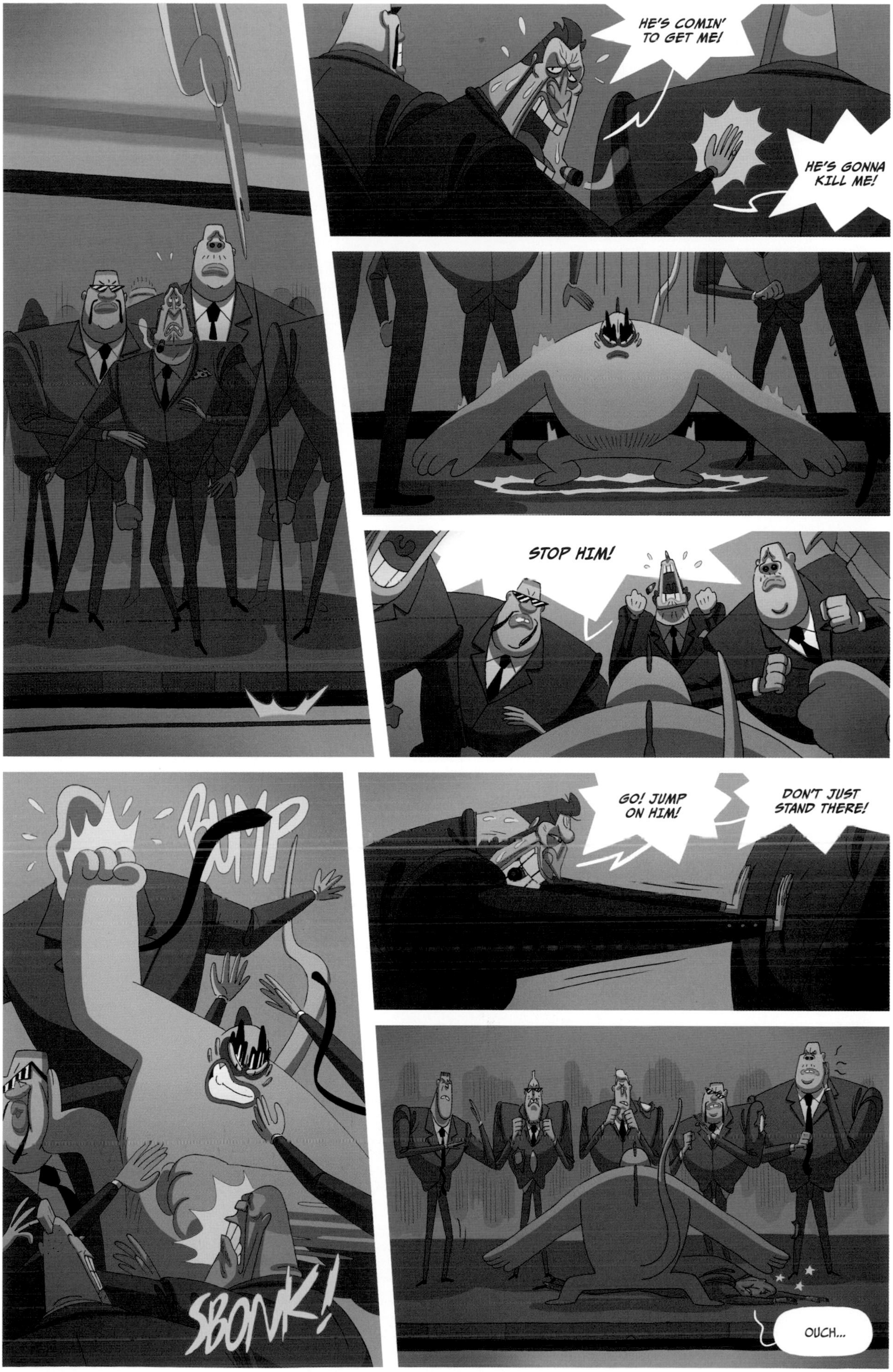
HE'S COMIN' TO GET ME!
HE'S GONNA KILL ME!
STOP HIM!
BUMP
SBONK!
GO! JUMP ON HIM!
DON'T JUST STAND THERE!
OUCH...

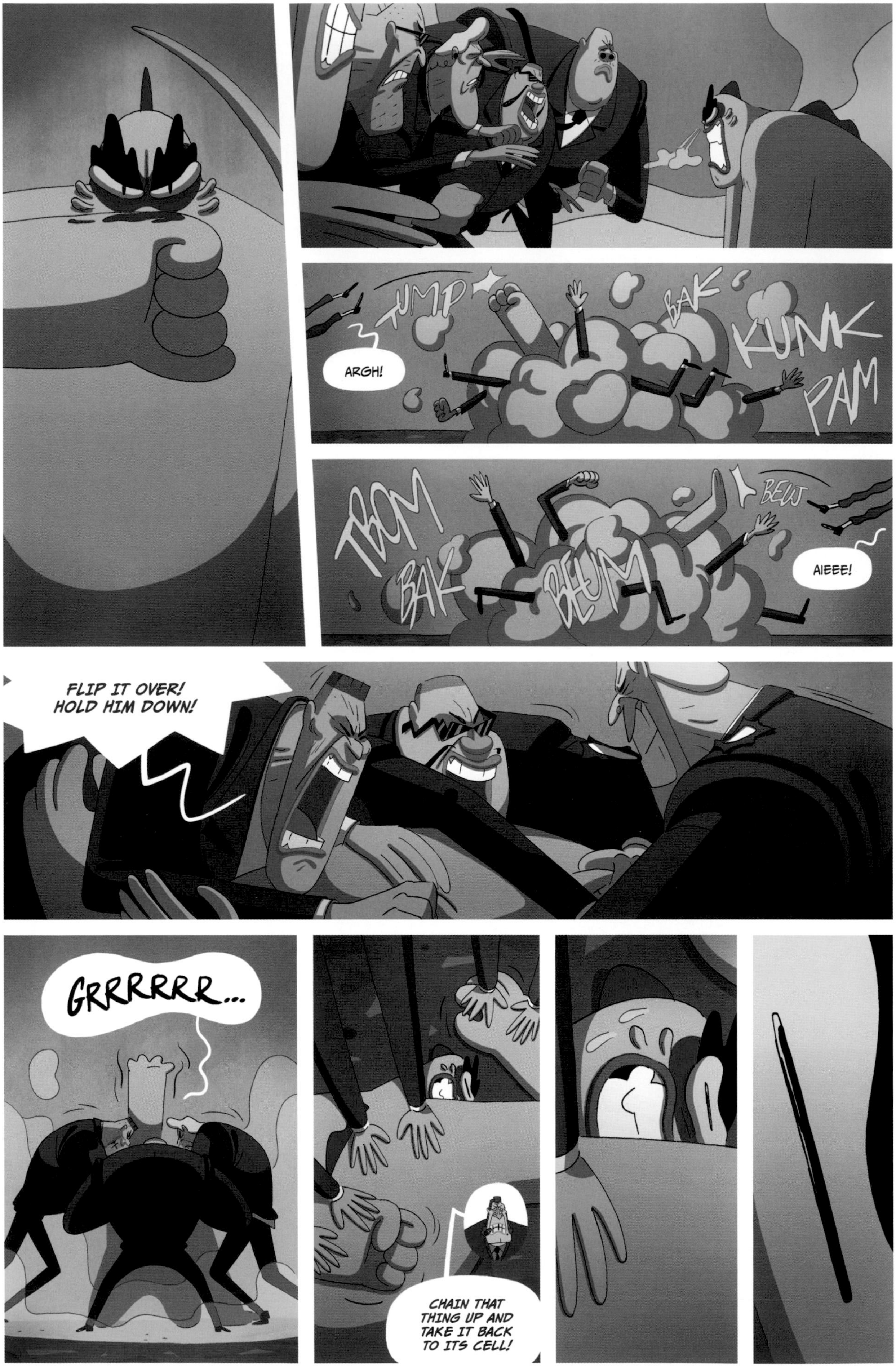
TUMP
BAK
KUNK
PAM
ARGH!
TBOM
BEW
BAK
BLUM
AIEEE!
FLIP IT OVER! HOLD HIM DOWN!
GRRRRRR...
CHAIN THAT THING UP AND TAKE IT BACK TO ITS CELL!

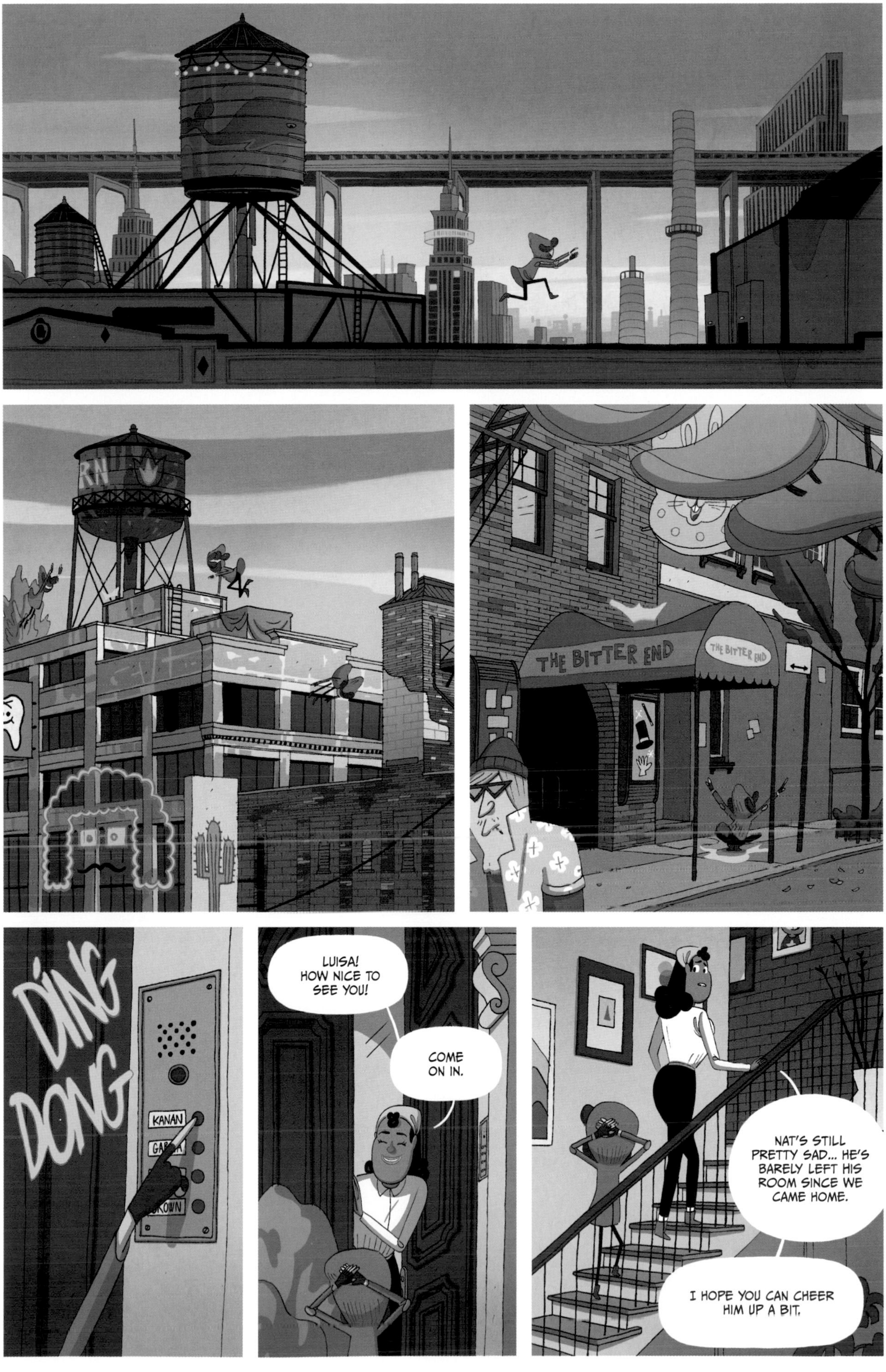
THE BITTER END
THE BITTER END
DING DONG
KANAN
LUISA! HOW NICE TO SEE YOU!
COME ON IN.
NAT'S STILL PRETTY SAD... HE'S BARELY LEFT HIS ROOM SINCE WE CAME HOME.
I HOPE YOU CAN CHEER HIM UP A BIT.

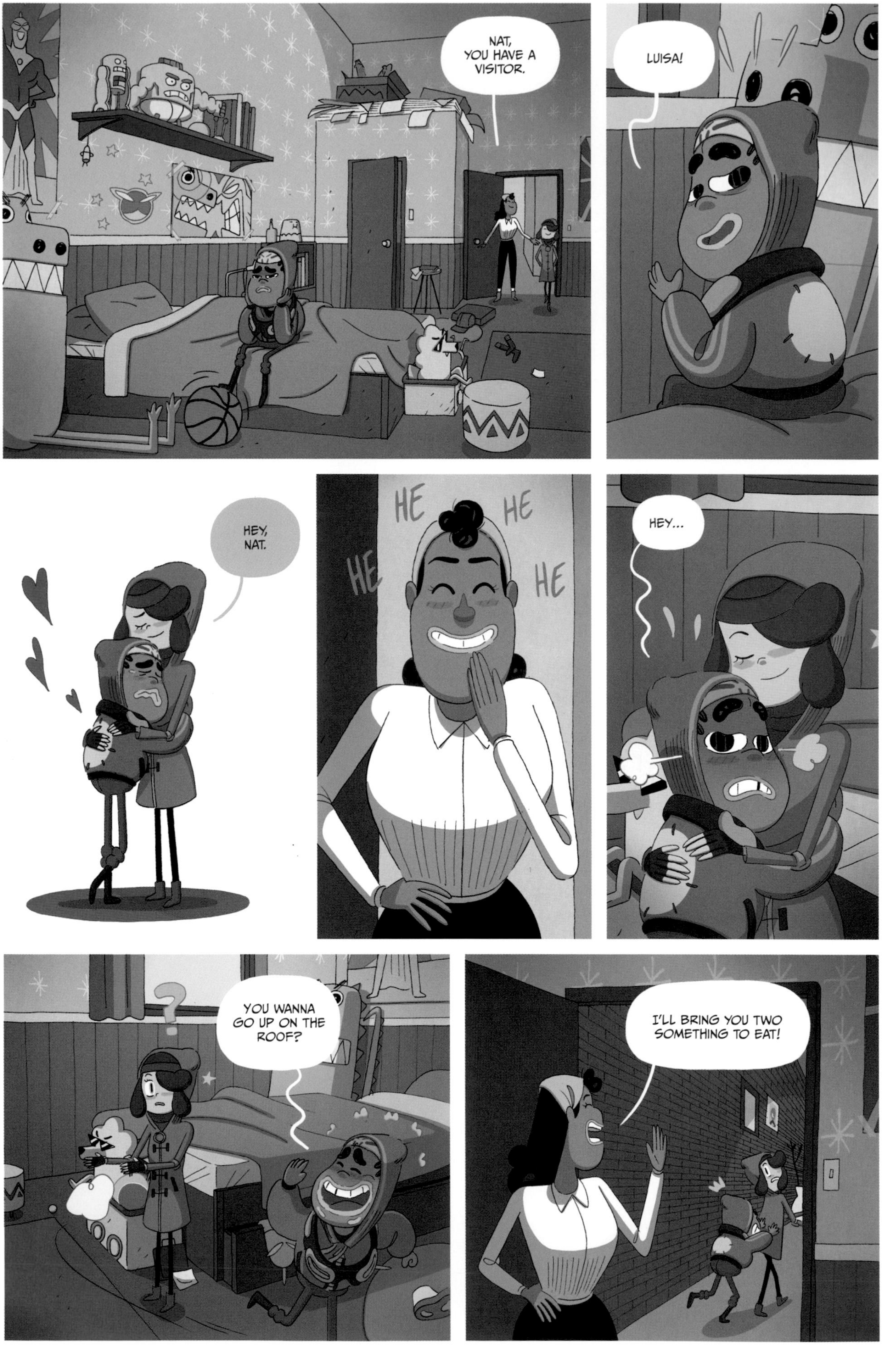
NAT, YOU HAVE A VISITOR.
LUISA!
HEY, NAT.
HE HE HE HE
HEY...
YOU WANNA GO UP ON THE ROOF?
I'LL BRING YOU TWO SOMETHING TO EAT!

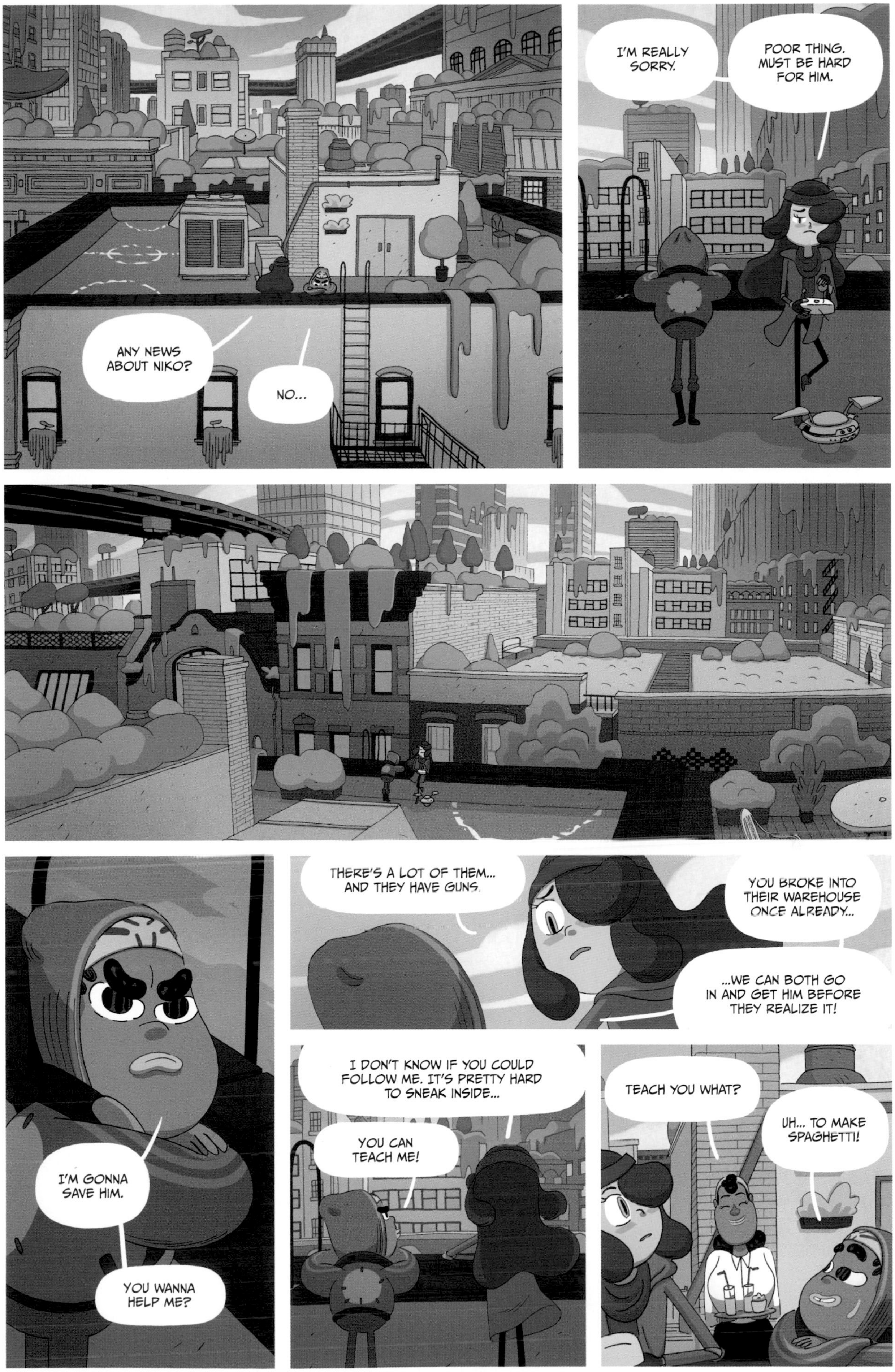
ANY NEWS ABOUT NIKO?
NO...
I'M REALLY SORRY.
POOR THING. MUST BE HARD FOR HIM.
I'M GONNA SAVE HIM.
YOU WANNA HELP ME?
THERE'S A LOT OF THEM... AND THEY HAVE GUNS.
YOU BROKE INTO THEIR WAREHOUSE ONCE ALREADY...
...WE CAN BOTH GO IN AND GET HIM BEFORE THEY REALIZE IT!
I DON'T KNOW IF YOU COULD FOLLOW ME. IT'S PRETTY HARD TO SNEAK INSIDE...
YOU CAN TEACH ME!
TEACH YOU WHAT?
UH... TO MAKE SPAGHETTI!

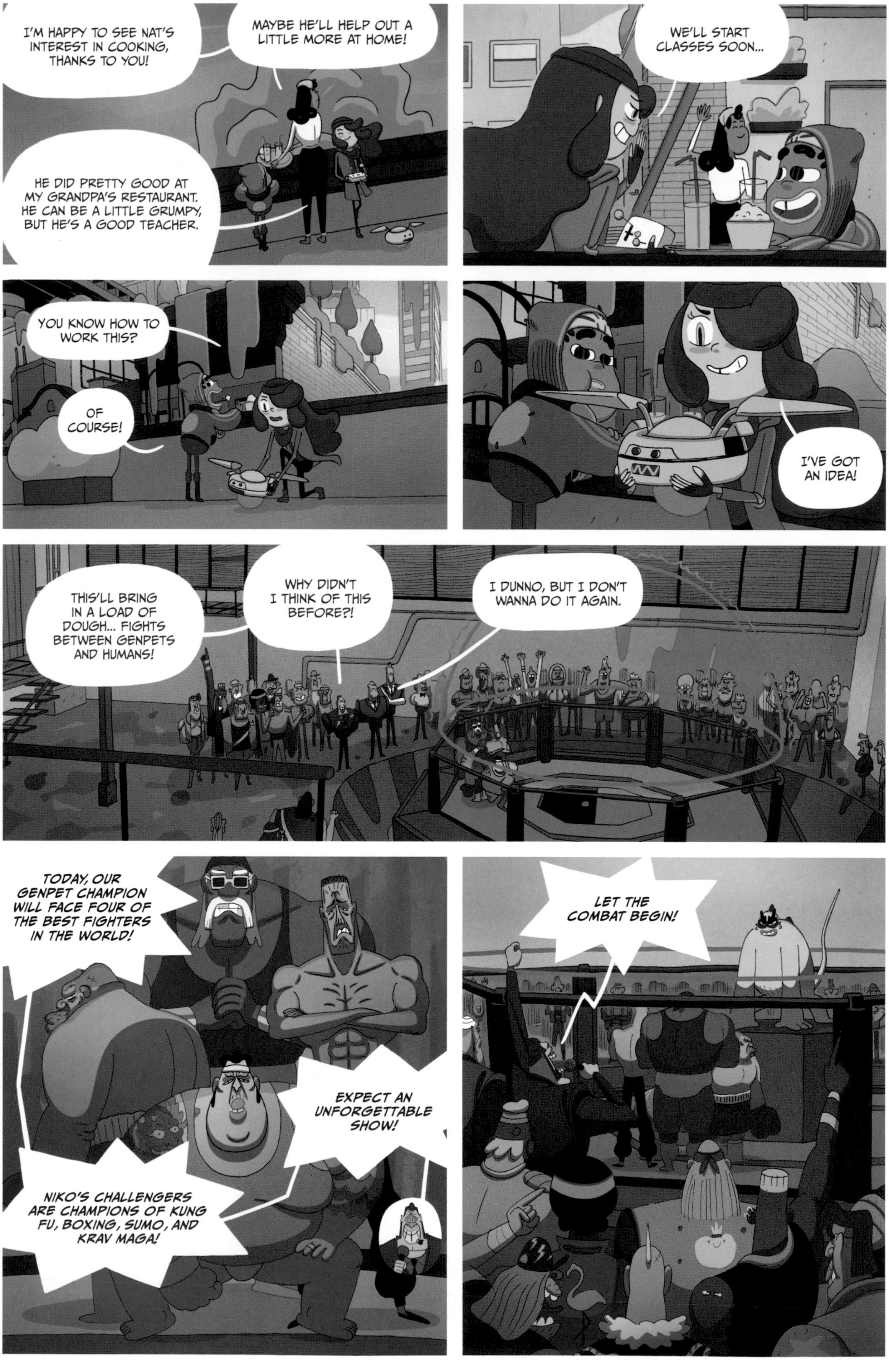
I'M HAPPY TO SEE NAT'S INTEREST IN COOKING, THANKS TO YOU!
MAYBE HE'LL HELP OUT A LITTLE MORE AT HOME!
HE DID PRETTY GOOD AT MY GRANDPA'S RESTAURANT. HE CAN BE A LITTLE GRUMPY, BUT HE'S A GOOD TEACHER.
WE'LL START CLASSES SOON...
YOU KNOW HOW TO WORK THIS?
OF COURSE!
I'VE GOT AN IDEA!
THIS'LL BRING IN A LOAD OF DOUGH... FIGHTS BETWEEN GENPETS AND HUMANS!
WHY DIDN'T I THINK OF THIS BEFORE?!
I DUNNO, BUT I DON'T WANNA DO IT AGAIN.
TODAY, OUR GENPET CHAMPION WILL FACE FOUR OF THE BEST FIGHTERS IN THE WORLD!
EXPECT AN UNFORGETTABLE SHOW!
NIKO'S CHALLENGERS ARE CHAMPIONS OF KUNG FU, BOXING, SUMO, AND KRAV MAGA!
LET THE COMBAT BEGIN!

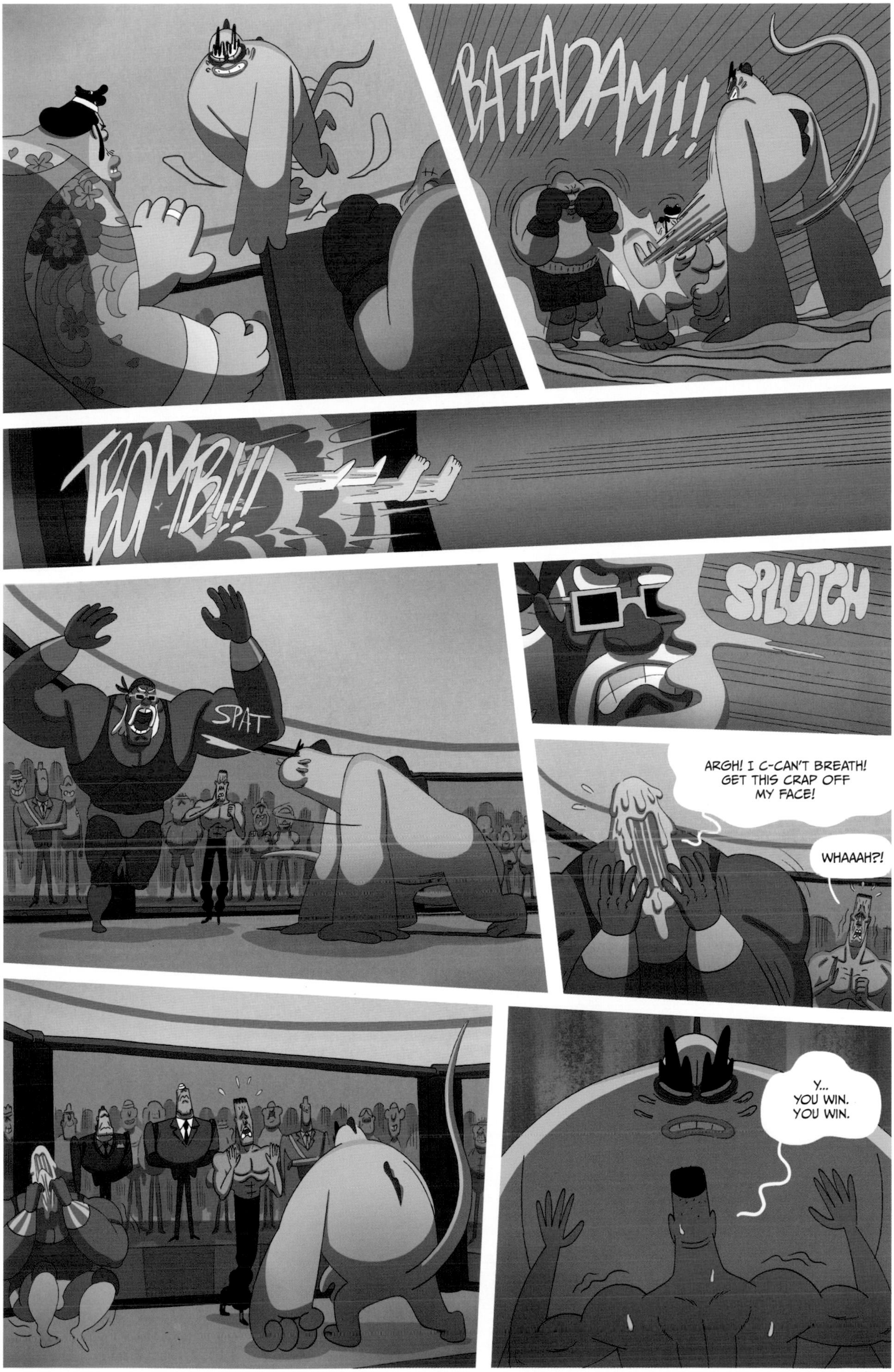
BATADAM!!
TBOMB!!!
SPLUTCH
SPAT
ARGH! I C-CAN'T BREATH! GET THIS CRAP OFF MY FACE!
WHAAAH?!
Y... YOU WIN. YOU WIN.

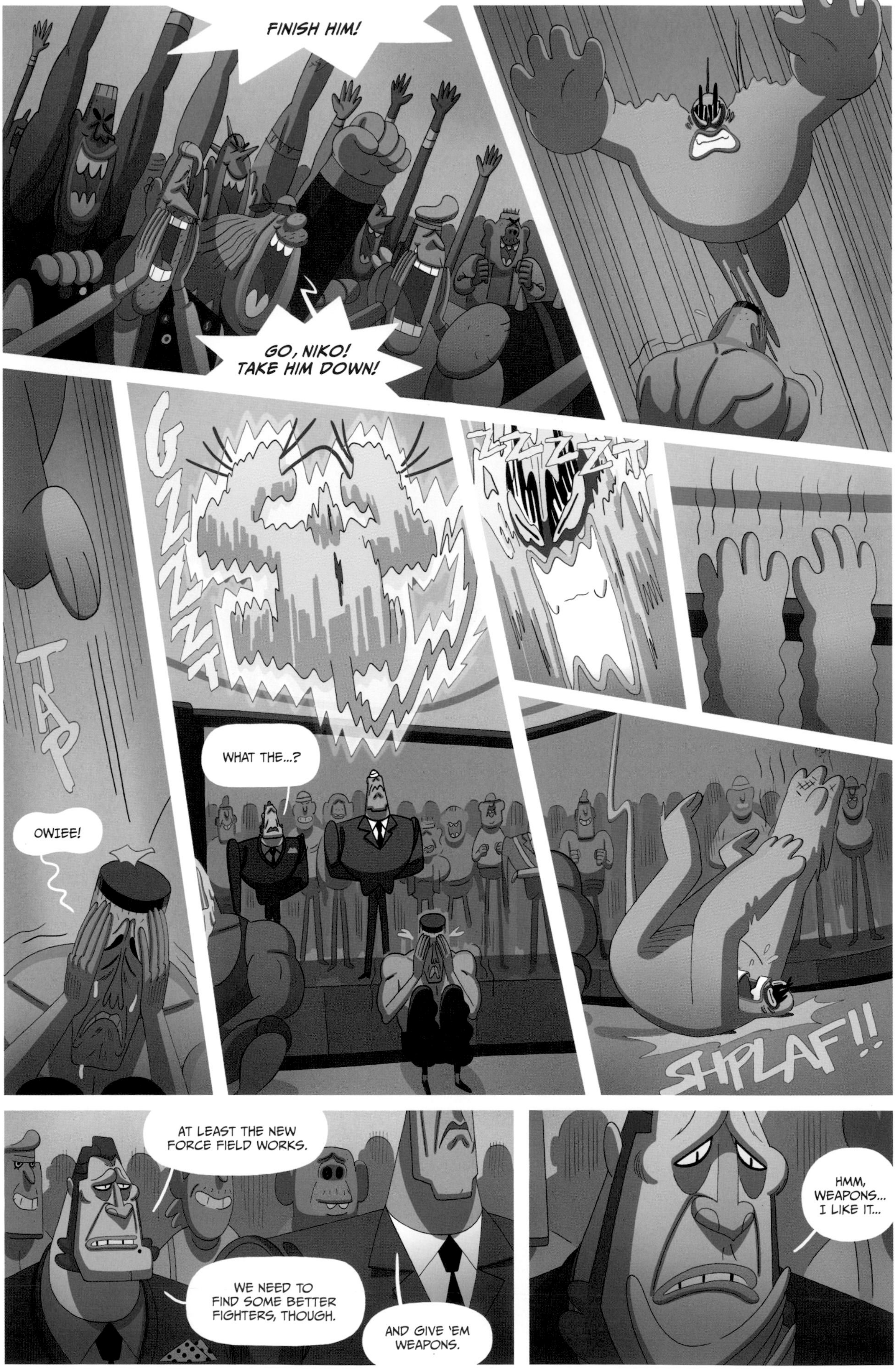
FINISH HIM!
GO, NIKO! TAKE HIM DOWN!
TAP
OWIEE!
GZZZZZT
ZZZZZZT
WHAT THE...?
SHPLAF!!
AT LEAST THE NEW FORCE FIELD WORKS.
WE NEED TO FIND SOME BETTER FIGHTERS, THOUGH.
AND GIVE 'EM WEAPONS.
HMM, WEAPONS... I LIKE IT...

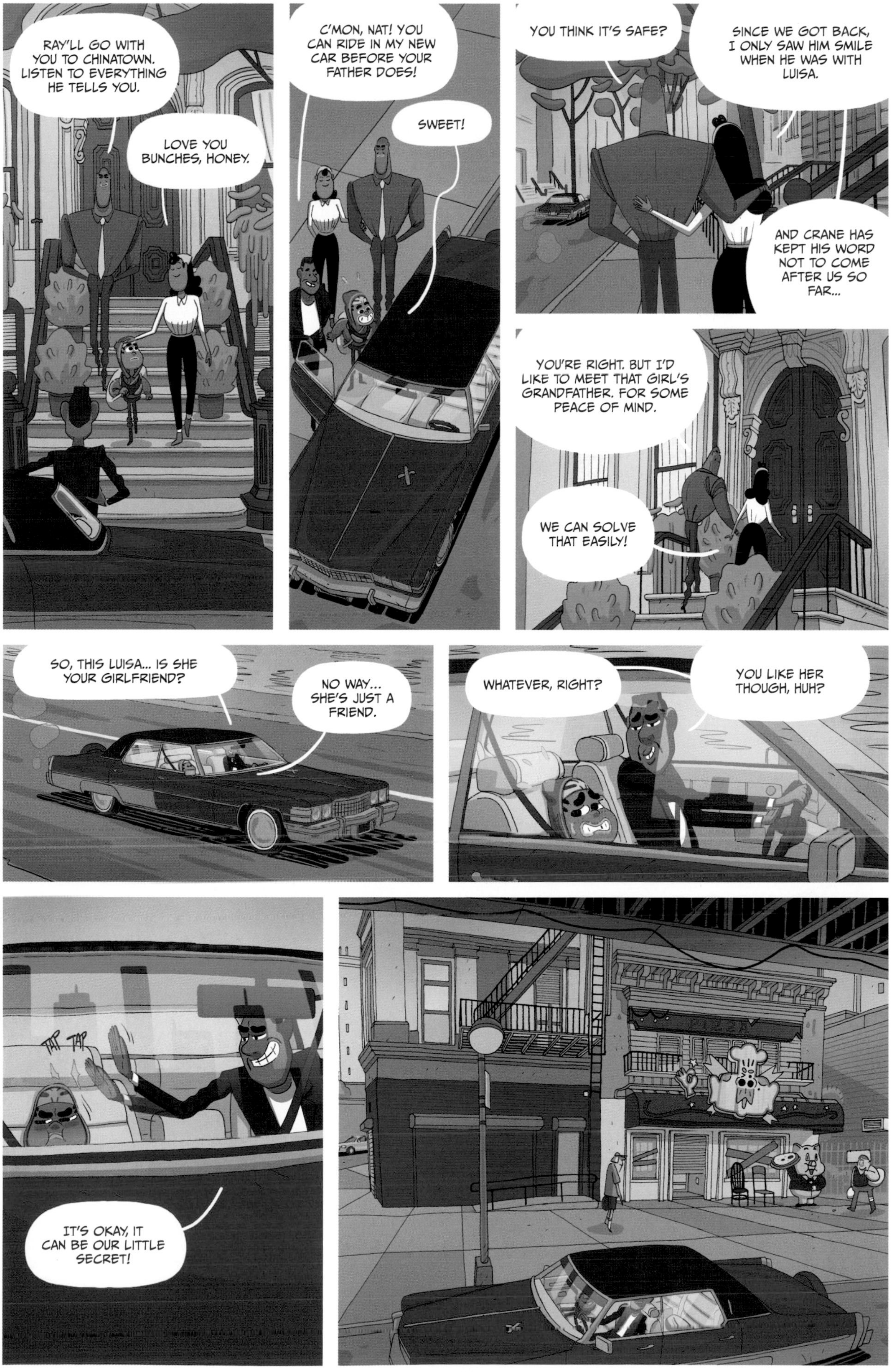
RAY'LL GO WITH YOU TO CHINATOWN. LISTEN TO EVERYTHING HE TELLS YOU.
LOVE YOU BUNCHES, HONEY.
C'MON, NAT! YOU CAN RIDE IN MY NEW CAR BEFORE YOUR FATHER DOES!
SWEET!
YOU THINK IT'S SAFE?
SINCE WE GOT BACK, I ONLY SAW HIM SMILE WHEN HE WAS WITH LUISA.
AND CRANE HAS KEPT HIS WORD NOT TO COME AFTER US SO FAR...
YOU'RE RIGHT. BUT I'D LIKE TO MEET THAT GIRL'S GRANDFATHER. FOR SOME PEACE OF MIND.
WE CAN SOLVE THAT EASILY!
SO, THIS LUISA... IS SHE YOUR GIRLFRIEND?
NO WAY... SHE'S JUST A FRIEND.
WHATEVER, RIGHT?
YOU LIKE HER THOUGH, HUH?
TAP TAP
IT'S OKAY, IT CAN BE OUR LITTLE SECRET!

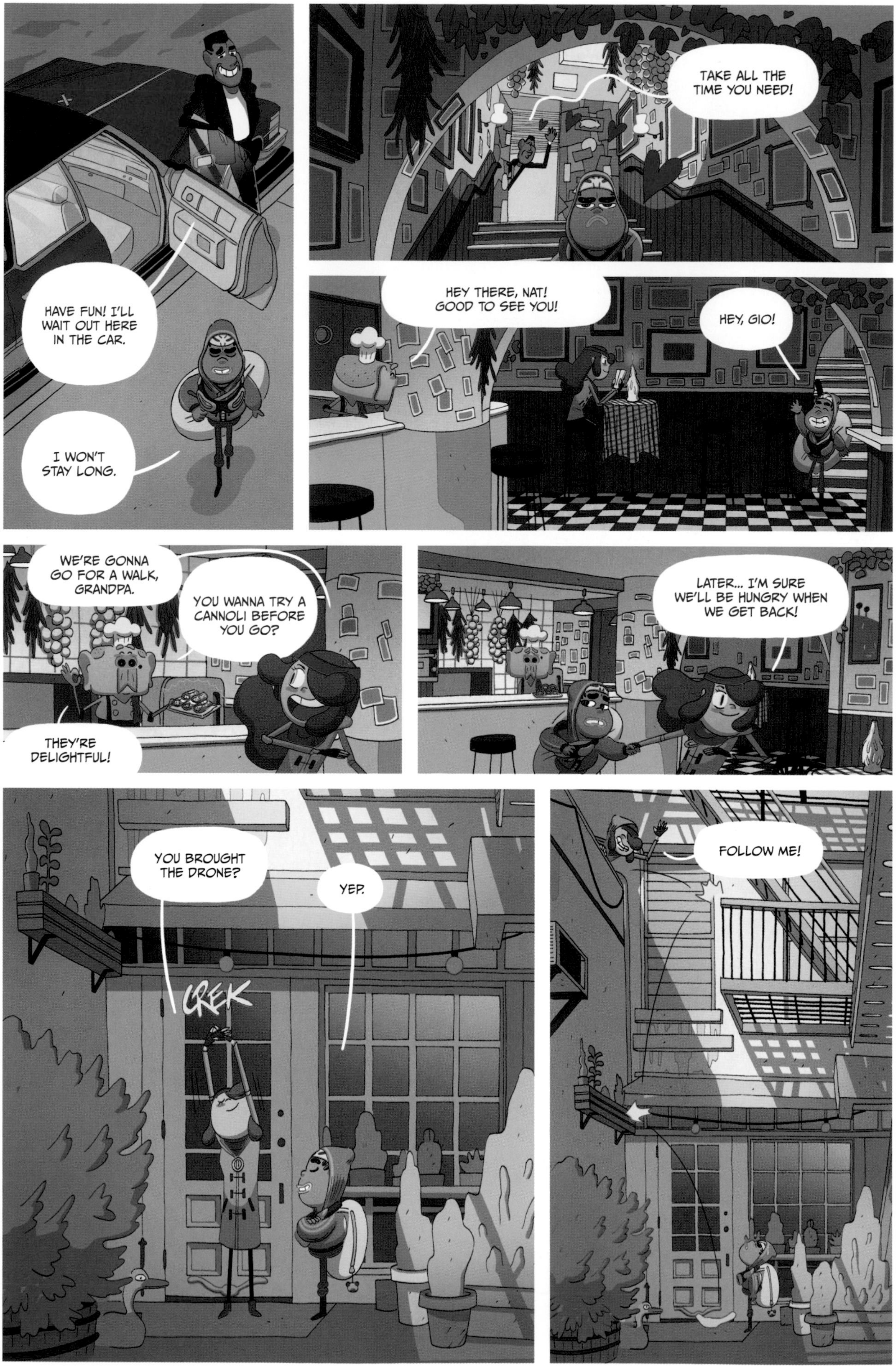
HAVE FUN! I'LL WAIT OUT HERE IN THE CAR.
I WON'T STAY LONG.
TAKE ALL THE TIME YOU NEED!
HEY THERE, NAT! GOOD TO SEE YOU!
HEY, GIO!
WE'RE GONNA GO FOR A WALK, GRANDPA.
YOU WANNA TRY A CANNOLI BEFORE YOU GO?
THEY'RE DELIGHTFUL!
LATER... I'M SURE WE'LL BE HUNGRY WHEN WE GET BACK!
YOU BROUGHT THE DRONE?
YEP.
CREK
FOLLOW ME!

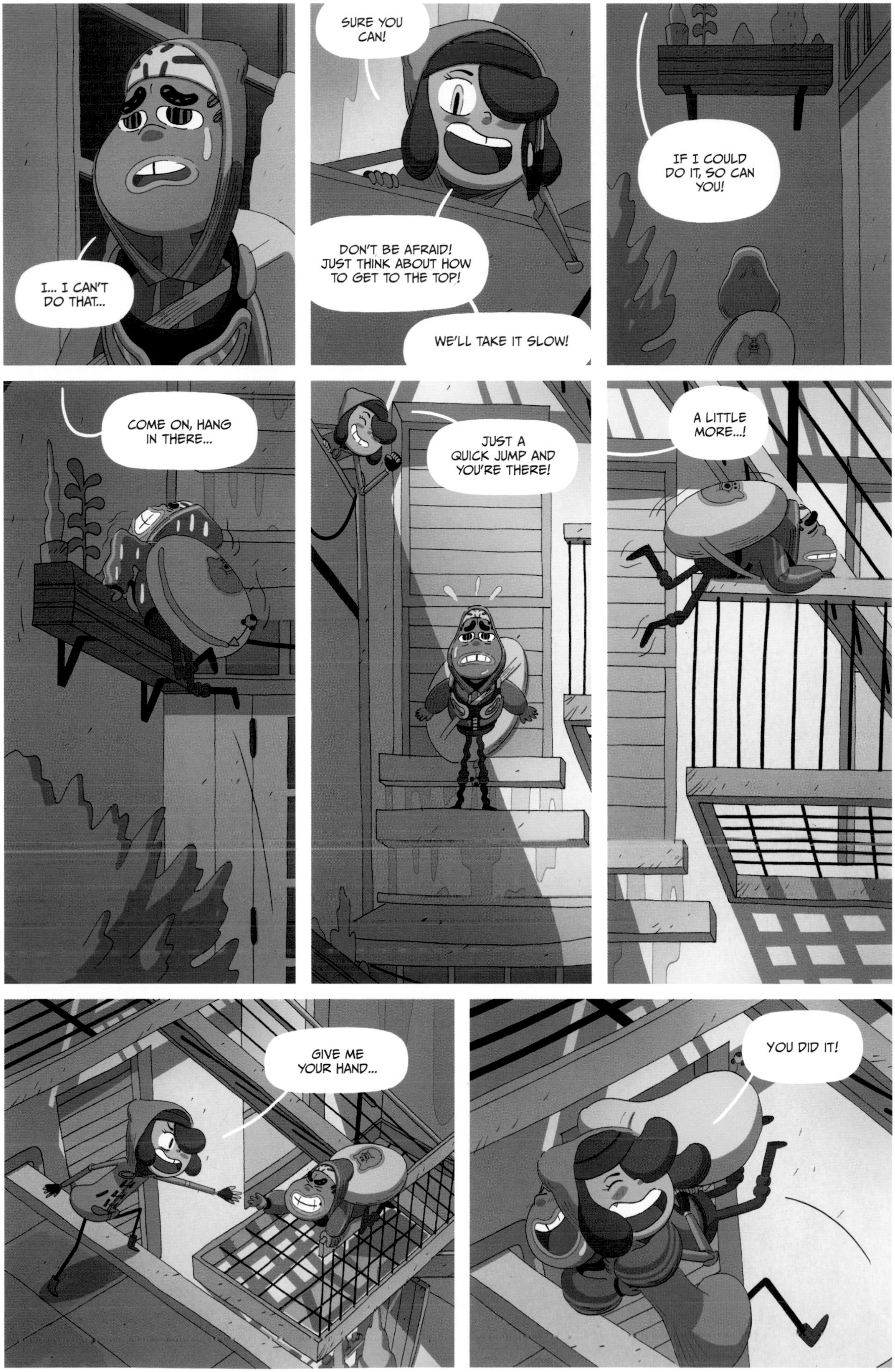
I... I CAN'T DO THAT...
SURE YOU CAN!
DON'T BE AFRAID! JUST THINK ABOUT HOW TO GET TO THE TOP!
WE'LL TAKE IT SLOW!
IF I COULD DO IT, SO CAN YOU!
COME ON, HANG IN THERE...
JUST A QUICK JUMP AND YOU'RE THERE!
A LITTLE MORE...!
GIVE ME YOUR HAND...
YOU DID IT!

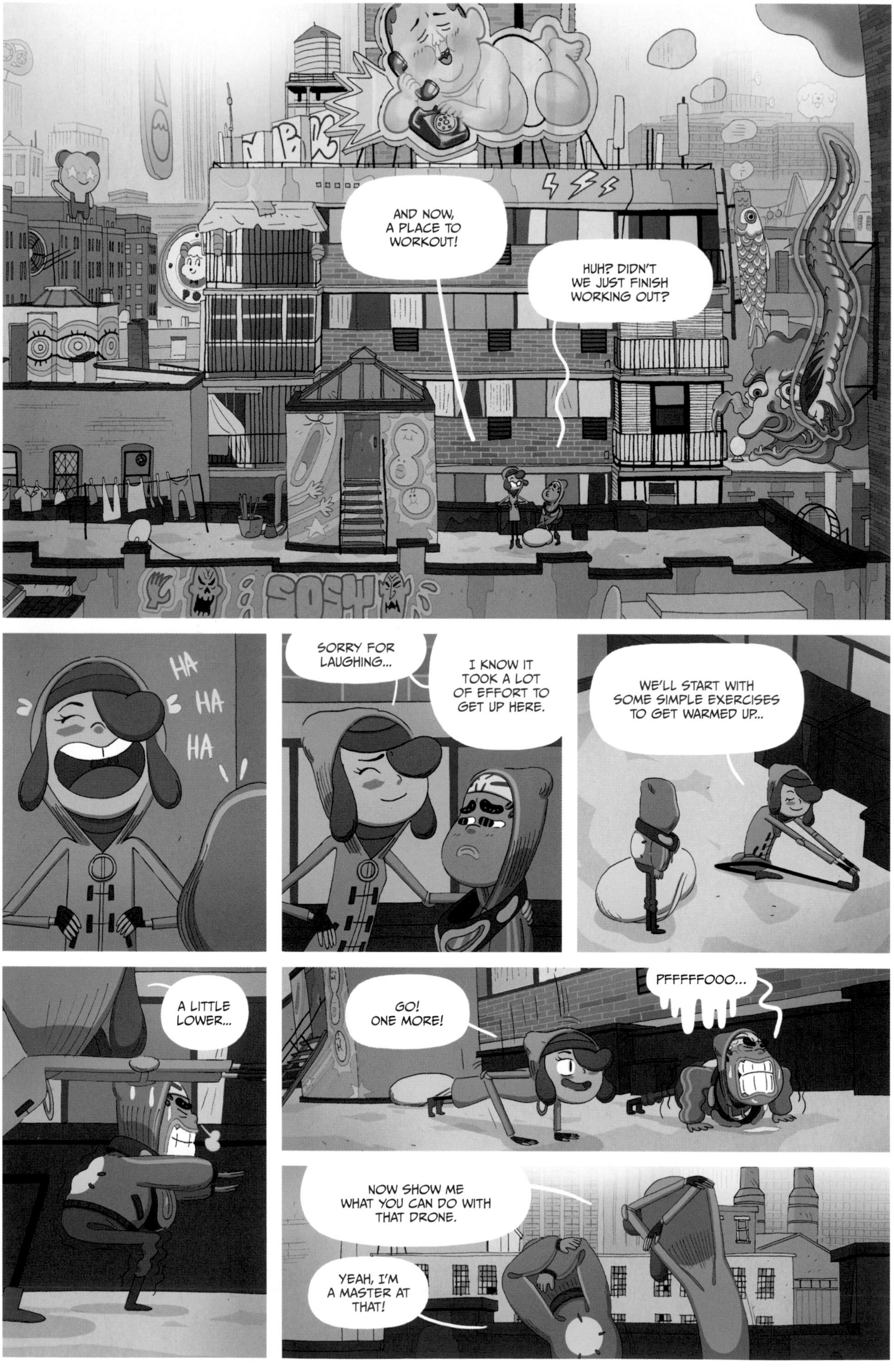
AND NOW, A PLACE TO WORKOUT!
HUH? DIDN'T WE JUST FINISH WORKING OUT?
HA HA HA
SORRY FOR LAUGHING...
I KNOW IT TOOK A LOT OF EFFORT TO GET UP HERE.
WE'LL START WITH SOME SIMPLE EXERCISES TO GET WARMED UP...
A LITTLE LOWER...
GO! ONE MORE!
PFFFFFOOO...
NOW SHOW ME WHAT YOU CAN DO WITH THAT DRONE.
YEAH, I'M A MASTER AT THAT!

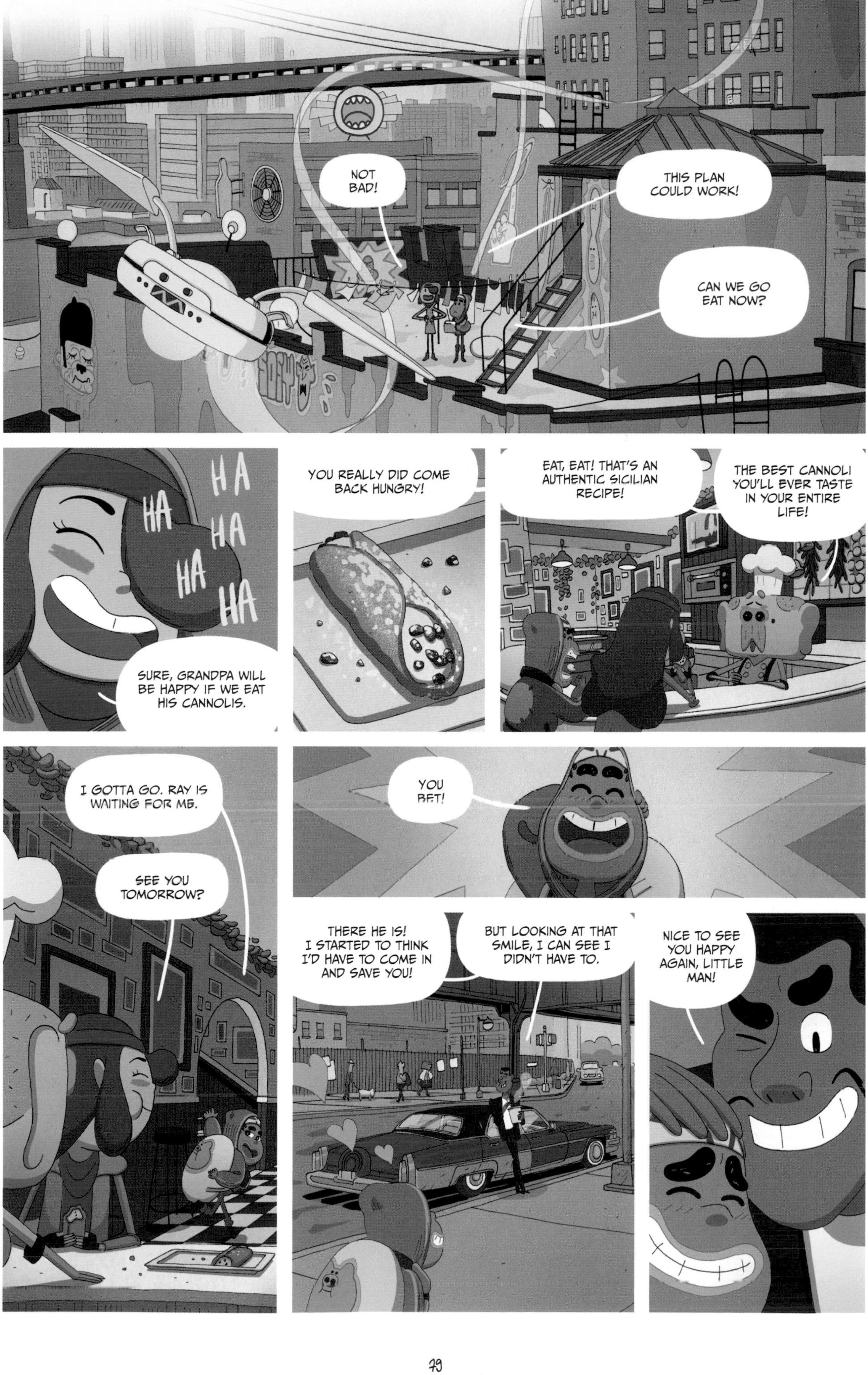

NOT BAD!
THIS PLAN COULD WORK!
CAN WE GO EAT NOW?
HA HA HA HA HA HA
SURE, GRANDPA WILL BE HAPPY IF WE EAT HIS CANNOLIS.
YOU REALLY DID COME BACK HUNGRY!
EAT, EAT! THAT'S AN AUTHENTIC SICILIAN RECIPE!
THE BEST CANNOLI YOU'LL EVER TASTE IN YOUR ENTIRE LIFE!
I GOTTA GO. RAY IS WAITING FOR ME.
SEE YOU TOMORROW?
YOU BET!
THERE HE IS! I STARTED TO THINK I'D HAVE TO COME IN AND SAVE YOU!
BUT LOOKING AT THAT SMILE, I CAN SEE I DIDN'T HAVE TO.
NICE TO SEE YOU HAPPY AGAIN, LITTLE MAN!

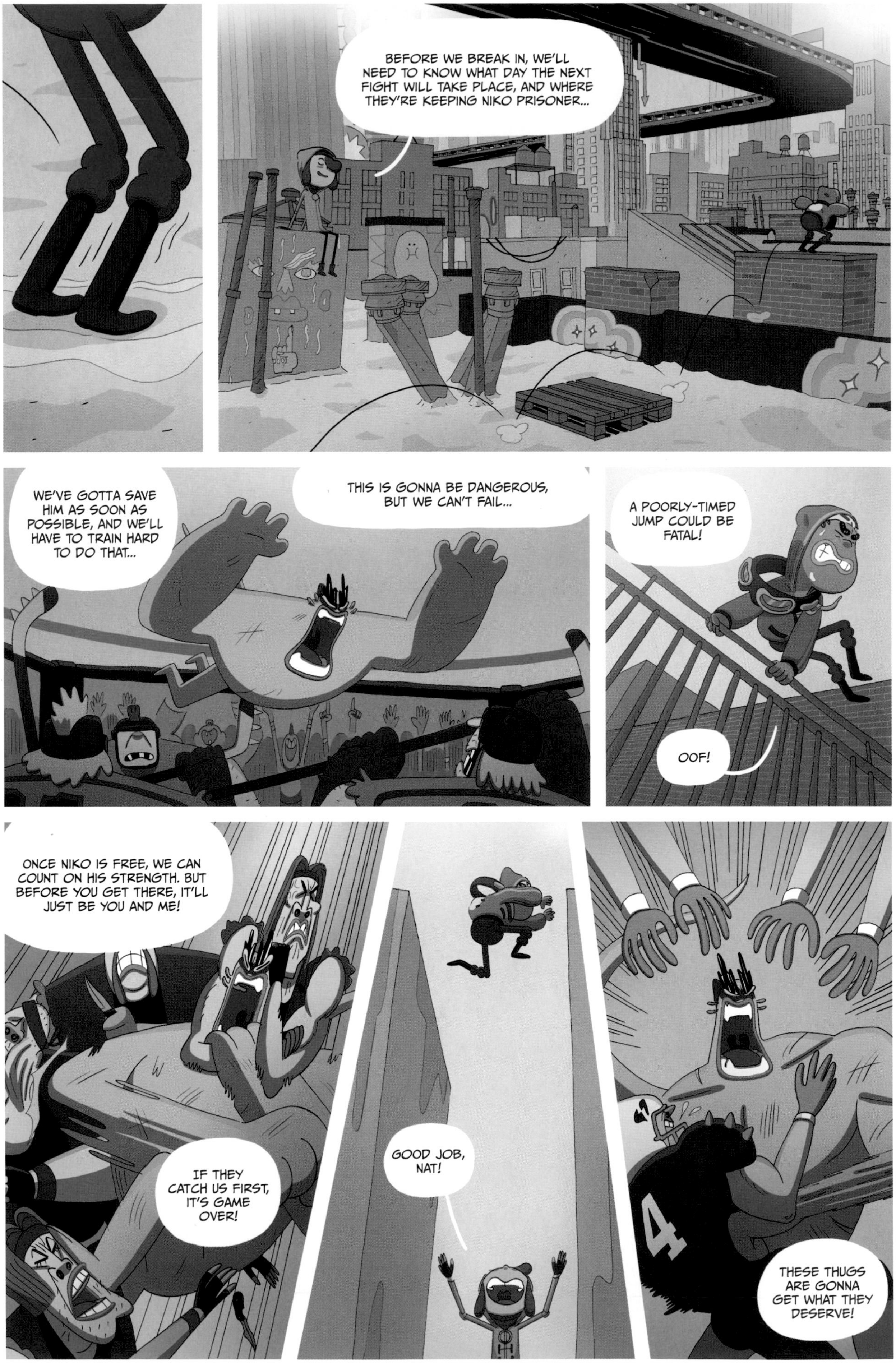
BEFORE WE BREAK IN, WE'LL NEED TO KNOW WHAT DAY THE NEXT FIGHT WILL TAKE PLACE, AND WHERE THEY'RE KEEPING NIKO PRISONER...
WE'VE GOTTA SAVE HIM AS SOON AS POSSIBLE, AND WE'LL HAVE TO TRAIN HARD TO DO THAT...
THIS IS GONNA BE DANGEROUS, BUT WE CAN'T FAIL...
A POORLY-TIMED JUMP COULD BE FATAL!
OOF!
ONCE NIKO IS FREE, WE CAN COUNT ON HIS STRENGTH. BUT BEFORE YOU GET THERE, IT'LL JUST BE YOU AND ME!
IF THEY CATCH US FIRST, IT'S GAME OVER!
GOOD JOB, NAT!
THESE THUGS ARE GONNA GET WHAT THEY DESERVE!

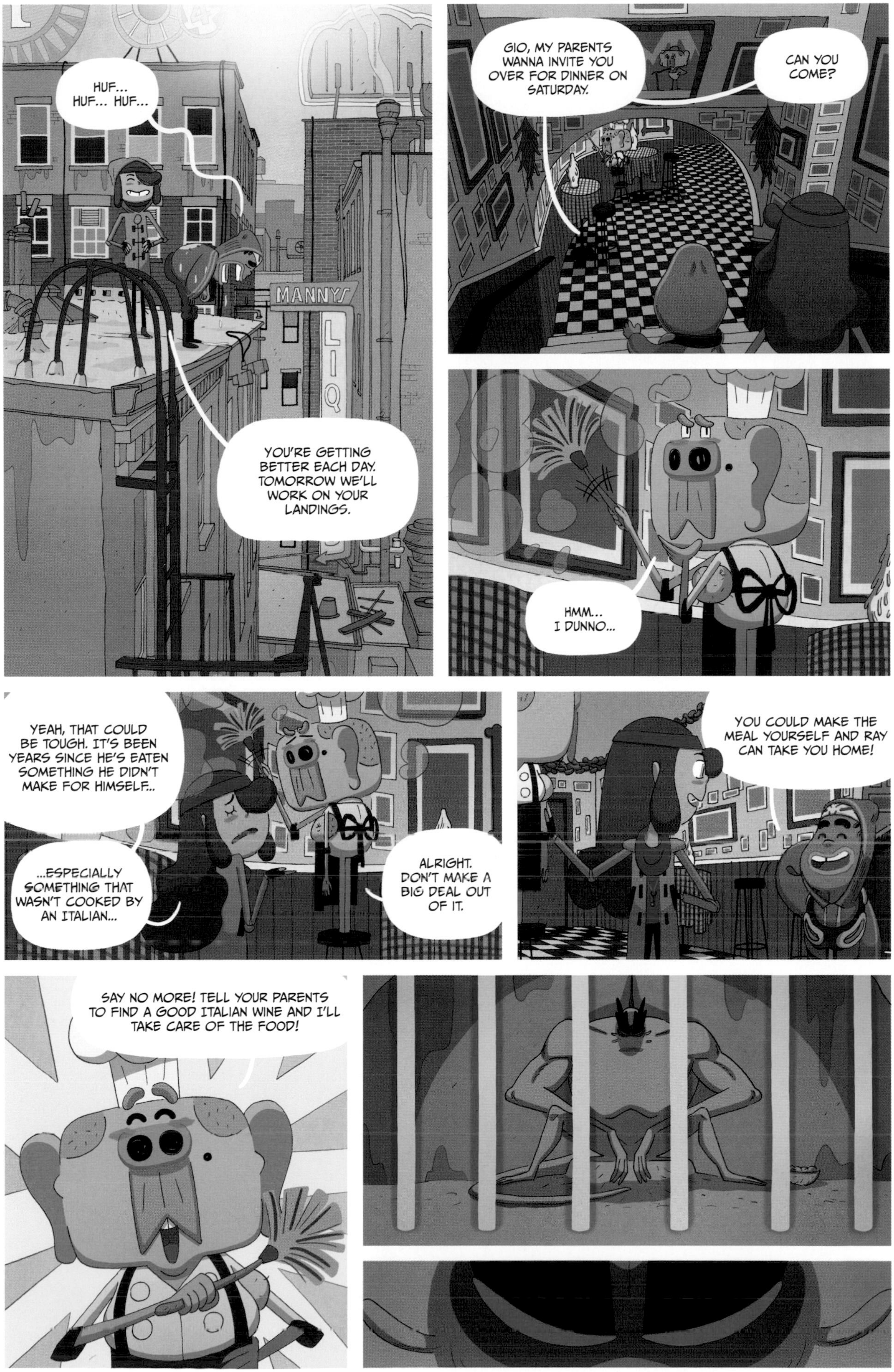
HUF... HUF... HUF...
YOU'RE GETTING BETTER EACH DAY. TOMORROW WE'LL WORK ON YOUR LANDINGS.
MANNY'S
LIQ
GIO, MY PARENTS WANNA INVITE YOU OVER FOR DINNER ON SATURDAY.
CAN YOU COME?
HMM... I DUNNO...
YEAH, THAT COULD BE TOUGH. IT'S BEEN YEARS SINCE HE'S EATEN SOMETHING HE DIDN'T MAKE FOR HIMSELF...
...ESPECIALLY SOMETHING THAT WASN'T COOKED BY AN ITALIAN...
ALRIGHT. DON'T MAKE A BIG DEAL OUT OF IT.
YOU COULD MAKE THE MEAL YOURSELF AND RAY CAN TAKE YOU HOME!
SAY NO MORE! TELL YOUR PARENTS TO FIND A GOOD ITALIAN WINE AND I'LL TAKE CARE OF THE FOOD!

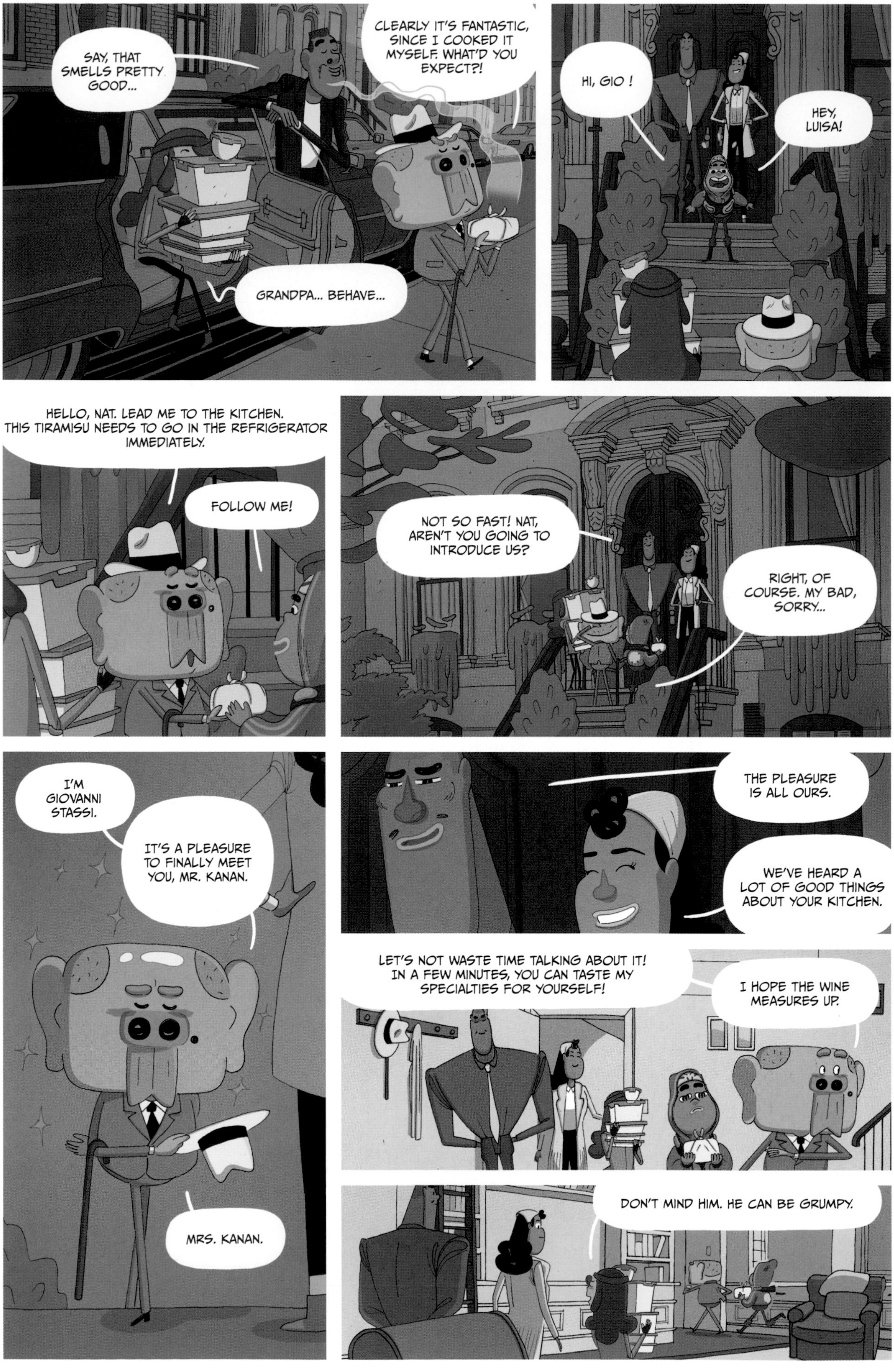
SAY, THAT SMELLS PRETTY GOOD...
CLEARLY IT'S FANTASTIC, SINCE I COOKED IT MYSELF. WHAT'D YOU EXPECT?!
GRANDPA... BEHAVE...
HI, GIO !
HEY, LUISA!
HELLO, NAT. LEAD ME TO THE KITCHEN. THIS TIRAMISU NEEDS TO GO IN THE REFRIGERATOR IMMEDIATELY.
FOLLOW ME!
NOT SO FAST! NAT, AREN'T YOU GOING TO INTRODUCE US?
RIGHT, OF COURSE. MY BAD, SORRY...
I'M GIOVANNI STASSI.
IT'S A PLEASURE TO FINALLY MEET YOU, MR. KANAN.
MRS. KANAN.
THE PLEASURE IS ALL OURS.
WE'VE HEARD A LOT OF GOOD THINGS ABOUT YOUR KITCHEN.
LET'S NOT WASTE TIME TALKING ABOUT IT! IN A FEW MINUTES, YOU CAN TASTE MY SPECIALTIES FOR YOURSELF!
I HOPE THE WINE MEASURES UP.
DON'T MIND HIM. HE CAN BE GRUMPY.

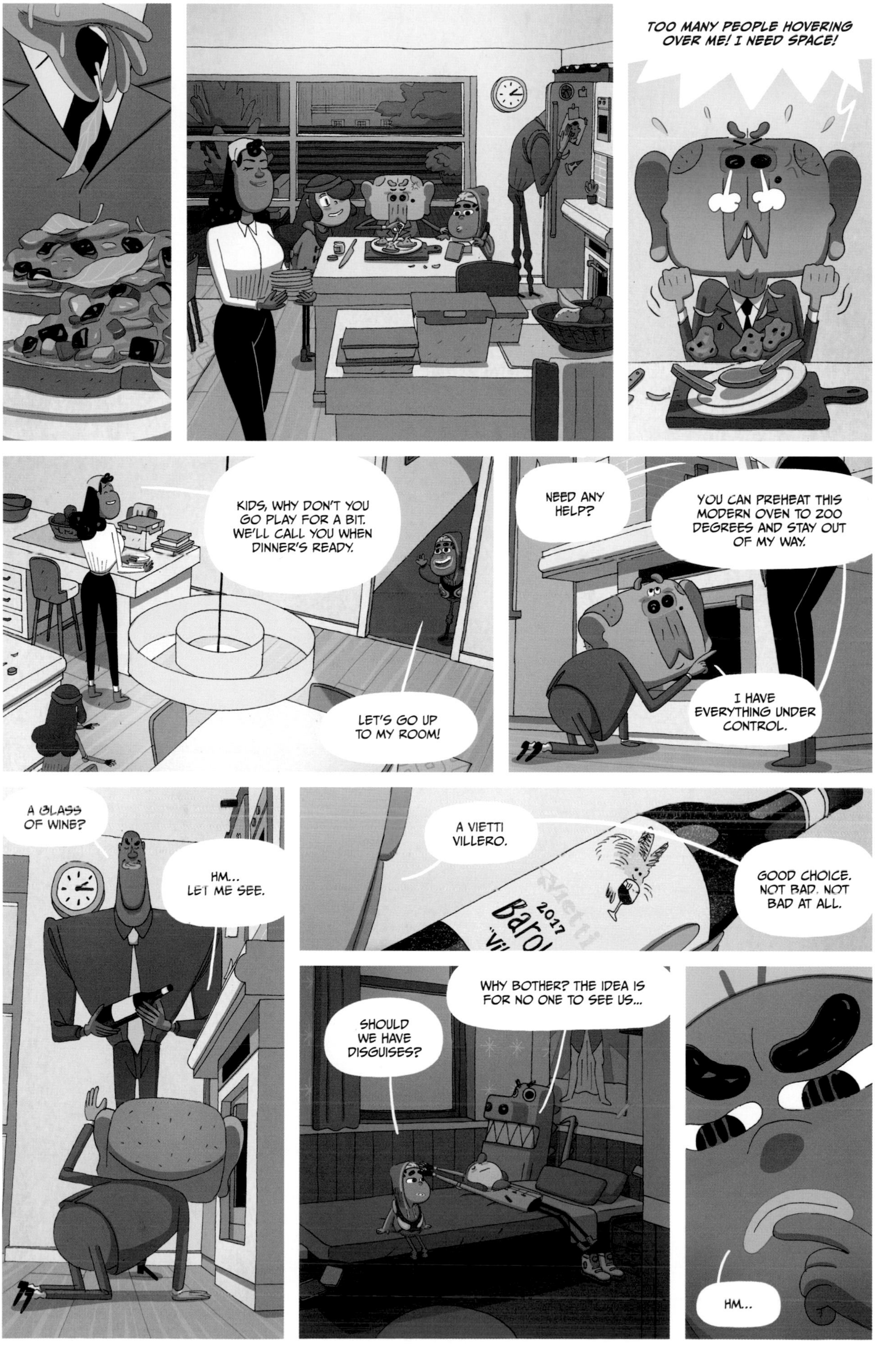
TOO MANY PEOPLE HOVERING OVER ME! I NEED SPACE!
KIDS, WHY DON'T YOU GO PLAY FOR A BIT. WE'LL CALL YOU WHEN DINNER'S READY.
LET'S GO UP TO MY ROOM!
NEED ANY HELP?
YOU CAN PREHEAT THIS MODERN OVEN TO 200 DEGREES AND STAY OUT OF MY WAY.
I HAVE EVERYTHING UNDER CONTROL.
A GLASS OF WINE?
HM... LET ME SEE.
A VIETTI VILLERO.
Vietti
2017
Barol
GOOD CHOICE. NOT BAD. NOT BAD AT ALL.
SHOULD WE HAVE DISGUISES?
WHY BOTHER? THE IDEA IS FOR NO ONE TO SEE US...
HM...

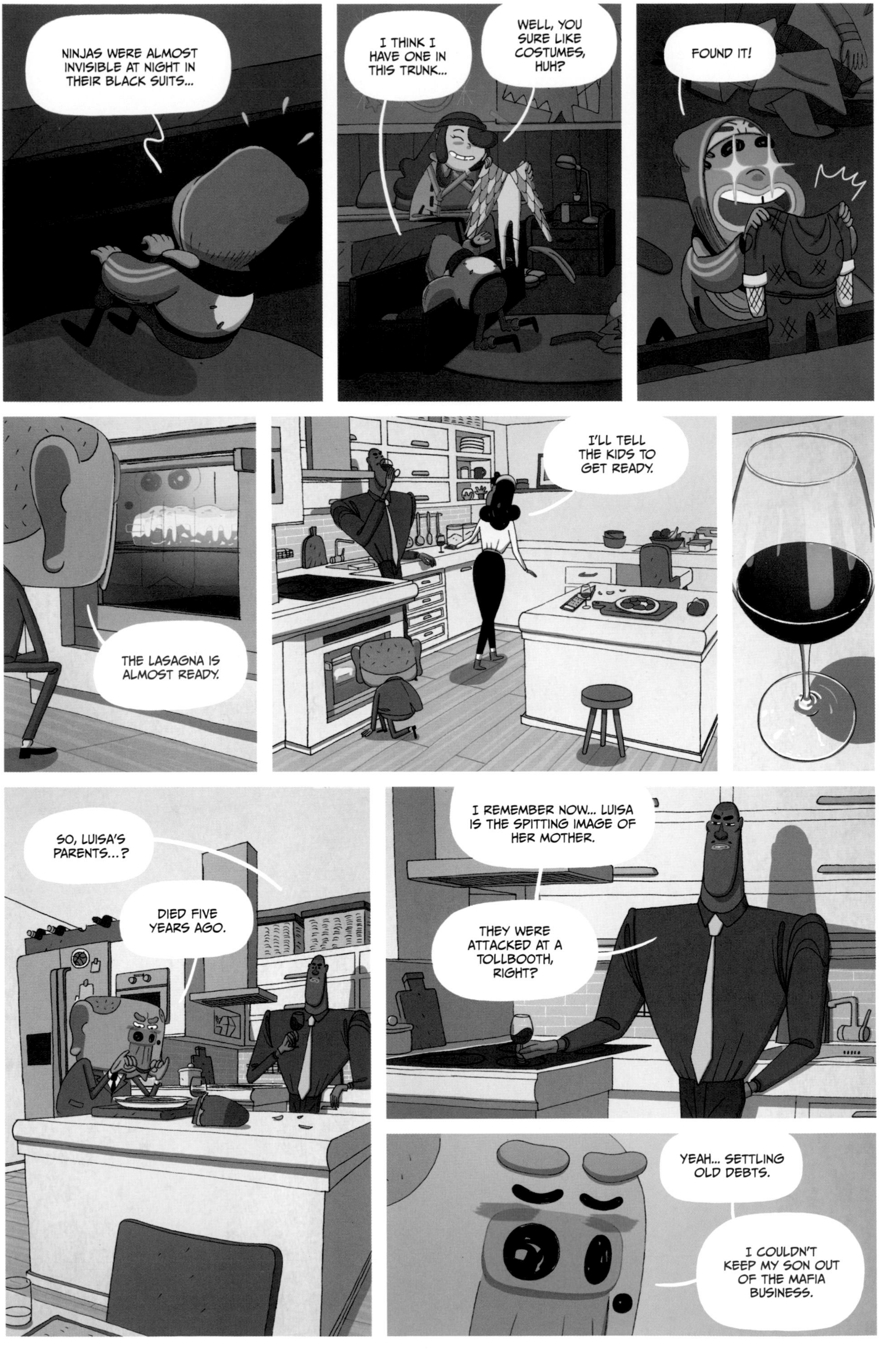
NINJAS WERE ALMOST INVISIBLE AT NIGHT IN THEIR BLACK SUITS...
I THINK I HAVE ONE IN THIS TRUNK...
WELL, YOU SURE LIKE COSTUMES, HUH?
FOUND IT!
THE LASAGNA IS ALMOST READY.
I'LL TELL THE KIDS TO GET READY.
SO, LUISA'S PARENTS...?
DIED FIVE YEARS AGO.
I REMEMBER NOW... LUISA IS THE SPITTING IMAGE OF HER MOTHER.
THEY WERE ATTACKED AT A TOLLBOOTH, RIGHT?
YEAH... SETTLING OLD DEBTS.
I COULDN'T KEEP MY SON OUT OF THE MAFIA BUSINESS.

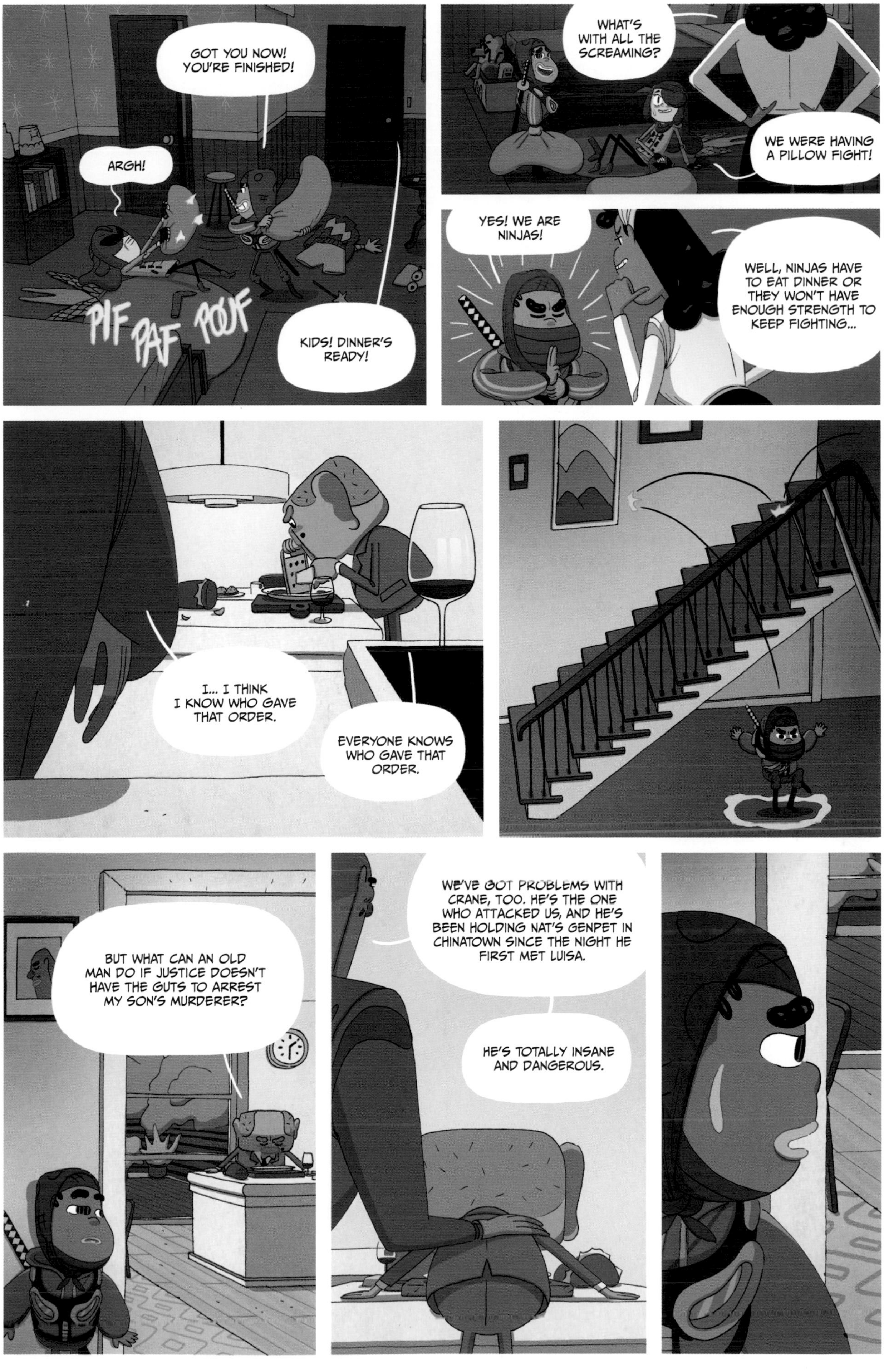
GOT YOU NOW! YOU'RE FINISHED!
ARGH!
PIF PAF POUF
KIDS! DINNER'S READY!
WHAT'S WITH ALL THE SCREAMING?
WE WERE HAVING A PILLOW FIGHT!
YES! WE ARE NINJAS!
WELL, NINJAS HAVE TO EAT DINNER OR THEY WON'T HAVE ENOUGH STRENGTH TO KEEP FIGHTING...
I... I THINK I KNOW WHO GAVE THAT ORDER.
EVERYONE KNOWS WHO GAVE THAT ORDER.
BUT WHAT CAN AN OLD MAN DO IF JUSTICE DOESN'T HAVE THE GUTS TO ARREST MY SON'S MURDERER?
WE'VE GOT PROBLEMS WITH CRANE, TOO. HE'S THE ONE WHO ATTACKED US, AND HE'S BEEN HOLDING NAT'S GENPET IN CHINATOWN SINCE THE NIGHT HE FIRST MET LUISA.
HE'S TOTALLY INSANE AND DANGEROUS.

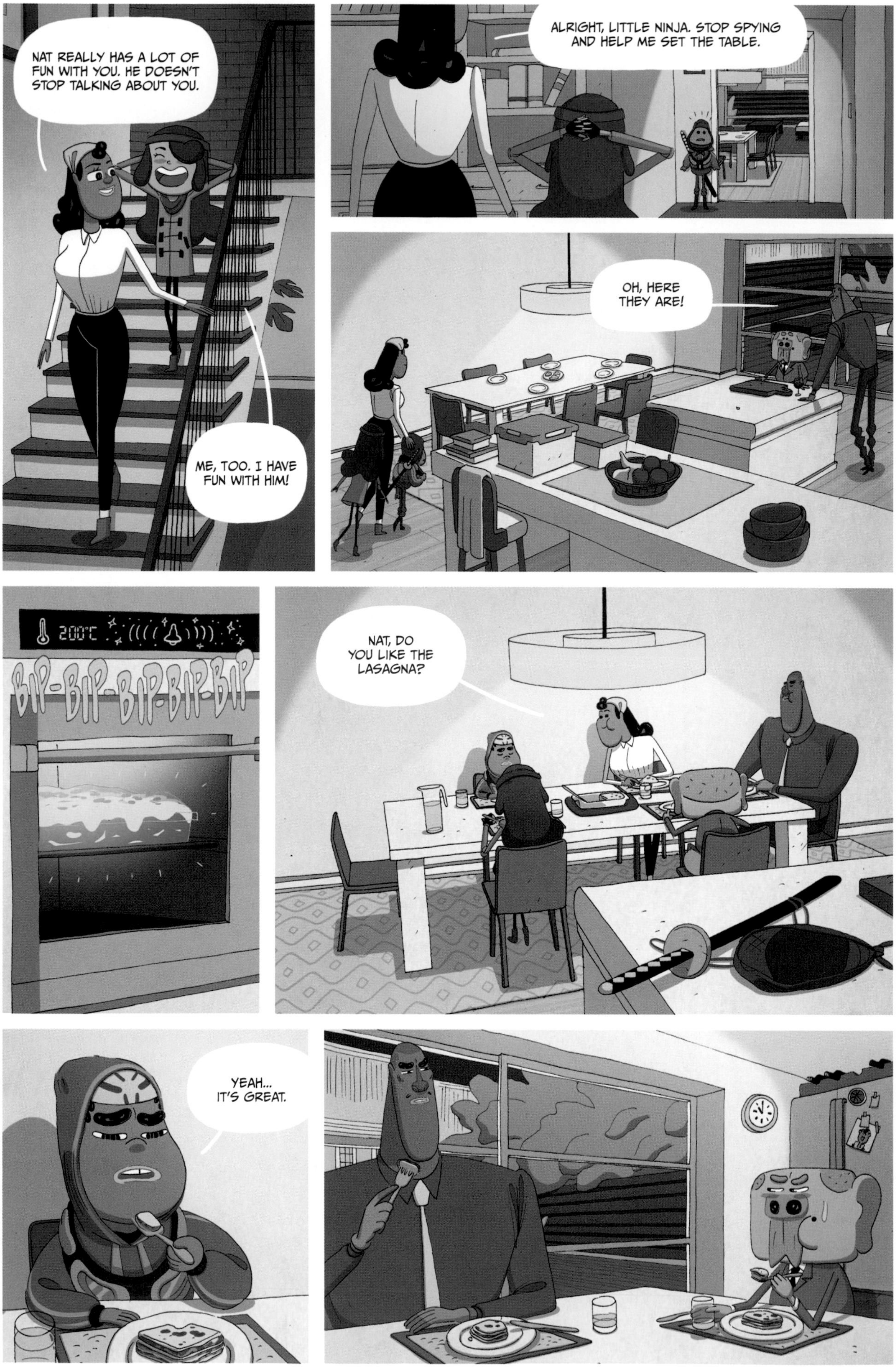
NAT REALLY HAS A LOT OF FUN WITH YOU. HE DOESN'T STOP TALKING ABOUT YOU.
ME, TOO. I HAVE FUN WITH HIM!
ALRIGHT, LITTLE NINJA. STOP SPYING AND HELP ME SET THE TABLE.
OH, HERE THEY ARE!
200°C
BIP-BIP-BIP-BIP-BIP
NAT, DO YOU LIKE THE LASAGNA?
YEAH... IT'S GREAT.

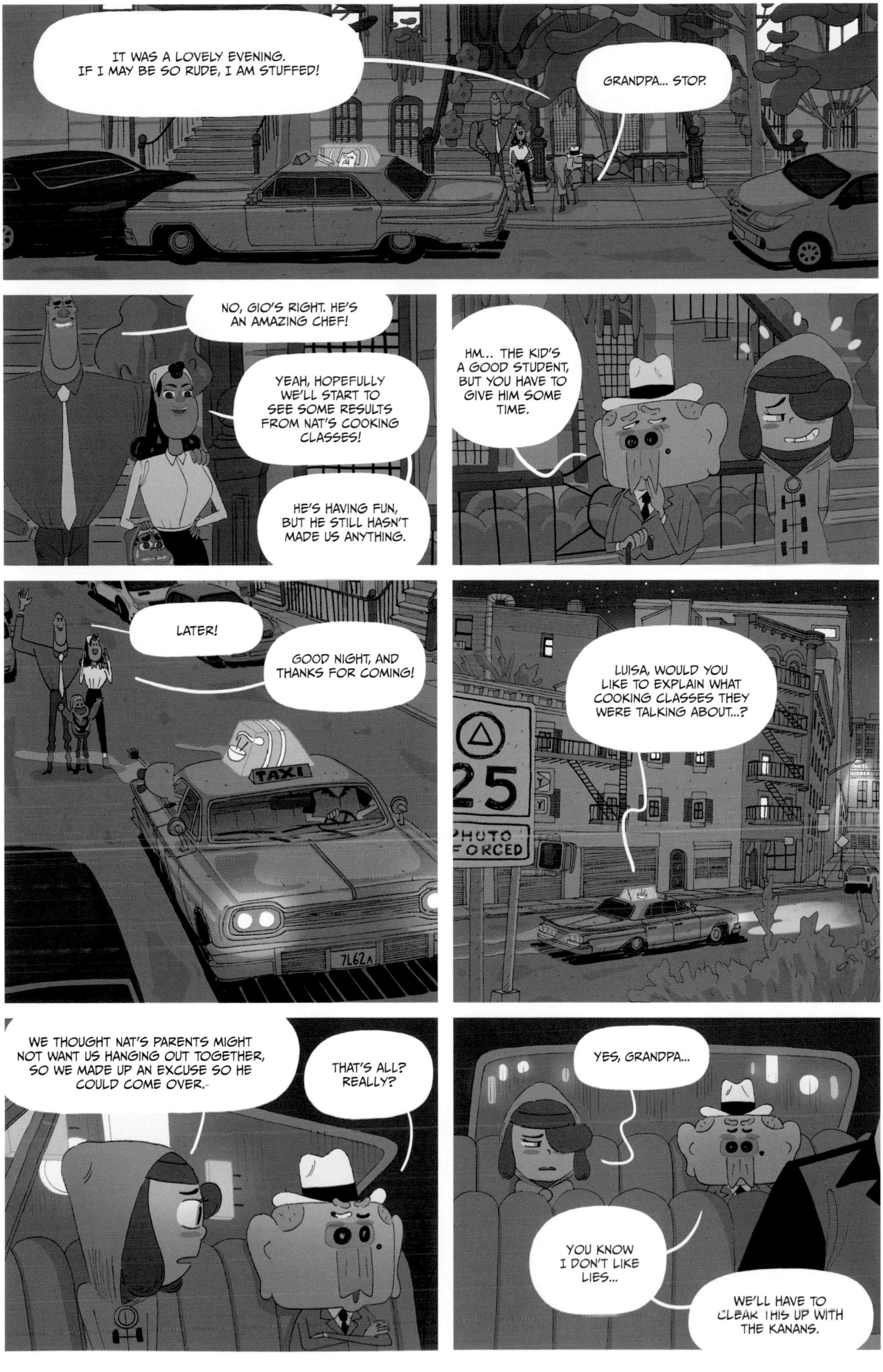
IT WAS A LOVELY EVENING. IF I MAY BE SO RUDE, I AM STUFFED!
GRANDPA... STOP.
NO, GIO'S RIGHT. HE'S AN AMAZING CHEF!
YEAH, HOPEFULLY WE'LL START TO SEE SOME RESULTS FROM NAT'S COOKING CLASSES!
HE'S HAVING FUN, BUT HE STILL HASN'T MADE US ANYTHING.
HM... THE KID'S A GOOD STUDENT, BUT YOU HAVE TO GIVE HIM SOME TIME.
LATER!
GOOD NIGHT, AND THANKS FOR COMING!
TAXI
7L62A
25
PHOTO
FORCED
LUISA, WOULD YOU LIKE TO EXPLAIN WHAT COOKING CLASSES THEY WERE TALKING ABOUT...?
WE THOUGHT NAT'S PARENTS MIGHT NOT WANT US HANGING OUT TOGETHER, SO WE MADE UP AN EXCUSE SO HE COULD COME OVER.
THAT'S ALL? REALLY?
YES, GRANDPA...
YOU KNOW I DON'T LIKE LIES...
WE'LL HAVE TO CLEAR THIS UP WITH THE KANANS.

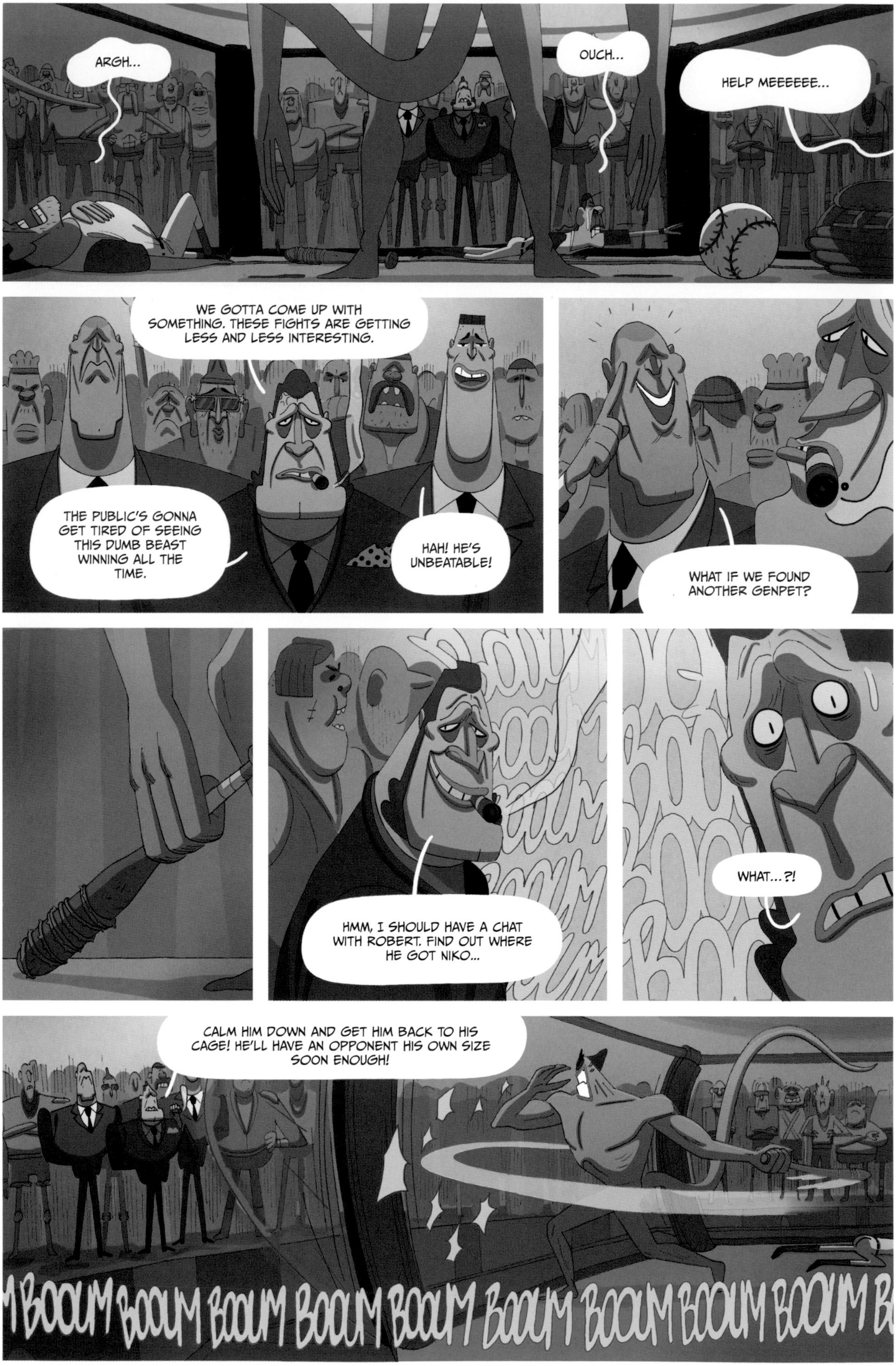
ARGH...
OUCH...
HELP MEEEEEE...
WE GOTTA COME UP WITH SOMETHING. THESE FIGHTS ARE GETTING LESS AND LESS INTERESTING.
THE PUBLIC'S GONNA GET TIRED OF SEEING THIS DUMB BEAST WINNING ALL THE TIME.
HAH! HE'S UNBEATABLE!
WHAT IF WE FOUND ANOTHER GENPET?
HMM, I SHOULD HAVE A CHAT WITH ROBERT. FIND OUT WHERE HE GOT NIKO...
WHAT...?!
CALM HIM DOWN AND GET HIM BACK TO HIS CAGE! HE'LL HAVE AN OPPONENT HIS OWN SIZE SOON ENOUGH!
BOOUM BOOUM BOOUM BOOUM BOOUM BOOUM BOOUM BOOUM BOOUM

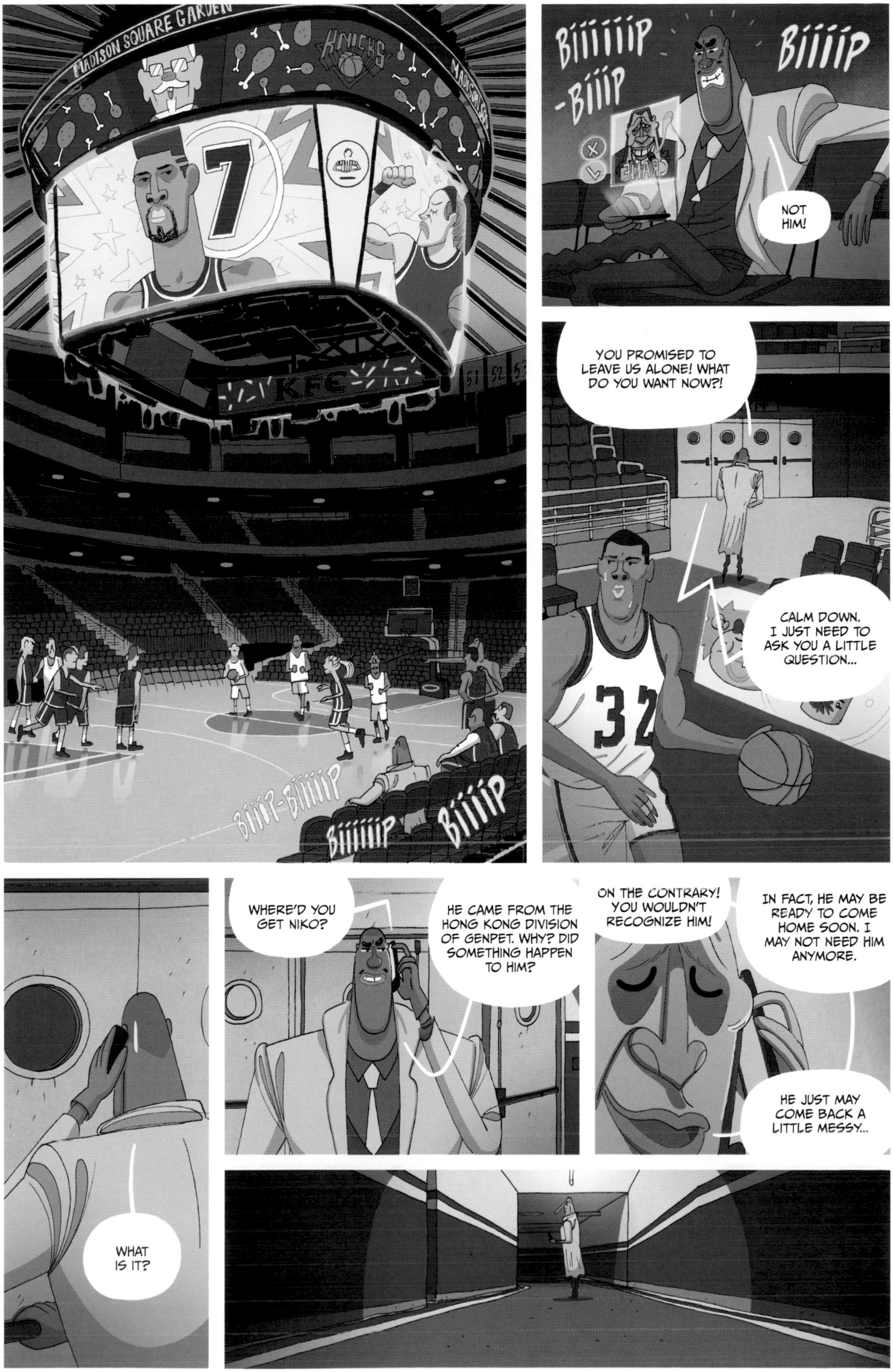
MADISON SQUARE GARDEN
KNICKS
KFC
BIIIP-BIIIIIP
BIIIIIIP
BIIIIP
BIIIIIIP
-BIIIP
BIIIIP
NOT HIM!
YOU PROMISED TO LEAVE US ALONE! WHAT DO YOU WANT NOW?!
CALM DOWN. I JUST NEED TO ASK YOU A LITTLE QUESTION...
WHAT IS IT?
WHERE'D YOU GET NIKO?
HE CAME FROM THE HONG KONG DIVISION OF GENPET. WHY? DID SOMETHING HAPPEN TO HIM?
ON THE CONTRARY! YOU WOULDN'T RECOGNIZE HIM!
IN FACT, HE MAY BE READY TO COME HOME SOON. I MAY NOT NEED HIM ANYMORE.
HE JUST MAY COME BACK A LITTLE MESSY...

I... I HAVE TO TELL YOU SOMETHING.

I HEARD MY DAD AND YOUR GRANDPA TALKING WHEN I CAME DOWN TO DINNER...

I THINK MY GRANDPA SUSPECTS SOMETHING. WE HAVE TO SAVE NIKO BEFORE HE TALKS TO YOUR PARENTS.

IF THEY DISCOVER OUR PLAN, WE WON'T BE ABLE TO SAVE HIM FROM CRANE'S CLUTCHES.

SO...?

CRANE'S RESPONSIBLE FOR YOUR PARENTS' DEATH, TOO.

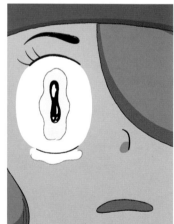

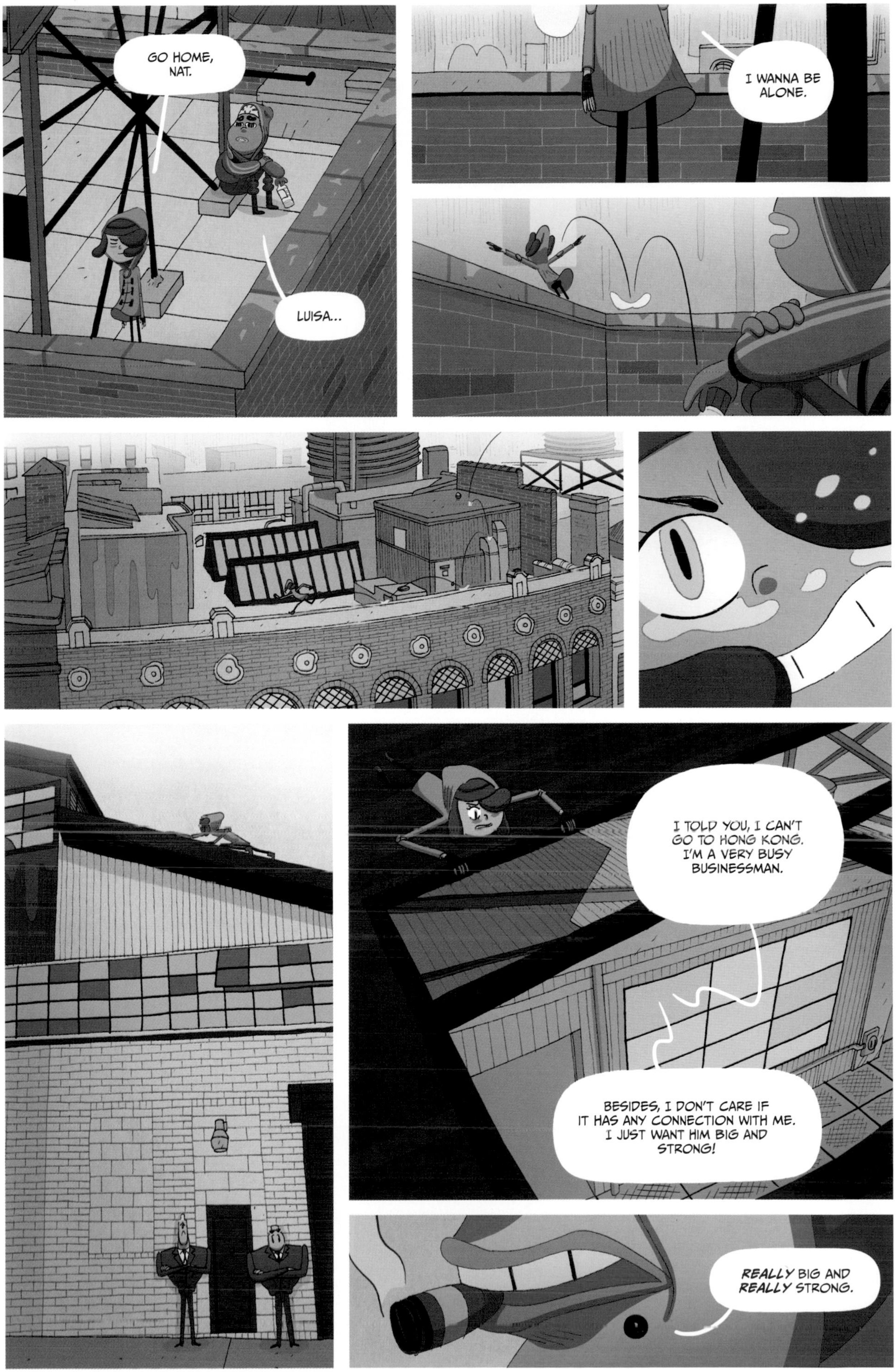
GO HOME, NAT.
LUISA...
I WANNA BE ALONE.
I TOLD YOU, I CAN'T GO TO HONG KONG. I'M A VERY BUSY BUSINESSMAN.
BESIDES, I DON'T CARE IF IT HAS ANY CONNECTION WITH ME. I JUST WANT HIM BIG AND STRONG!
REALLY BIG AND *REALLY* STRONG.

YOU DON'T UNDERSTAND... IF THE GENPET HAS NO CONNECTION WITH IT'S OWNER, IT WILL NOT FOLLOW ANYONE'S ORDERS. IT WOULD BE VERY DANGEROUS!

ESPECIALLY WITH THE FEATURES YOU ARE REQUESTING.

THAT'S THE POINT! IT'S SUPPOSED TO BE DANGEROUS!

DEADLY!

I DON'T WANT IT TO PLAY TEA PARTY!

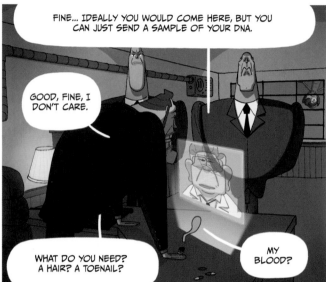

FINE... IDEALLY YOU WOULD COME HERE, BUT YOU CAN JUST SEND A SAMPLE OF YOUR DNA.

GOOD, FINE, I DON'T CARE.

WHAT DO YOU NEED? A HAIR? A TOENAIL?

MY BLOOD?

A HAIR WILL SUFFICE. SEND IT AS SOON AS POSSIBLE.

IT'LL BE IN HONG KONG FIRST THING TOMORROW.

PLING

GENTLEMEN, THANKS TO SOMETHING AS INSIGNIFICANT AS THIS TINY STRAND OF HAIR, IN TWO WEEKS WE'LL SEE THE BEST FIGHT IMAGINABLE. WE'LL WITNESS...

...THE END OF NIKO'S REIGN!

YOU'RE IN FOR A BIG SURPRISE...

92

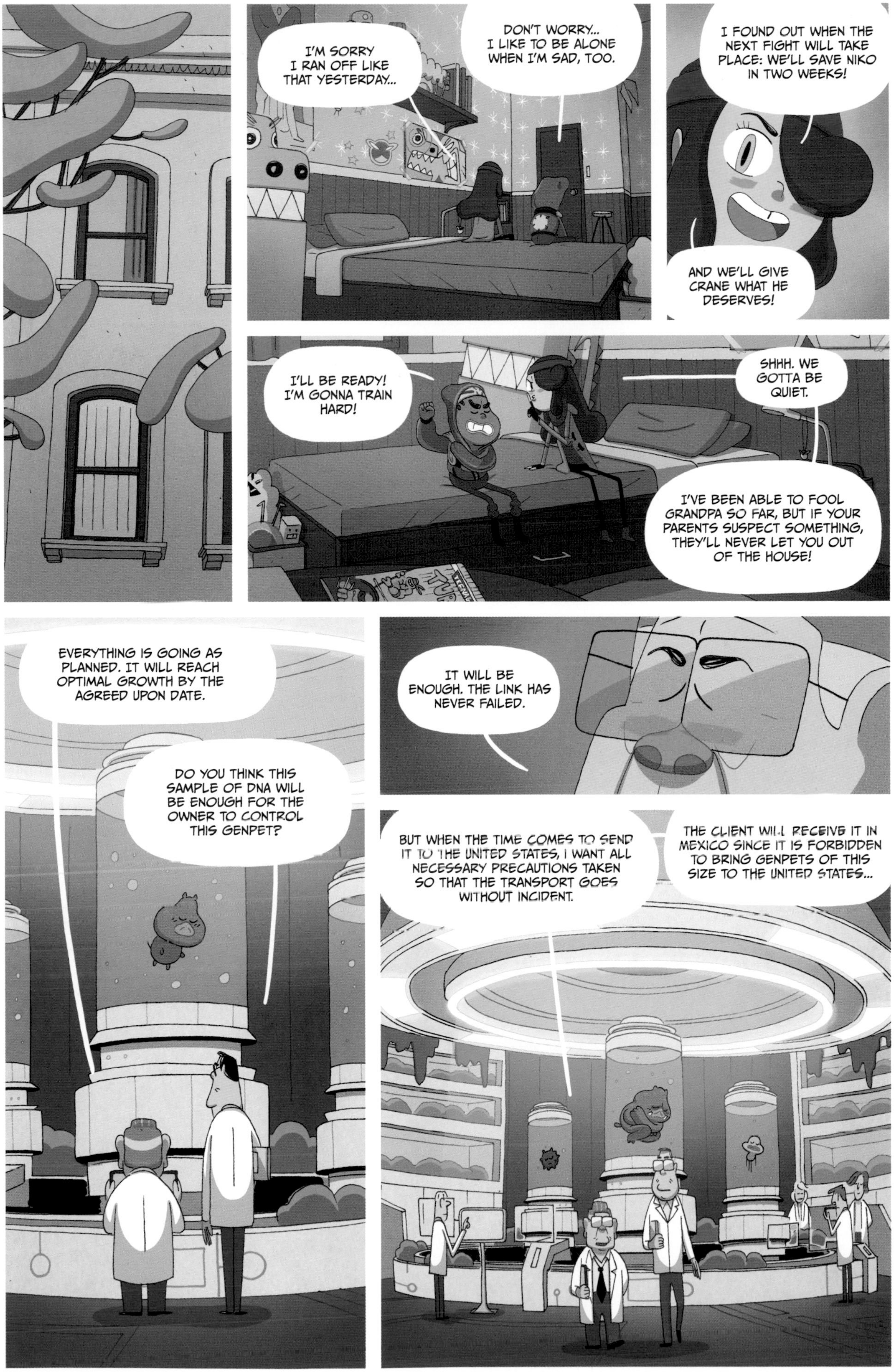

I'M SORRY I RAN OFF LIKE THAT YESTERDAY...
DON'T WORRY... I LIKE TO BE ALONE WHEN I'M SAD, TOO.
I FOUND OUT WHEN THE NEXT FIGHT WILL TAKE PLACE: WE'LL SAVE NIKO IN TWO WEEKS!
AND WE'LL GIVE CRANE WHAT HE DESERVES!
I'LL BE READY! I'M GONNA TRAIN HARD!
SHHH. WE GOTTA BE QUIET.
I'VE BEEN ABLE TO FOOL GRANDPA SO FAR, BUT IF YOUR PARENTS SUSPECT SOMETHING, THEY'LL NEVER LET YOU OUT OF THE HOUSE!
EVERYTHING IS GOING AS PLANNED. IT WILL REACH OPTIMAL GROWTH BY THE AGREED UPON DATE.
DO YOU THINK THIS SAMPLE OF DNA WILL BE ENOUGH FOR THE OWNER TO CONTROL THIS GENPET?
IT WILL BE ENOUGH. THE LINK HAS NEVER FAILED.
BUT WHEN THE TIME COMES TO SEND IT TO THE UNITED STATES, I WANT ALL NECESSARY PRECAUTIONS TAKEN SO THAT THE TRANSPORT GOES WITHOUT INCIDENT.
THE CLIENT WILL RECEIVE IT IN MEXICO SINCE IT IS FORBIDDEN TO BRING GENPETS OF THIS SIZE TO THE UNITED STATES...

SIGN HERE AND THE MONSTER'S YOURS.

IT'S EVEN SCARIER THAN THE PHOTOS...

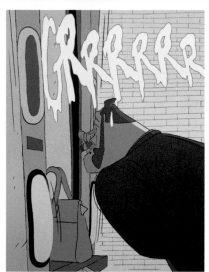

GRRRRRR

WHY'S HE GROWLING AT ME? SHOULDN'T HE BE HAPPY TO SEE ME?

GIVE HIM SOME TIME. YOU TWO JUST MET.

AT THIS RATE, WE'LL BE PLANNING YOUR WEDDING PRETTY SOON...!

THAT'S NOT FUNNY.

HELLO, NAT! LUISA'S WAITING FOR YOU UPSTAIRS.

HEY, GIO!

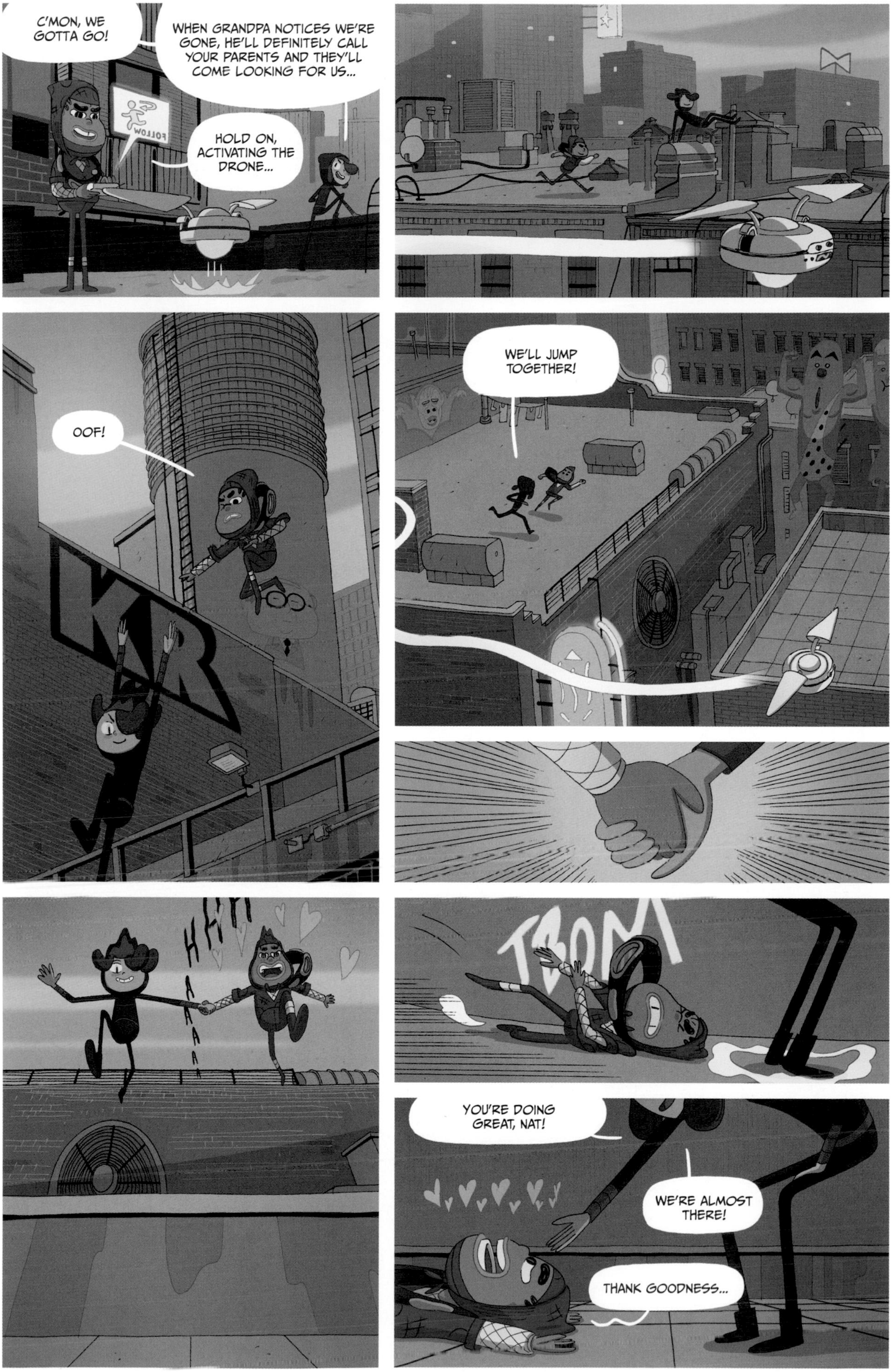
C'MON, WE GOTTA GO!
WHEN GRANDPA NOTICES WE'RE GONE, HE'LL DEFINITELY CALL YOUR PARENTS AND THEY'LL COME LOOKING FOR US...
HOLD ON, ACTIVATING THE DRONE...
OOF!
WE'LL JUMP TOGETHER!
TBOM
YOU'RE DOING GREAT, NAT!
WE'RE ALMOST THERE!
THANK GOODNESS...

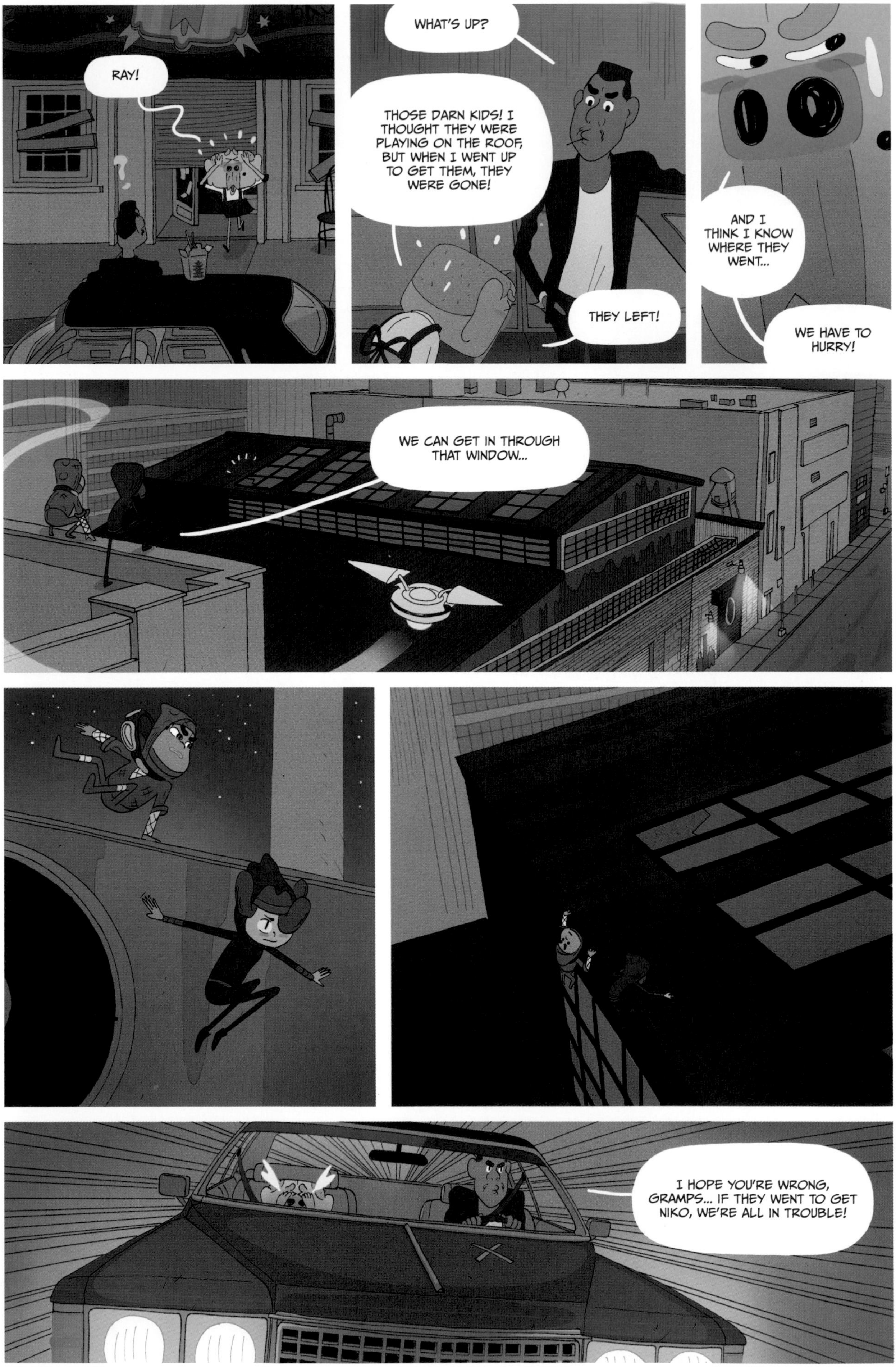
RAY!
WHAT'S UP?
THOSE DARN KIDS! I THOUGHT THEY WERE PLAYING ON THE ROOF, BUT WHEN I WENT UP TO GET THEM, THEY WERE GONE!
THEY LEFT!
AND I THINK I KNOW WHERE THEY WENT...
WE HAVE TO HURRY!
WE CAN GET IN THROUGH THAT WINDOW...
I HOPE YOU'RE WRONG, GRAMPS... IF THEY WENT TO GET NIKO, WE'RE ALL IN TROUBLE!

MY TURN TO PLAY NOW!
WHAT WAS THAT?
ANOTHER PIGEON THAT GOT STUCK IN HERE, MAYBE?
DO YOU SEE ANYTHING?
NOTHING YET...
HE SHOULD BE HERE!
NO, THAT'S NOT HIM...
I FOUND HIM! I MEAN... I THINK ITS HIM. HE'S SKINNY!
HE LOOKS SICK OR SOMETHING...

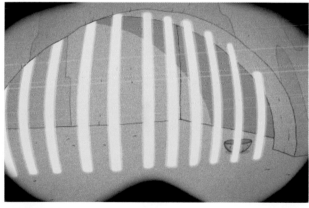

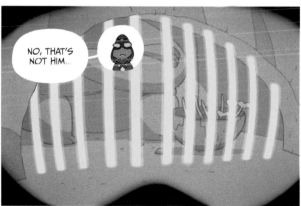

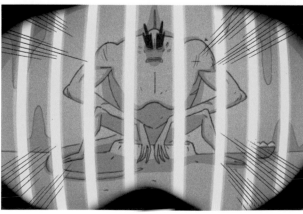

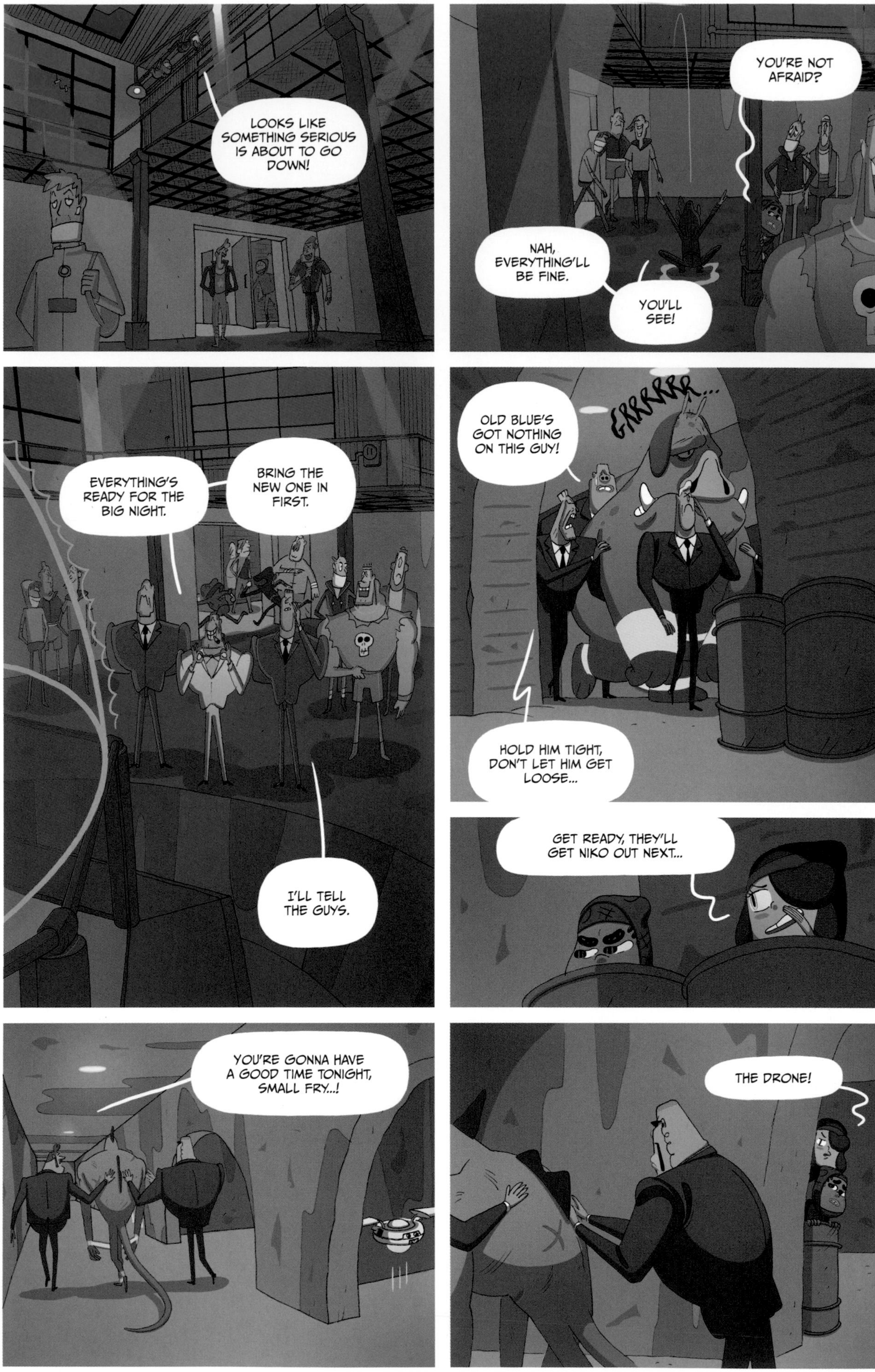
LOOKS LIKE SOMETHING SERIOUS IS ABOUT TO GO DOWN!
YOU'RE NOT AFRAID?
NAH, EVERYTHING'LL BE FINE.
YOU'LL SEE!
EVERYTHING'S READY FOR THE BIG NIGHT.
BRING THE NEW ONE IN FIRST.
I'LL TELL THE GUYS.
GRRRRRR...
OLD BLUE'S GOT NOTHING ON THIS GUY!
HOLD HIM TIGHT, DON'T LET HIM GET LOOSE...
GET READY, THEY'LL GET NIKO OUT NEXT...
YOU'RE GONNA HAVE A GOOD TIME TONIGHT, SMALL FRY...!
THE DRONE!

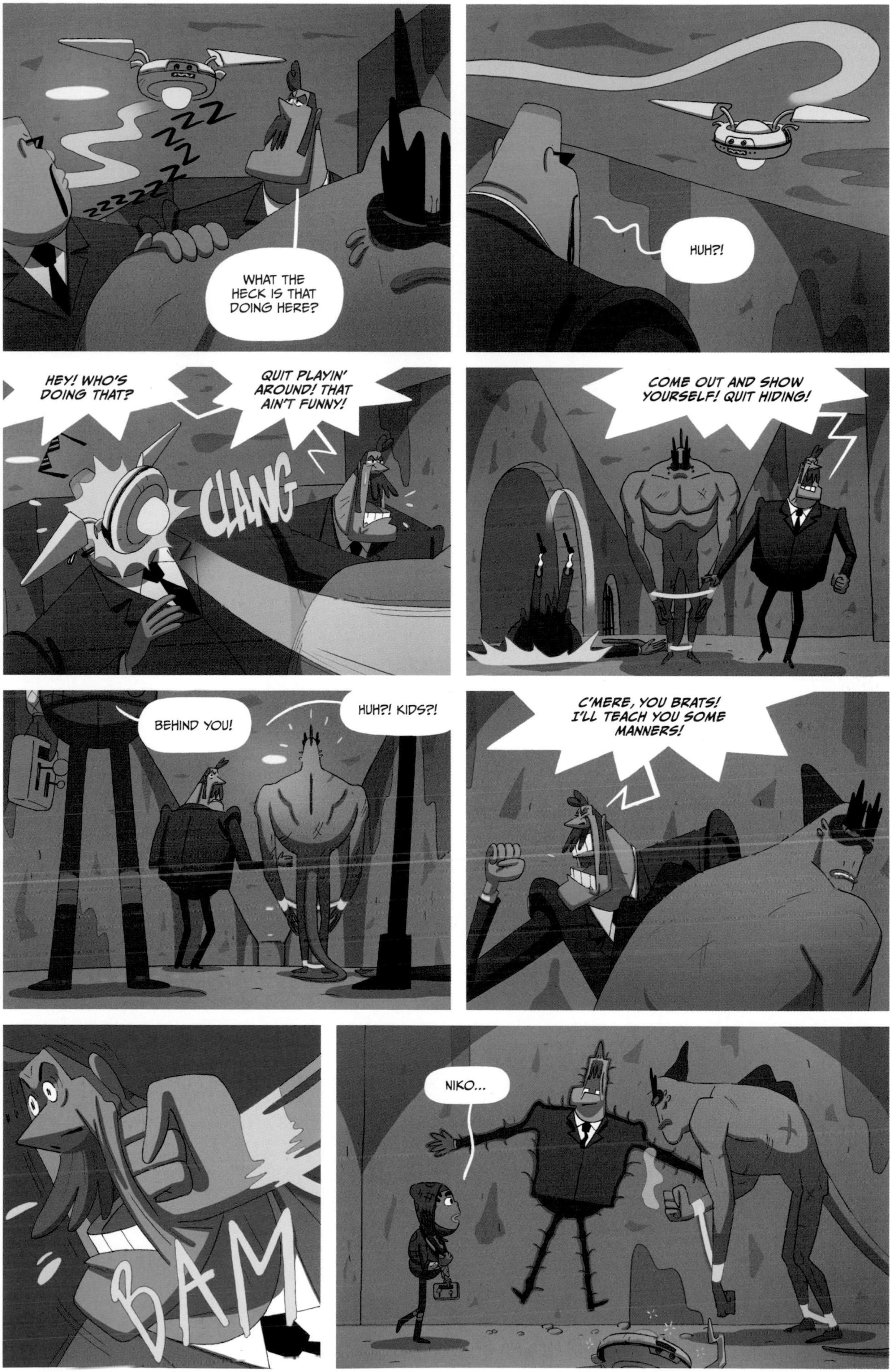
ZZZ
ZZZZZZ
WHAT THE HECK IS THAT DOING HERE?
HUH?!
HEY! WHO'S DOING THAT?
QUIT PLAYIN' AROUND! THAT AIN'T FUNNY!
CLANG
COME OUT AND SHOW YOURSELF! QUIT HIDING!
BEHIND YOU!
HUH?! KIDS?!
C'MERE, YOU BRATS! I'LL TEACH YOU SOME MANNERS!
BAM
NIKO...

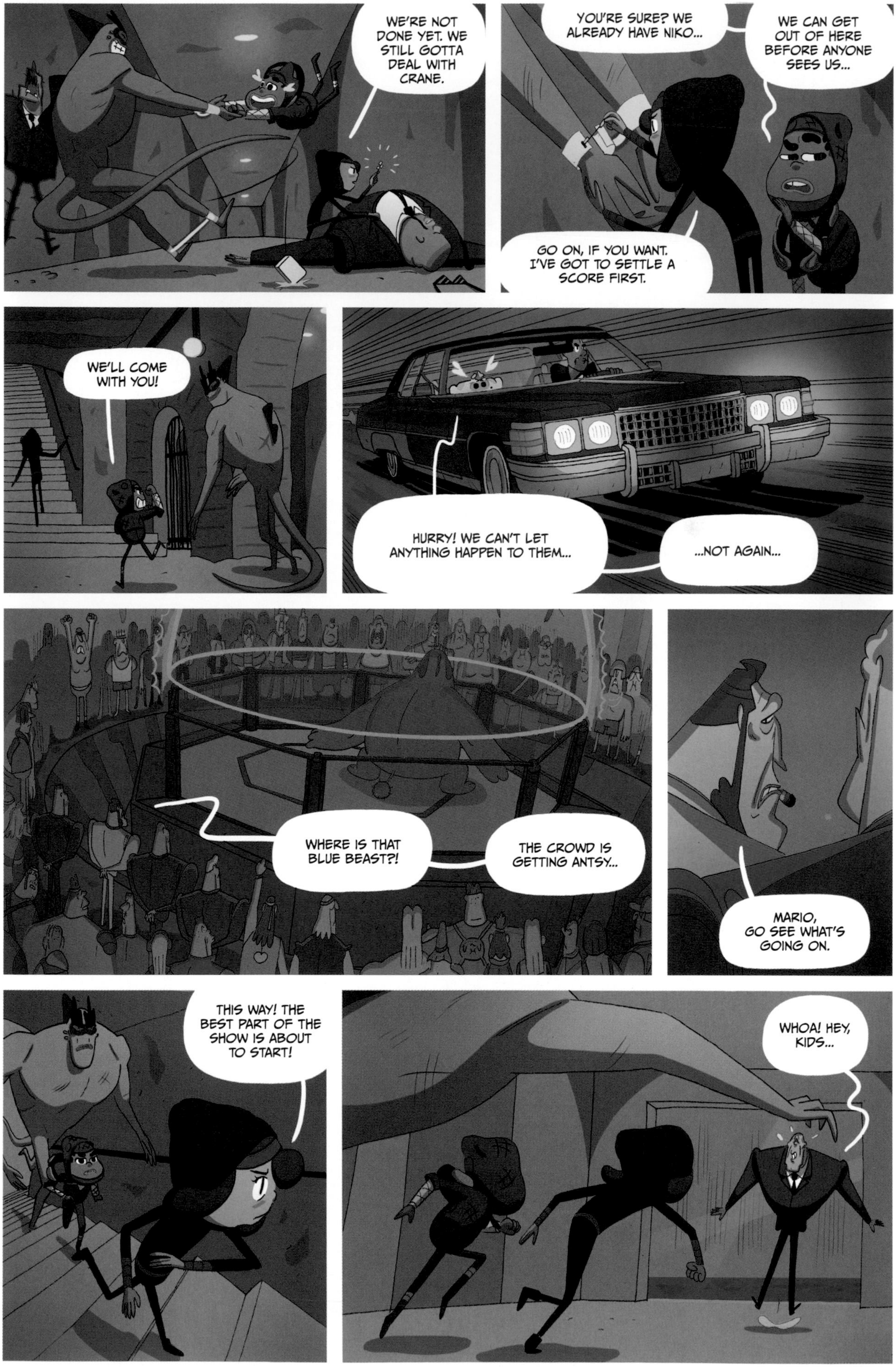
WE'RE NOT DONE YET. WE STILL GOTTA DEAL WITH CRANE.
YOU'RE SURE? WE ALREADY HAVE NIKO...
WE CAN GET OUT OF HERE BEFORE ANYONE SEES US...
GO ON, IF YOU WANT. I'VE GOT TO SETTLE A SCORE FIRST.
WE'LL COME WITH YOU!
HURRY! WE CAN'T LET ANYTHING HAPPEN TO THEM...
...NOT AGAIN...
WHERE IS THAT BLUE BEAST?!
THE CROWD IS GETTING ANTSY...
MARIO, GO SEE WHAT'S GOING ON.
THIS WAY! THE BEST PART OF THE SHOW IS ABOUT TO START!
WHOA! HEY, KIDS...

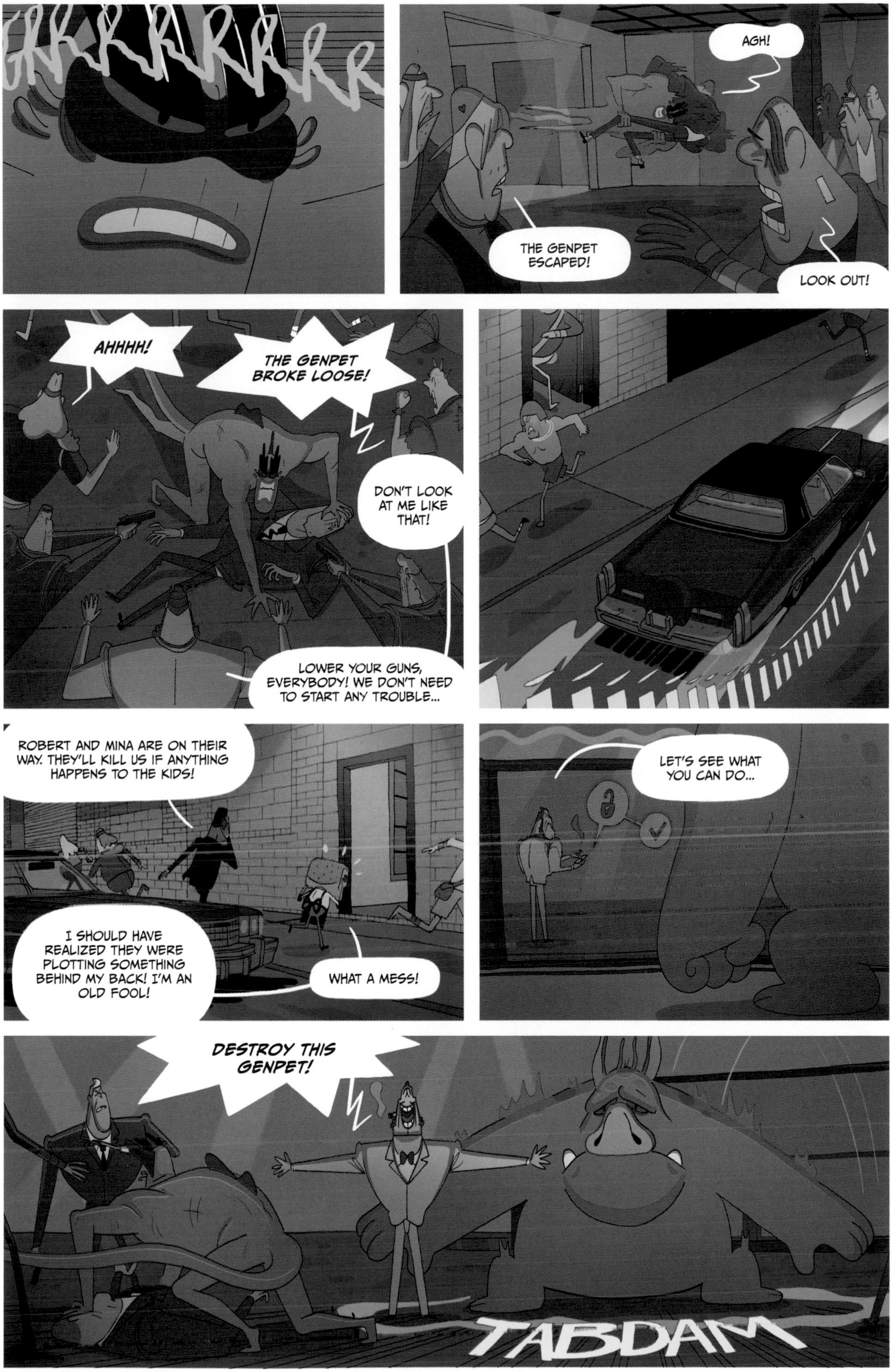
GRRRRRRRRRR
AGH!
THE GENPET ESCAPED!
LOOK OUT!
AHHHH!
THE GENPET BROKE LOOSE!
DON'T LOOK AT ME LIKE THAT!
LOWER YOUR GUNS, EVERYBODY! WE DON'T NEED TO START ANY TROUBLE...
ROBERT AND MINA ARE ON THEIR WAY. THEY'LL KILL US IF ANYTHING HAPPENS TO THE KIDS!
I SHOULD HAVE REALIZED THEY WERE PLOTTING SOMETHING BEHIND MY BACK! I'M AN OLD FOOL!
WHAT A MESS!
LET'S SEE WHAT YOU CAN DO...
DESTROY THIS GENPET!
TABDAM

NO!

AH, NOW I RECOGNIZE YOU!

I DIDN'T SEE IT THE OTHER NIGHT... YOU'RE STASSI'S DAUGHTER!

WHAT'D I DO TO GET SO LUCKY?!

HA HA HA HA HA HA HA

LET ME TAKE CARE OF NIKO FIRST AND I'LL GET TO YOU NEXT!

YOU AREN'T DOING ANYTHING TO NIKO!

AS PRETTY AS YOUR MOTHER AND AS TOUGH AS YOUR FATHER...

NOW, GET OUTTA MY WAY!

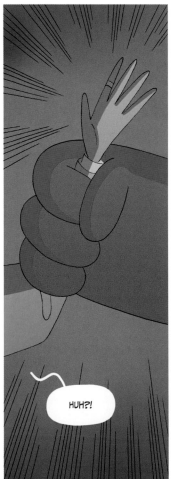

HUH?!

PAF

BOSS! YOU OKAY?

HOW IS THIS POSSIBLE...?

THAT THING'S SUPPOSED TO OBEY ONLY ME! *ME!*

TOO BAD.

YOU HAVE NO IDEA HOW EASY IT IS TO REPLACE ONE HAIR WITH ANOTHER...

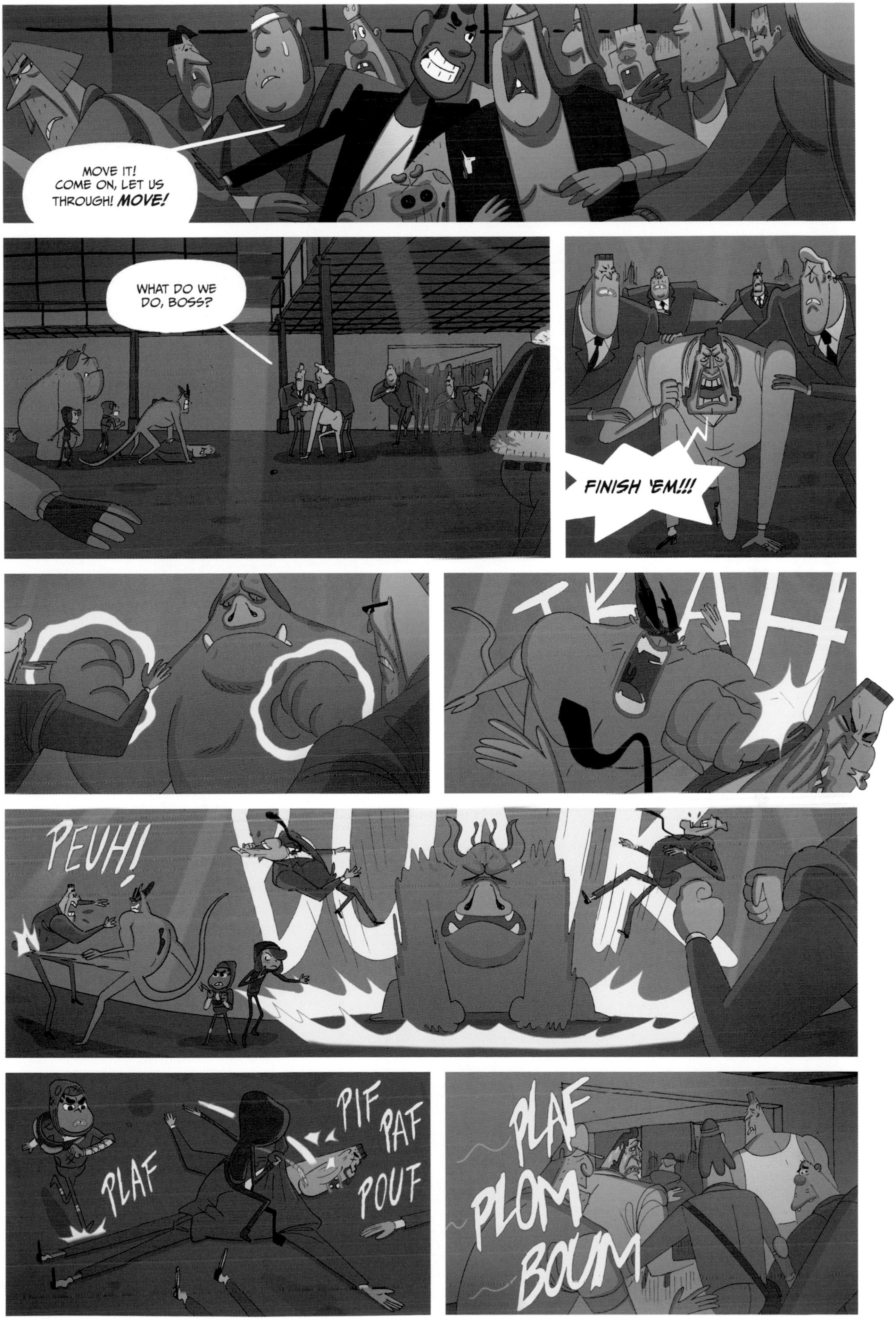
MOVE IT! COME ON, LET US THROUGH! MOVE!
WHAT DO WE DO, BOSS?
FINISH 'EM!!!
PEUH!
PLAF
PIF
PAF
POUF
PLAF
PLOM
BOUM

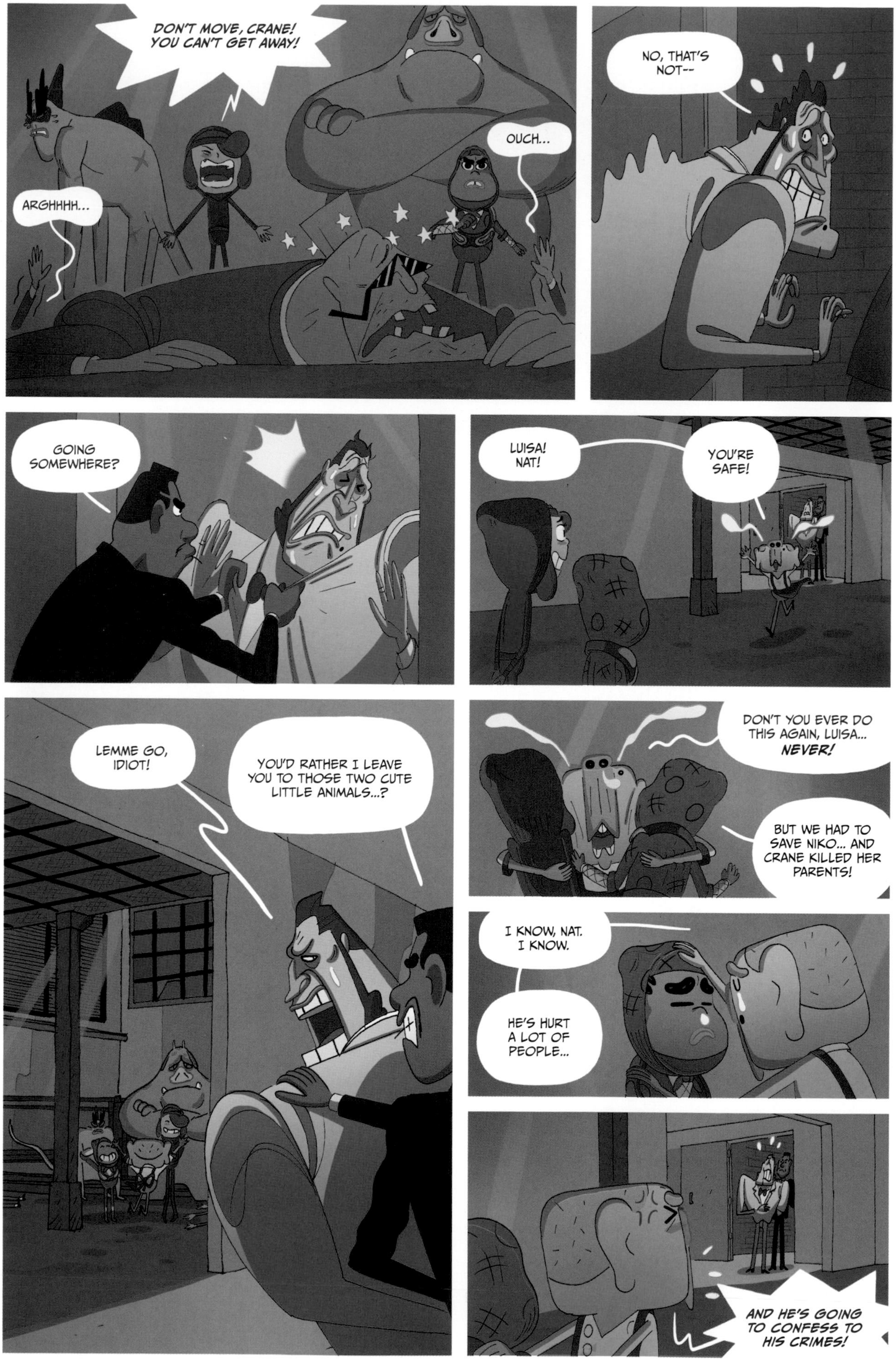
DON'T MOVE, CRANE! YOU CAN'T GET AWAY!
OUCH...
ARGHHHH...
NO, THAT'S NOT--
GOING SOMEWHERE?
LUISA! NAT!
YOU'RE SAFE!
LEMME GO, IDIOT!
YOU'D RATHER I LEAVE YOU TO THOSE TWO CUTE LITTLE ANIMALS...?
DON'T YOU EVER DO THIS AGAIN, LUISA... NEVER!
BUT WE HAD TO SAVE NIKO... AND CRANE KILLED HER PARENTS!
I KNOW, NAT. I KNOW.
HE'S HURT A LOT OF PEOPLE...
AND HE'S GOING TO CONFESS TO HIS CRIMES!

YOU THINK HE'LL STAY LOCKED UP?

I HOPE SO, FELLA.

WHERE'S NAT?!

WHERE ARE THE KIDS?!

SHHH! THE CHILDREN ARE FINE...

...BUT WE THOUGHT IT'D BE BETTER IF THE POLICE DIDN'T SEE THE TWO GENPETS...

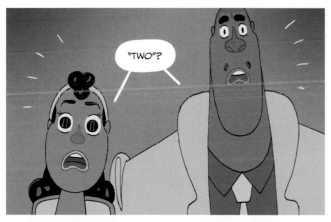

"TWO"?

HA HA HA HA HA HA HA HA HA HA HA HA

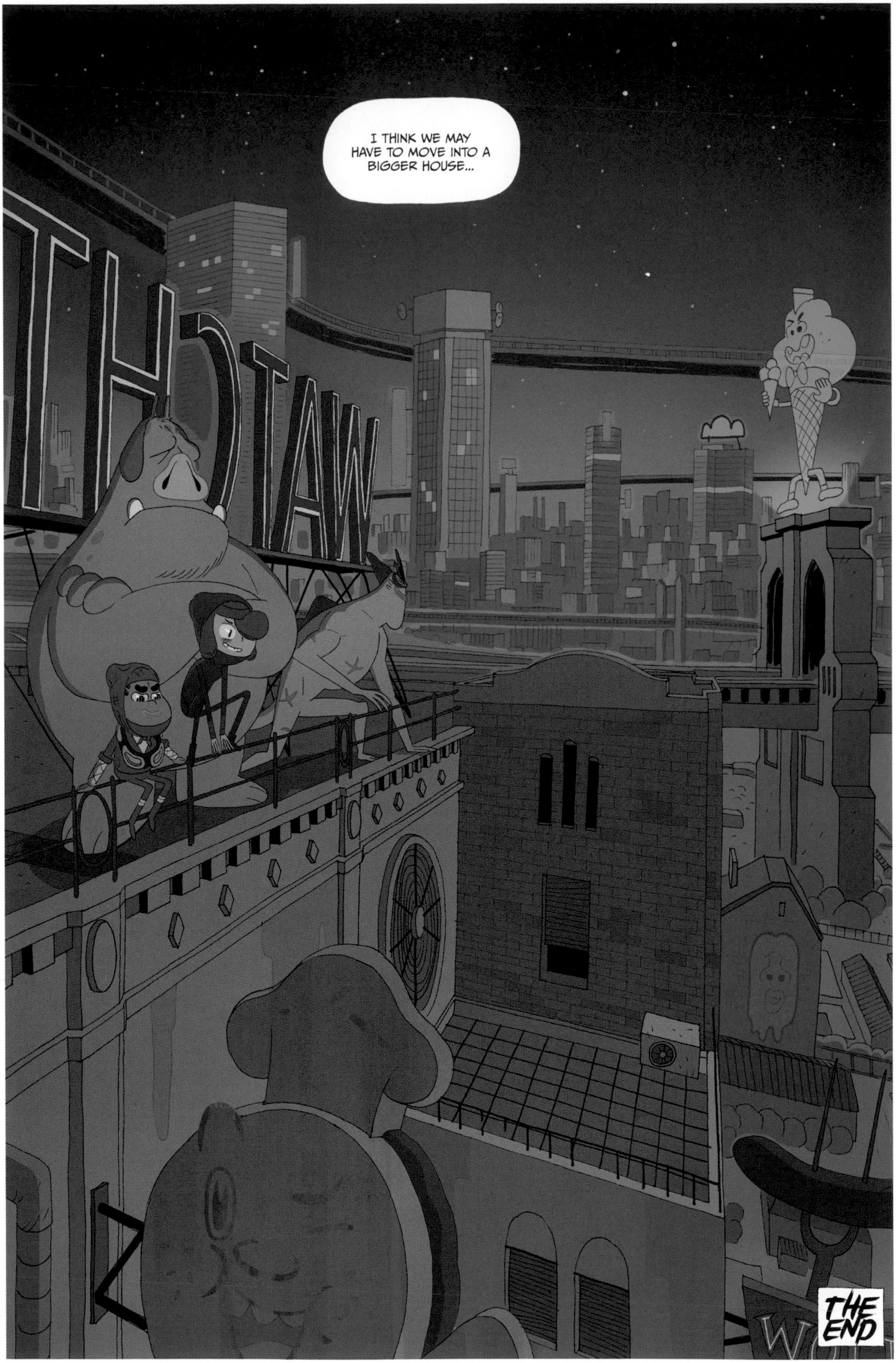
I THINK WE MAY HAVE TO MOVE INTO A BIGGER HOUSE...
THE END

CHARACTER DESIGNS

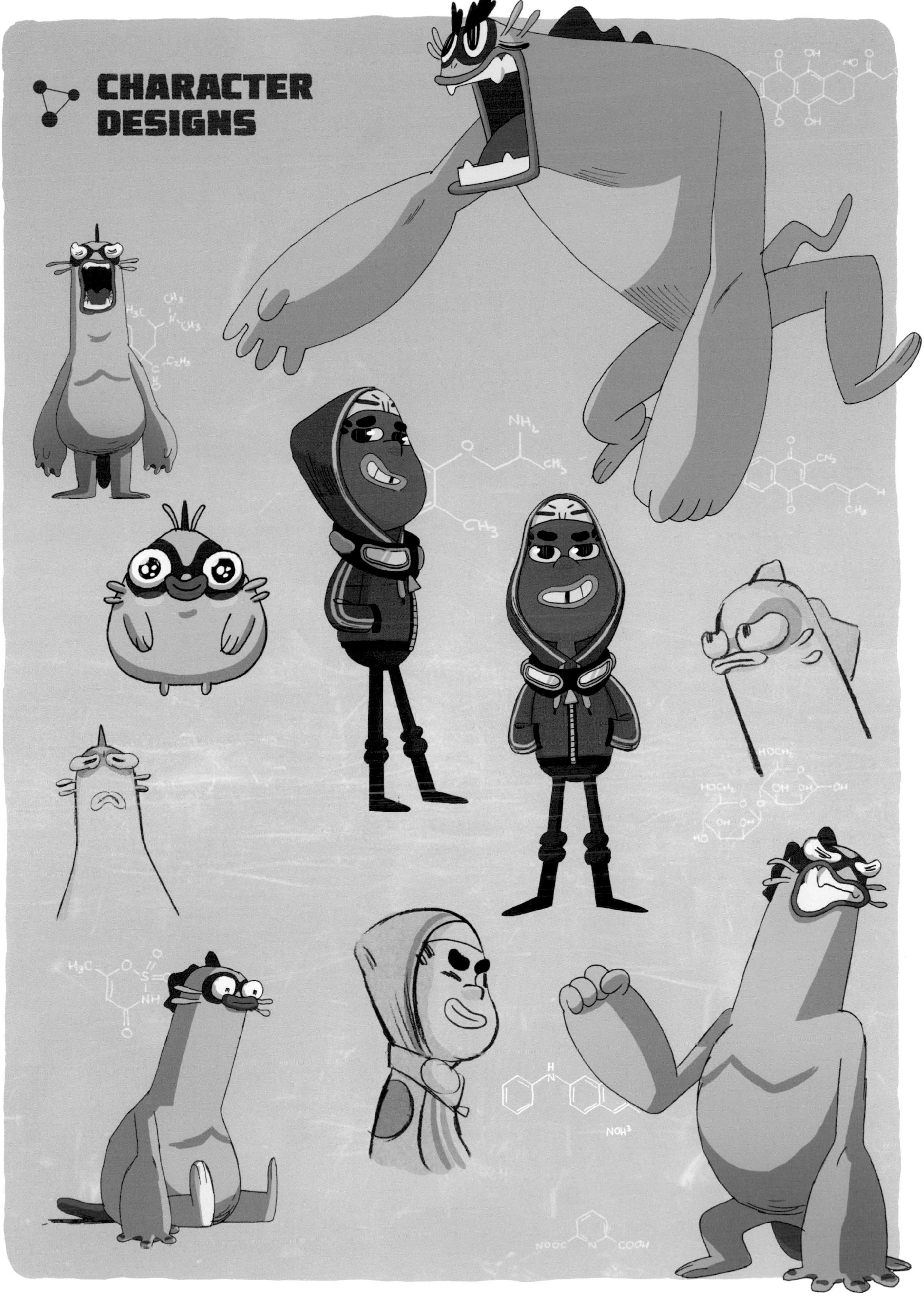

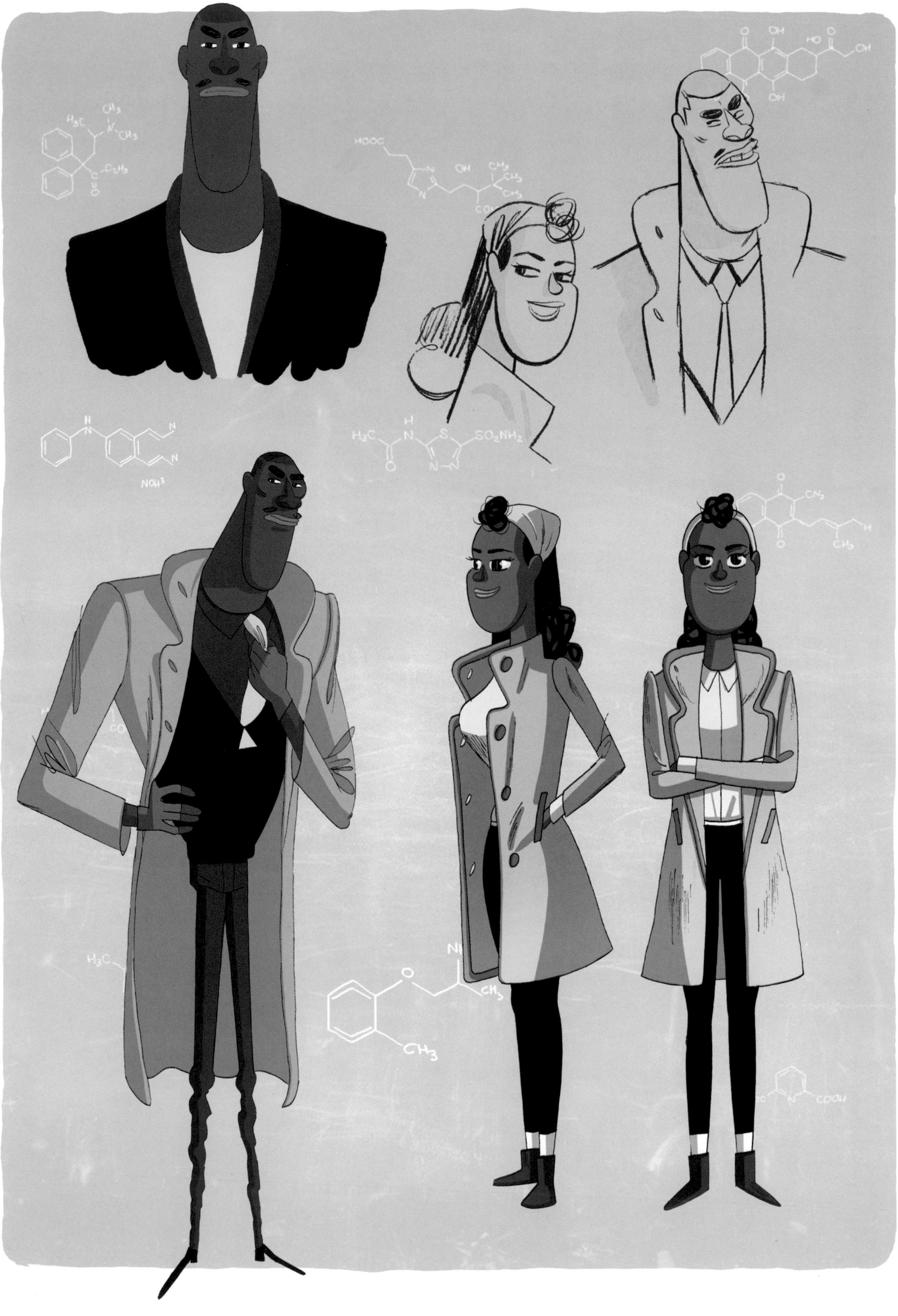
HOOC
OH
H_3C
SO_2NH_2
NOH^3
CH_3
COOH

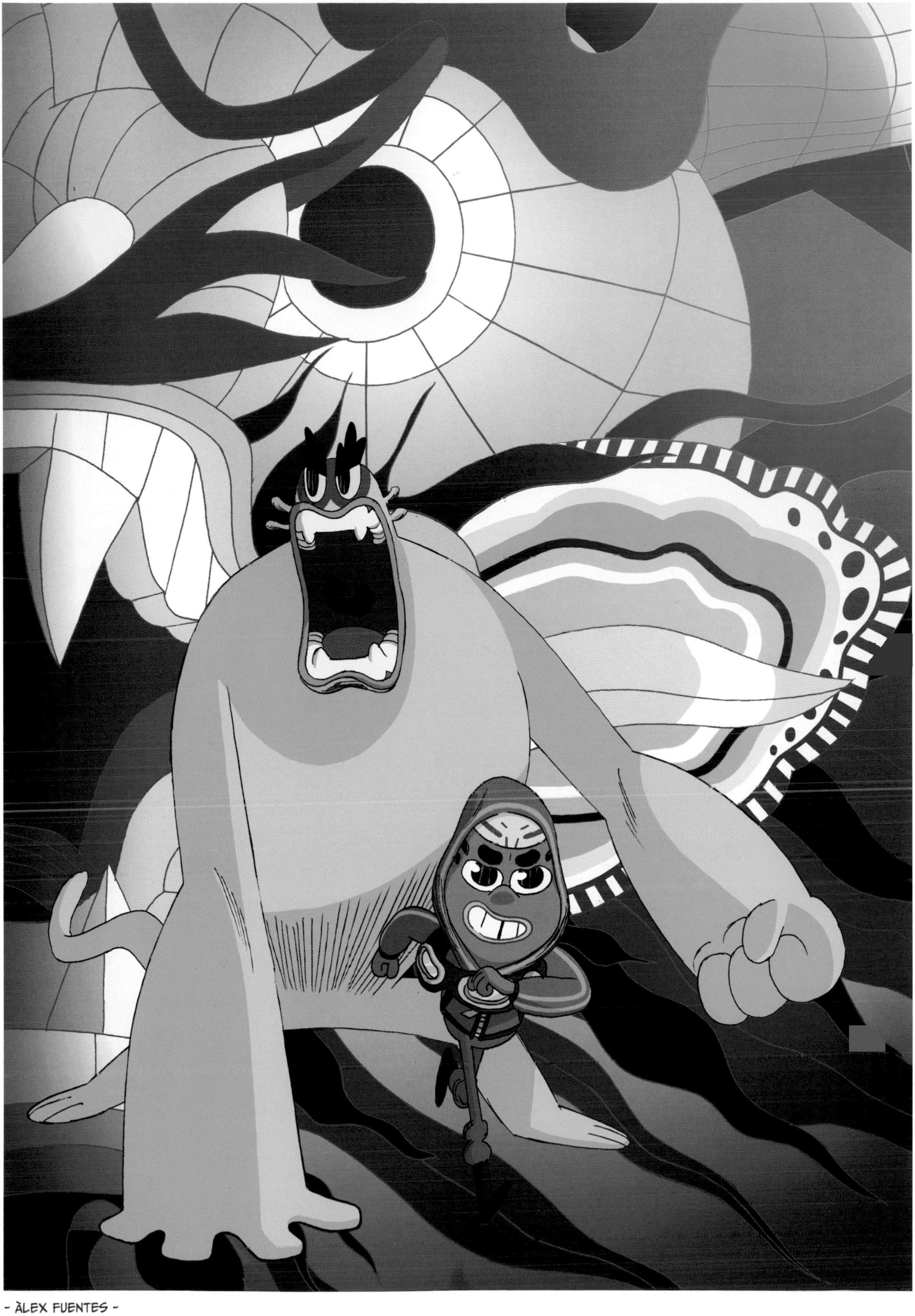

- ÀLEX FUENTES -

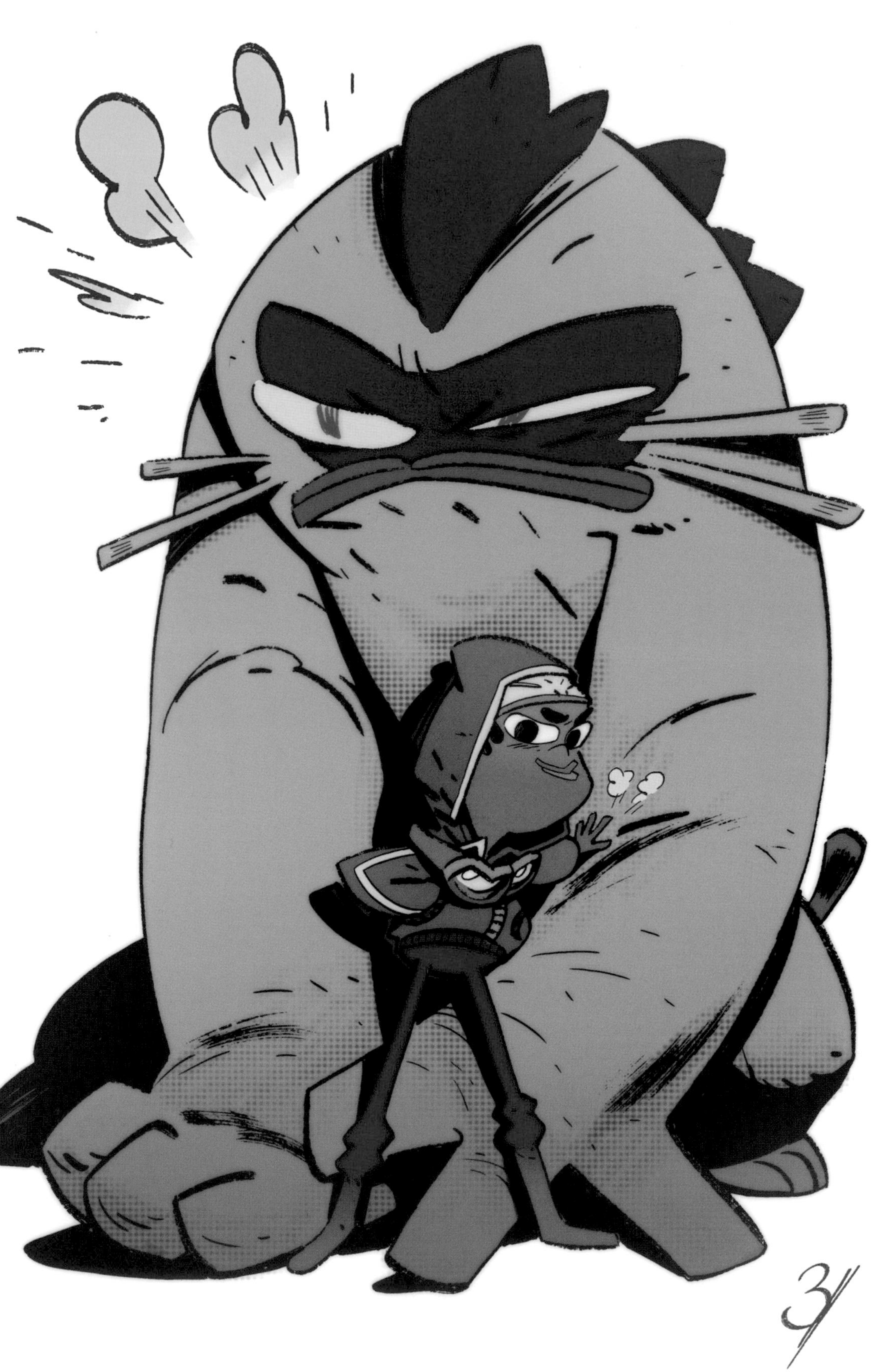

- ENRIQUE FERNÁNDEZ -

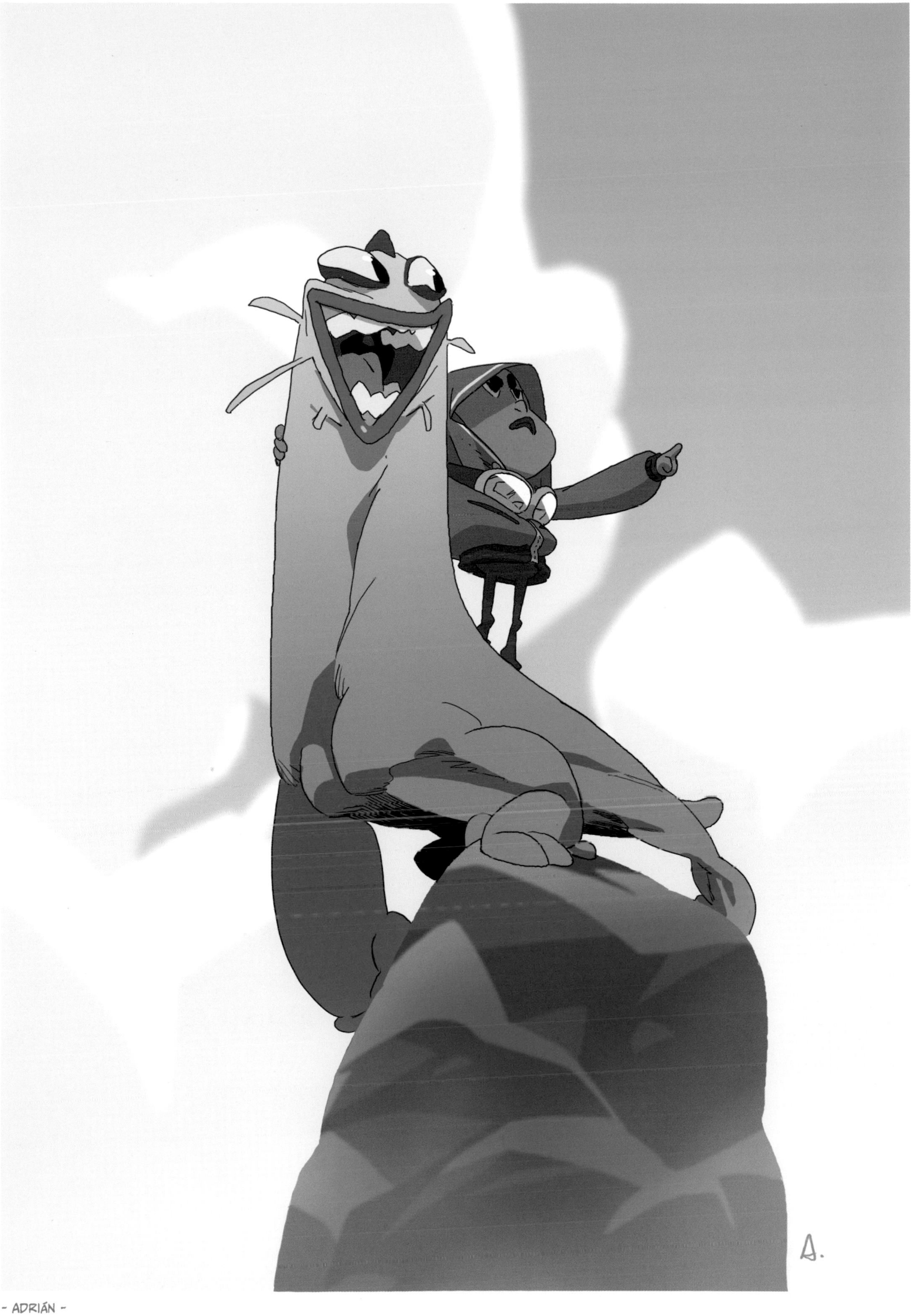
A.

- ADRIÁN -

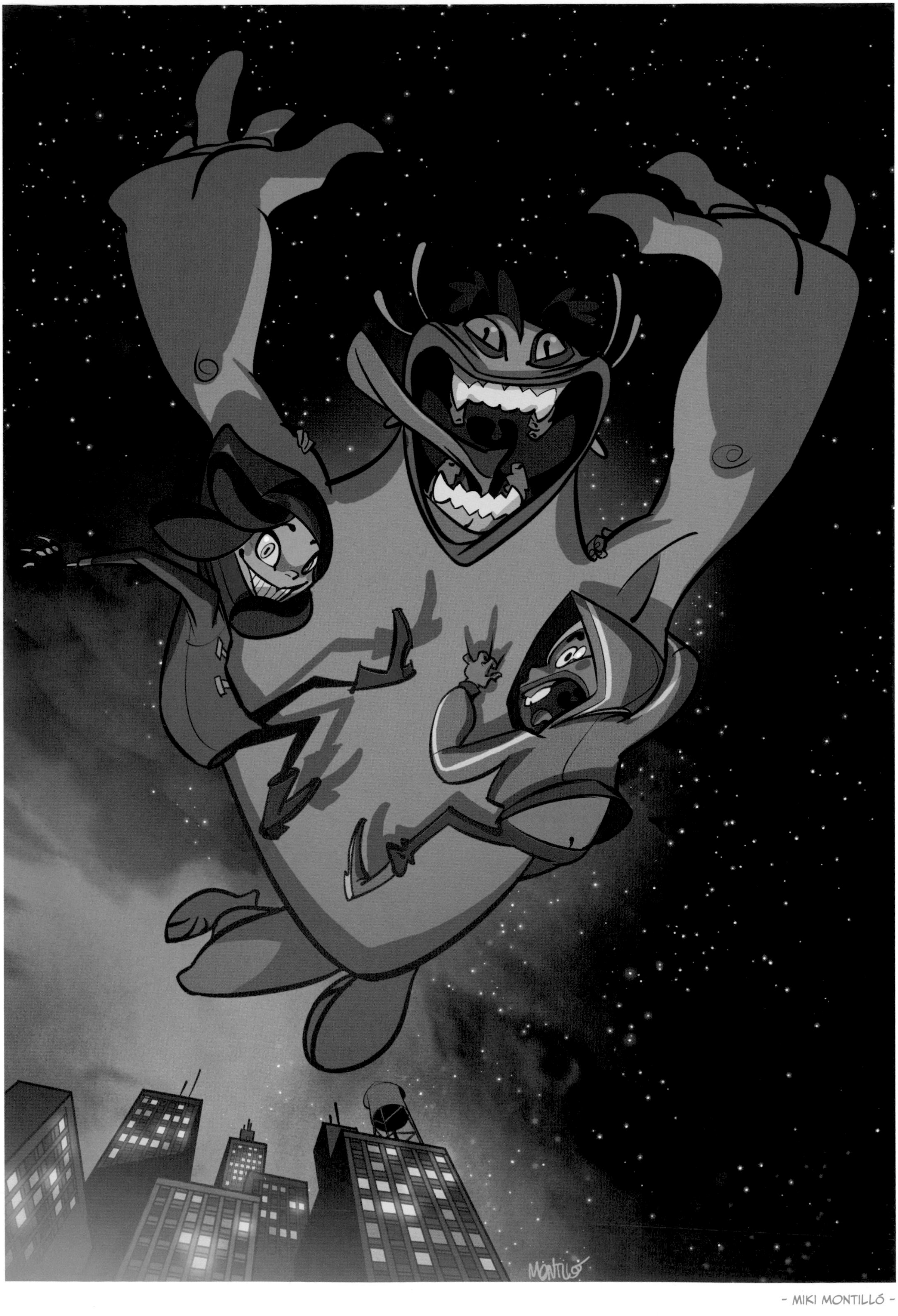
MONTILLÓ

- MIKI MONTILLÓ -